POINT APOCALYPSE

A NOVEL BY
ALEX BOBL

Point Apocalypse
Alex Bobl
Second Edition
Published by Magic Dome Books, 2017
Copyright © Alex Bobl 2013
Cover Art © Vladimir Manyukhin 2013
English translation copyright © Irene Woodhead 2013
Editor: Neil P. Mayhew
All Rights Reserved
ISBN: 978-80-88231-04-2

This book is entirely a work of fiction.
Any correlation with real people or events is coincidental.

TABLE OF CONTENTS:

PART ONE

Chapter One. The Jumpgate...1

Chapter Two. The Ferry Boat...20

Chapter Three. Questions..30

Chapter Four. The Raiders...48

Chapter Five. The Trigger Code...69

Chapter Six. New Identity...84

Chapter Seven. Comrades in Misery..97

Chapter Eight. King of the Forest...115

PART TWO

Chapter One. The River..135

Chapter Two. God Loves the Infantry...149

Chapter Three. Jim..168

Chapter Four. Walking Around the Devil's Barn................................178

Chapter Five. Long Time No See..188

Chapter Six. Metropolis...201

Chapter Seven. The Tables Turn...216

PART THREE

Chapter One. The Dream Is One Step Away.......................................233

Chapter Two. No Way Out..243

Chapter Three. An Important Link..258

Chapter Four. As the Crow Flies...280

Chapter Five. Point Apocalypse..296

PART ONE

CHAPTER ONE
THE JUMPGATE

DARKNESS. Light. Hundreds of bare feet slapping the tiled floor around me. Pitch dark again. Blinding light - I squeezed my eyes shut for a moment but kept moving amid the naked figures. Cold water jets pelted us from the walls; people yelped, someone slipped and fell flat on the floor.

"No huddling together! Keep moving!" the invisible loudspeakers barked in Russian. "Form columns! Line up, I said!"

The controller just had to be new. Trying too hard, the idiot. I'd love to know who'd authorized his access.

The stench of bleach hit my nose.

"Move it!" the voice hollered. "Don't stop, keep walking! Listen and obey orders!"

They dimmed the light. Strings of lamps flickered and blinked under the ceiling. Someone cussed to my right. The guy in front of me jerked back and somebody else pushed him onto me. I fended him off with my elbow, hitting his shoulder. More swearing drowned out the jets' hissing.

"Everyone shut up!" the speakers barked. "The culprits will-"

The speakers crackled and screeched. The lights flickered and went out. The shower stopped, too. For a few seconds, the crowd continued in the dark, their bare feet slapping on the tiles.

"Serves him right, the asshole," said a voice behind me.

I didn't know whether he meant the controller who'd loudspeakered us around or whoever had tried to start the fight.

"Hey, what is it?" a voice said. "I'm afraid of the dark."

"Get your filthy hands off me!" another voice demanded. "And keep 'em to yourself!"

"You better watch yours!"

"You what?"

What followed sounded like a slap in someone's face and a suppressed yell followed by a struggle. Far behind my back, I heard more angry voices. I raised my fists, pressed my elbows to my sides and lowered my head. The tribunal had decided to have my acceleratory implants removed so it was time I learned to make do without them. As long as they didn't knock me off my feet, I had a fair chance of fighting them off provided I had enough space.

The crowd poured toward the walls like overflowing jelly. I kept walking, all the while sensing there was no one left in front of me. The speakers were dead. The corridor filled with noises and voices.

When was the controller going to switch to the

auxiliary power? There had to be a good hundred people at the jumpgate. What were they waiting for? If they didn't do it soon, people could panic causing a stampede. And I couldn't hurry the things up for fear of triggering it.

I threw my arm to one side and swiped a face whispering, "Out of my way!" I was about to add a kick but reconsidered: I might miss and fall flat on the tiles.

The glow of lamps snaking down the corridor imprinted themselves on my retinas. I kept walking, slowly. Now I had no one left at my sides, either - only some wheezing at a safe distance behind me.

Then the lights went back on. The water jets hit the crowd with a hum and sent people flying to the center of the corridor. I jumped over a slumped figure and escaped someone's crooked fingers digging into my shoulder. A burly man with a beard raised his fist and stepped in my way. I thumped his solar plexus.

The shower stopped.

"Everybody freeze!" the speakers howled. "Stay where you are!"

I lowered my hands and glanced over my shoulder. Behind me, two Asians stopped in their tracks back-to-back. Could be Chinese, or... you could never tell. They all looked the same to me. Could be clones for all I knew.

"Form three ranks," this was a different Russian voice, cold and emotionless. Apparently, a more experienced officer had replaced the hollering greenhorn. "In ten seconds I'll turn on the shower. Those failing to comply will be eliminated. Ten, nine..."

He wasn't joking. We were at the Fort Commander's complete mercy. They could kill us whenever they pleased, then dump our bodies from the cliffs into the ocean to save the energy costs on the return transfer. His threat worked: we were still convicts with fewer rights than slaves, so people started getting back onto their feet and falling in. The bearded guy I'd knocked down grunted and tried to prop himself up with his elbows but failed. He pushed with his forehead against the floor.

"Seven, six..." the speakers kept on.

I grabbed the man's elbow and jerked him upright.

"Four, three... Leave the corridor once the disinfection is complete. Wait for orders to enter the airlock then proceed to the mind check. Start moving from your right, in single file."

The bearded man doubled up with his hand pressed to his stomach and teetered. I squeezed his elbow making sure he didn't collapse under the water jet.

"The shower's on - now."

I raised my face to the ceiling and closed my eyes. The cold torrent stank of chemicals as it lashed against my body.

The first cleaning cycle was followed by thirty seconds of warm disinfecting foam. They turned it off and then put the water back on, the pressure slightly less this time. Having washed off the foam, the drying systems kicked in, turning the air in the corridor as hot as a sauna. The sterilization lamps on the ceiling lit up, and I held my breath watching the red light flicker over the exit.

I ended up in the right column with only two men in front of me. That was good. I'd be through with the mind check quick enough.

A siren wailed announcing the end of the disinfection. The red light over the exit went out and the main lights came back on. At the end of the corridor, a steel door whirred as it sunk into the wall exposing the airlock.

The men stirred, their voices low.

"By the right, in single file!" the speakers spewed.

A tall old man happened to be the first by the airlock door. He started for it, stopped and gave a cautious look over his shoulder.

"By the right, in single file, toward the door, forward march!" repeated the voice from the ceiling.

"Get on with it, granddad," a square man from the second rank nudged. "Don't hold everybody up."

His bulging back and arm muscles were pockmarked with what looked like bullet holes, skin tight and wrinkled around them. Only these were no bullet wounds. They'd removed enhancing implants from his shoulder muscles. The modified man must have been a heavy laborer - most likely a pit worker at one of the Arctic mines. The mines and the Army - two places you had no business to be in Russia without muscle enhancers.

"Next," the voice echoed down the corridor once the first convict had cleared the airlock.

The miner stepped into the opening, swaying. Judging by his lack of coordination, he must have suffered the removal surgery pretty recently. I could see he hadn't adjusted to it yet. I knew by myself the first few days were the hardest.

"Next."

As I crossed the airlock, my head span around. My spine and shoulder blades started prickling in places where I'd once had my combat modules installed. The invisible rays of electromagnetic detectors searched every inch of my body, then switched off. The prickling ceased. I walked past the guardhouse to my left behind a one-way mirror and stepped into a narrow portal facing the door to the mind check room where the miner had just entered.

"Nex-" the controller didn't finish the word.

An alarm wailed. I stepped aside and looked back. The Asian who'd followed me still had a few more paces to clear the airlock. He ran, then stumbled, dropping to his knees and grasping at his blackened chest. His mouth opened, his screams inaudible above the howling of the alarm, fire and blood splattering through a hole in his chest.

The controller blocked the camera and turned off the alarm. For a few seconds, I stood still by the closed door. Then I shook my head and squatted down.

The jumpgate seemed to be rife with emergency situations. Something was going on. First the power failure in the disinfection corridor, then they'd replaced the controller, and now this Asian with his implant...

I tried to second-guess the actions of the duty officers. Handling this kind of emergency couldn't take more than a couple of minutes at a top security facility like this one. They'd now remove the body, make a radio announcement and resume the scan.

The dead man had to be Chinese, by the looks of it. They just couldn't help pushing their luck. Their wetware people were still beyond competition; so apparently, they had fixed their man with a micro container housing the implant. They must have delivered it to the carrier after the trial but before his transfer to the Fort. It looked as if they wanted to try and see if they could get a modified man through to Pangea.

Again, I shook my head. Impossible. Once the judgment was made, they removed all neuromodules and stimulators while still on Earth. After convicts were convoyed to the Kola Peninsula, they were checked again - and for all I knew, their medical staff were quite unpurchasable.

I reached behind my back and scratched a hollow under my shoulder blade where a somatic module used to sit. Those thingies could affect the work of the endocrine glands ejecting hormones like adrenaline. I propped my elbows on my knees, my hands hanging down, and looked up at the ceiling. Almost immediately, I glimpsed the black button of a camera between two of the lamps.

It looked as if the Chinese had had his implant installed right before being shipped here. But how? This wasn't as easy as inserting a night-vision lens! This was proper surgery affecting the whole body. All right, imagine they'd done it somehow, but how on earth had they expected the implanted Asian to pass the three-level safety system? The Fort was notorious for its multiple checks. Every room on the base had infrared cameras in it; the airlock was jam-packed with sensors, plus the ultrasound scanner in the portal. I reached again and scratched my back. It itched like hell. They must have put the scanner on full.

I heard voices in the mind check block. The door slid sideways into its frame. I stood up, clasped my hands behind my back and turned to the wall.

"Center," a voice said behind my back, "There's a convict in the portal."

"As if I can't see," the speaker answered overhead. "Put him through."

"Isn't it better he cleans up in the airlock first? Saves us the troub-"

"Put him through," the controller snapped.

I chuckled. So much for me mopping it up for them.

They yanked my shoulder to make me face the door.

"Quit sneering, you piece of-!" the guard snarled

pointing his pulse rifle at my chest.

He was in full gear. A composite vest hugged his torso above his protection suit, its square plates concealing his shoulders. Elbow guards and gloves protected his arms. High carbon fiber boots and a tactical helmet with a mirrored anti-laser visor completed the look.

"Move it!"

The condenser on the end of its barrel swayed pointing at the doorway into the block. It breathed with cold.

I walked through.

"Attention all," the controller said. "Clearance emergency situation. Penetration attempt."

Electric drives buzzed behind my back. The door closed, clanging its magnetic locks. The voice in the loudspeakers distanced, barely heard now, and then stopped altogether.

The mind check block looked a bit like an upended tumbler with its black matt walls of unknown mineral. I stepped into the middle and said out loud,

"Mark Posner. Convicted of the murder of a Federal Security agent. Proven guilty."

Mind checks are quick and absolutely painless. You don't feel a thing apart from the cold coming from the walls: the procedure calls for low temperatures of about -20F.

I'd done it a hundred times. In the Army school, then every time I'd moved to a new station, and the last time, before the Tribunal. In other words, every time the situation called for a quick identity check. Never had problems. But today... everything seemed to be going ass backwards.

They didn't let me out. They didn't open the door.

What the hell's going on here? An equipment malfunction? Couldn't be. They'd already restored the power in the corridor. The airlock detectors had caught the implanted Chinese. The communications between the guards and the loudspeakers were working. The doors seemed to be in order. Two of the convicts - the old man and the miner - had already cleared the mind check.

I shuffled my feet and huddled wishing to be back with those still in the warm disinfection corridor. What took the controller so long? Had he found something fishy with my mind map? But what if-

Then I realized. I could see the face of the base commander as the controller reported my identity...

The FSA - Russia's Federal Security Agency - didn't forgive those who murdered their agents. But before, they hadn't had a chance to get to me: I'd been kept in the Army detention center and tried by a military tribunal. The military and the FSA come from different planets as far as their structures and objectives are concerned. And now the Feds had their chance. The jumpgate base was under their jurisdiction. I wouldn't have been surprised if the commander had received special instructions regarding my arrival.

"Repeat check," resounded overhead. "State your name."

"Mark Posner."

"Sentence?'"

I repeated it fast and clear, like a parade report.

Another pause. The FSA men were overdoing it. Why repeat a scan if you're about to kill a convict? Why pile up evidence? I wouldn't. The control systems now had two scan results filed in their computers. Someone would have to delete them now.

My teeth chattered. My shoulders shuddered with the cold.

"Hello? Center?" I ventured, knowing that the controller wouldn't break instructions by speaking to a convict. "Stop fucking around! I'll freeze to death in here!"

I was shaking. Clouds of cold mist poured out of my mouth. The FSA men had to be dragging it out on purpose. They had to be trying to freeze me to death by lowering the temperature to -95F, the lowest possible in the block. No messy reports: they'd write me off as a mind check equipment malfunction. One convict frozen to death, no big deal.

"Hello!" I exhaled.

My nose stung, my eyes watered. I couldn't control my shaking any more.

"Hello!" I stepped forward and raised a fist to slam the door. It slid aside. I tumbled out, nearly tripping over myself, and started doing vigorous squats. The miner and the tall old man stared at me, uncomprehending. Both stood by the gate at the end of a long dark concrete corridor waiting to be issued their fatigues and shipped to the Continent.

After a dozen squats, I hugged my shoulders rubbing the chapped skin.

"I say," the miner started, "What the hell happened in there?"

I didn't answer. I had no wish to speak to him. The miner and the old man exchanged glances. Both had already put on their pale synthetic clothes and light plastic shoes.

The rags were disposable crap, you had to give them that. Instant-made as you waited, they lasted no longer than condoms. While a convict cleared the airlock, the scanners took his measurements and sent them to a thermoplastic machine next door. As the convict left the mind check, he received a perfectly useless set of fatigues: in less than a week, the fabric would crack and shred under Pangea's scorching sun, and the shoes would fall apart.

The miner turned his stare to me. "How long are they going to keep us in here, d'you know?"

I didn't bother to answer. A plastic bag containing my clothes slid out of the wall into a tray underneath. I tore it open and unfolded a pair of pants and a long-sleeved T-shirt. The shoes fell onto the floor. I stuffed the packaging into a bin under the machine and got dressed as quickly as I could, then pulled the shoes on and tore out the tongues. Now they could pass for a pair of sandals. I Velcroed them, crossed the corridor and sat in the far corner with my eyes half-shut.

" Are you mute, man? D'you understand what I'm saying?"

"Fuck off," I barked back glancing at him out of the corner of my eye.

The miner stuck out a square jaw and headed for me, muscles bulging under his clothes. The man was strong but stupid, going for a stranger like a dumbass cyber trooper.

I unglued my back from the wall and spread my shoulders preparing to spring up and knock him down with a good kneeing. The old man tried to call him back. When the miner didn't stop, the old boy hurried after him, grabbed the man's hand and pulled him back to the gate. I could hear him whisper that I was trouble, that he'd seen the implant scars on my back which was a sure sign I was an FSA man and my body language betrayed FSA training, too, so the miner should leave me well alone. Even better, he whispered, wait for the other inmates to arrive and tell them about me.

The old man turned to look at me. Our eyes met. He shut up and I leaned back against the wall. The old guy had an eye for that sort of thing. He'd been right about my modules and training. But he'd got the crux of the matter wrong as I had nothing to do with the FSA whatsoever. But who was I to explain that my implants had been of the Army type? Only an experienced neurotech could tell the difference.

Now I had to keep my eyes open. If the miner and the old guy shared their suspicions with the rest, I'd never make it to the Continent. The moment I stepped onto the ferry, I'd be dead meat. They could even try and take me out while still on the pier. That way, I'd never even have a chance to become a local. A Pangean deportee.

They started whispering again, softly this time, so I couldn't hear a word.

The mind check door opened letting out the second Asian. Wonder if he knew about his predecessor's implant? They could be accomplices. Not that the base commander cared. His job was shipping, not investigating: sending convoys both ways, from the Kola Peninsula to Pangea and back. No, that wasn't all: the commander wasn't supposed to allow new technologies to leak onto the Continent. And he had a well-equipped garrison and weaponry to help him do just that.

A clothes bag slid into the tray by the door. The Chinese took it, cool as a cucumber, tore the shrink film and started dressing. Before he could pull up his pants, another inmate cleared the lock. In half a minute, yet another one came out. The transfer was under way. In just over an hour, the two-hundred-strong gang would be ready for shipping.

The Chinese got dressed and crouched by the exit staring at the floor. I looked up. The ceiling sported the Fort's colors: two bolts of lightning crossed under a two-headed eagle.

Then I heard a quiet pop. My ears started hurting as if the air pressure in the room had dropped. Startled, I looked around. Neither the Chinese nor the others showed any signs of discomfort - in fact, they didn't appear to have noticed anything at all. My head, however, started hissing and crackling. What the hell was going on?

The back of my head ached in the recently healed hole which had once housed the memory chip. A quiet hiss again, then a woman's indifferent voice sounded inside my head,

Pangea: a continent lying along the equator. Is bounded by the ocean. The length of coastline, over thirty thousand kilometers. Status: an inland prison. No natural resources discovered. The climate...

My ears popped. The voice distanced itself but didn't disappear completely, reciting information on the Continent's climate, mountain ranges, rivers, plains, plateaus and settlements. I remembered a lot of the data from my army school days.

When the voice abated, I opened my eyes, confused. The lock corridor was now filled with people. Most had dressed and sat by the walls; some talked. Foreigners stuck together closer to the mind check exit. A few men by the gate surrounded the miner and the old man. They argued casting occasional glances in my direction.

I rubbed my forehead and winced. My head was

booming. I had to concentrate. I was Mark Posner - Private Posner, sentenced to life in exile for murdering a Federal Security agent. I'd been tried and sentenced by the military tribunal, then undergone an agonizing surgery as they'd removed my combat implants. They'd transferred me with the rest to the Kola Peninsula jumpgate - and there I was at the Pangean base, a.k.a. the Fort, that occupied a rocky island not far from the mainland, a.k.a. Pangea Anomalis - the only body of land amid the ocean that covers this world's entire surface.

That was all fine and dandy, but what was the information software doing in my head in the first place? This wasn't an implant - this was a basic program that someone had bothered to neuron-zip and which had now unzipped in my brain all by itself. You would think I'd know, wouldn't you? How could you install a piece of software into a man's head without him knowing, anyway? After the tribunal, they hadn't had the opportunity: it required sedation, and I... wait a second... when those military surgeons...

A voice put an end to my rationalizing. The old boy, the miner and a couple of bystanders stopped arguing.

'Hey there, buddy," the miner headed for me.

I stood up and, keeping an eye on him, walked toward the foreigners clustering nearby. Another man joined the miner: middle-aged with sunken cheeks and a sallow, unhealthy complexion.

"Wait up," he said in a low voice and rubbed his pointy chin. "We need to talk."

I backed off and cast a glance around. No one seemed to sneak up on me from behind. The sallow-faced man fixed his calm gaze on me while the miner stuck out his chin, menace in his glare. Behind them stood the old man and three more guys, fit and tall, all three younger than myself, square-shouldered like new recruits on parade. And their faces... but of course! They had to be clones! A custom-hatched brood: apparently, the mining foreman had donated his sample to sequester and force-grow apprentice triplets for himself. Force-grown clones looked at a lifespan of thirty years at best; wonder what the foreman and his brood had done to justify a Pangean exile? They must have protested by demanding better wages and working conditions. Dangerous thing to do in Russia these days. Ever since the new president had come to power after the Civil War, he'd been hunting down rioters and separatists. With Army support, he'd created the Federal Security Agency, banned trade unions and dissolved rival political parties. Any kind of protest could be qualified under the new Threat To The State law and the protester himself sentenced to life in exile, all thanks to Pangea whose discovery had solved the prison overcrowding problem.

The only known portal to Pangea was on the Kola Peninsula which had prompted a commercial approach as Russia started accepting convicts from other countries. The rapidly depleting oil supplies together with a chain of world crises had triggered a wave of riots and civil wars in virtually every country on the globe, filling foreign prisons to the roofs with unhappy undesirables.

I hesitated, unsure whether striking up a conversation with them was a healthy thing to do. I could wait for the line-up call or just blend in with the crowd.

"I think I know who you are," the man said. "But I'm not a hundred percent sure."

The day seemed to be rich in surprises.

"If I could have a look at your back, that would

eliminate many questions," he added.

"Negative," I decided to bid for time until the line-up call. "Any more suggestions?"

"None."

"Think well."

The sallow-faced man gave me a vaguely guilty look. "Then you're toast."

The miner and two of the clones were an easy job: they stood too close to each other leaving themselves little space to maneuver. The others could take a bit of time but overall, I should meet the combat training standards. But what would I gain - getting sent to the cooler?

That was one place I shouldn't be in. If I picked the fight, I'd give FSA agents the perfect excuse to lock me up and take me out at their leisure.

"Pointless dragging it out," the sallow face said. "We're attracting attention. You don't need it."

He rubbed his pale sunken cheek and added,

"Fighting is no good, either."

"Know your implants?"

He shrugged. On brief reflection, I said, "Back off."

I walked to the gate, all the time knowing this wasn't the best alternative, but I had no other option. I turned to the clones and the old man, "Gather around. We don't need the others to gawk."

When they shielded me from unwanted stares, I pulled the T-shirt up and glanced back at the man. "Well?"

"I told you, didn't I?" the old man glared at me. "Look at all them scars!"

Sallow face raised his hand, silencing him. Then he came closer as did the miner. Cold fingers touched my back and shoulder blade points and traced my spine down to the small of my back.

"You can get dressed... Private."

I turned to him straightening my T-shirt and stated, "You're a neurotech."

"So he's not an-" the old man stopped short.

"No," sallow face offered me his hand. "I'm Wladas Chabrov. Chartered neurotech."

I paused, then shook his hand. "I'm Mark."

Wladas nodded. No words needed: only chartered specialists had access to the military. He could see at once the placement and purpose of my implants. The miner, however, took time to take it in.

"Name, rank, sentence?" he asked me like the mind check operator.

"Quiet, Petro!" the neurotech mouthed.

I glanced at the faces surrounding me. The clones watched me, still uptight. The old man fidgeted, his wrinkly hands trembling.

"Relax, Misha," Wladas touched the old man's shoulder and went on in a quiet voice, "Everyone, relax. Mark could have killed us all here in his own sweet time. With or without implants, his combat potential is high enough. I'd say, a couple units? Two point five, maybe?"

His words fell on deaf ears as our professional mumbo jumbo meant nothing to lay people.

"Allow me to translate," I said. "Combat potential is what we call a soldier's qualification levels. All of you put together might average two combat units. Not even. My potential equals three combat units. Four, with implants installed."

As I said it, I realized that Wladas had just given me another check. FSA agents used a different qualification system. Had I been one of them, I'd have explained it differently.

His mouth twitched suppressing a sneer.

"What makes you stick together?" I asked.

They ordered us to line up. The crowd began to fall into ranks, quickly and efficiently this time. The miner, the neurotech and myself were in the first file, followed by the triplets. One of them shouldered away the Chinese who tried to wriggle in with us.

"He's weird," Wladas said.

"Yeah," I watched as the Asian took his place in the third file next to old Misha. "His buddy has croaked in the air lock. Maybe not his buddy. They could've had nothing to do with each other."

"I saw it."

"So what do you think?"

"Nothing," Wladas shrugged. "No one can smuggle an implant to Pangea. The Asians tailgated you through the disinfection corridor like you had honey on your ass. One definitely did. The other could just be hanging around for all we know. We even tried to pick a fight with them - no way," he rubbed his cheek. "They didn't buy it. And you were deaf to the world, you! Schlepping along like a cyber trooper."

Aha. So they'd kept an eye on me. Tried to get into a fight. Now what would they need me for? Or - why did he need me?

"You didn't answer my question," I glanced back at the triplets. Their glares were lasering a hole in my head.

"They're Petro's clones," Wladas whispered.

"I've worked that out. Are they miners?"

"They are. I helped them adapt after implant removal on the way here."

It made sense. A certified neurotech meets a few

fellow convicts in transit. He helps them. The tribulations of trial and prison followed by deportation can be too much even for a specially trained man. Some clam up, others seek contact hoping for some support or try to secure a place in the prison hierarchy. If you looked around you could see that the crowd consisted of smaller affinity groups. They tried to stick together knowing they had to survive the ultimate tribulation: life on Pangea. The old man didn't look as if he belonged in Wladas' group, but I left it till later.

"Why did you follow me?" I asked. Their attention worried me a lot. First the Chinese exploded in the air lock, then the mind block freeze, followed by the software in my head. I couldn't help connecting the morning's events looking for a trend and an explanation.

"It was Misha. He's a political prisoner, been rioting against the system. He pointed you out. His idea was, you were an FSA agent. Planted by the Feds to stir the shit. We meant to check you out in the corridor but couldn't. The Asians were constantly in our way."

"Which was-?"

"They just didn't let us close. Like they were covering you or something."

I didn't have time to think it over. The electric motors whirred within the walls pulling the doors in front of us open. The white-hot midday sun hit our eyes. I shielded my face with my hand and squinted at the thin strip of rocky land past the gate. Beyond it, the surf washed against the shore driving turquoise waves onto the rocks. The sky far overhead was clear and equally turquoise. The wind smelled of brine as it splattered me in the face. The ocean lay before me. Far beyond, rose the shores of Pangea.

CHAPTER TWO
THE FERRY BOAT

"FORWARD march!" bawled from our right.

Four Feds guarded the exit. They wore heavy Centurion suits with integrated exoskeletons and jetpacks on their backs. The men held combined weapon systems. Diodes gleamed on their television sight units mounted on the barrel housing, ready for action. The red dot of a laser sight slid across my chest and jumped onto Wladas. I could almost see target markers flash as the ballistic calculators sent their data back to the guards' helmets, and nearly ducked aside to escape the estimated field of fire. I put out one leg and swayed to my left.

"Keep in line!" the nearest guard barked.

I stepped back cursing my army instincts. A Fed with corporal's insignia walked in front. On his shoulder I could see two dark stripes covered with some strange substance. It emitted a colored light when seen through an infrared device: same as the army friend-or-foe system. The other three stayed put but didn't lower their weapons.

The corporal led us to the pier. The sun was at its

zenith - and it wasn't our Earth sun, either, but a blinding ball of fire, scaringly larger and whiter than the one we're all used to.

The tall L-shaped pier projected a good fifty meters into the sea. There, safe from the bulging waves, was moored the ancient hulk of a ferry boat. The ocean breathed fresh and vital. This wasn't the continent yet: there, the further you were from the sea, the harder it was to breathe. The desert air tasted dry and bitter, and the swamps left a sweet and sticky aftertaste of toxic vapors...

I got out of step, then realized that my brain had soaked up the information from the software unpacking in my head. I'd never been to Pangea before and couldn't have known any of those desert and swamp things.

I relaxed and marched on with the other inmates. I licked my salty lips, took a deep breath and shielded my face from the sun. Far beyond, several miles away from the base, the Continent Anomalous stretched out its brown southern shore.

The continent non-existent on Earth, one that had come to life during a daring scientific experiment. It had been nearly forty years since Boris Neumann, the then-emerging prodigy of military physics, had carried out trials of a new type of non-lethal weapon. Supposedly non-lethal, that is. His electronic bomb was designed to scorch soldiers' implants which was why the Feds only equipped their special forces' men with them. From what I heard, these days the Feds tended to experiment with chemicals to see if they could affect the human brain - so that they could abandon neuromodules altogether. Anyway, what had happened was that they'd exploded an electronic bomb at their Kola Peninsula test site. But its air blast emitters, instead of targeting the enemy's simulation command center complete with working communications system and a tracking station, had born down into nothing creating a wormway that led to Pangea Anomalis.

I'd no idea why Neumann had dubbed it so. Never asked myself why. I'd heard, of course, that Pangea was the name given to the ancient protocontinent that had broken apart creating the Earth's continents as we knew them. Only the Earth's Pangea had been enormous, and Pangea Anomalis was half the size of Australia although its wild life looked similar to that on Earth.

Pangean tigers live in prides hunting not by night but during daylight, the Information's voice resounded in my head. I kept walking trying not to betray the fact that I had an illegal piece of software working in my head. The Information kept going on about the tigers: apparently, if you intruded into their territories, they would hunt you down and kill you. My brain was soaking up the data. My head boomed, blood pulsating in my temples and sending a hammering pain to the back of my neck.

Then, blurred and unstable at first, a map came into my mental view.

Sketchy but clear, it collided with reality and hindered my perceptions. I stumbled, causing the corporal to swing around. His weapon system's barrel jerked toward me.

"Keep in line!" I heard from under the mirrored visor.

Finally, the map faded away. I gave a sigh of relief. The corporal led the group onto the pier and ordered us to stop, then walked down the gangway onto the ferry's lower deck. It was barred all around and formed a large cage slightly rocking with the waves. The corporal crossed the cage inside, looked around, then headed back and started climbing the steep stairs that lead to the captain's bridge.

The ferry was quite big - bulky and squat - with spots of rust here and there. Two sailors stood aft, wearing light-colored canvas shorts and orange safety vests. Positioning themselves under the arm of the crane, they argued with a third crew member overhead who was tugging at the levers of the hoist trying to land a rusty ten-ton container onto the slipway.

A fat bald man came out of a deckhouse that rather resembled a riveted armored pillbox. He scratched his suntanned belly which hung above white shorts, stretched and yawned, then noticed the prisoners' column down at the pier. For a couple of seconds he stared at us, as if unable to grasp what he was seeing, then grabbed at the railing and leant over the stairs. The corporal shouted something, and the fat one hurried toward the sailors lurking under the crane.

"I have a funny feeling they brought us out earlier than usual," Wladas said.

"Could be," I agreed. "The sky above the base is getting dark."

"Where do you see that?" the burly miner said next to me. "It couldn't be clearer."

"Petro, wait. You don't know about this," Wladas turned to me. "I can see it, too. It's getting very murky right above the Fort. Have you any idea what's going on?"

The island was oblong, by the looks of it. The fort that had been built around the portal was surrounded by towering walls that ran the island's entire perimeter. Above it protruded a few segments of ancient parabolic dishes. I knew too little about Neumann's experiment: just bits of trivia of what had happened forty years ago. The wave from the electronic bomb that had created the wormway to Pangea had also caused the test site to collapse, together with its tropospheric station and part of the Kola Peninsula. Later, they had erected the inward-sloping wall around the base. Keeping the wormway stable demanded a shitload of power so they'd been forced to build a nuclear power station right on the base. The concrete top of its reactor peeked above the wall to our left. Rusty mesh parabolic dishes, several hundred square meters each, stood on tall steel supports behind the walls. The dishes had been mounted close to the center of the island and were oriented toward the cardinal points at opposing angles to each other. They were the only old installations left intact. The rest had been encased in steel and concrete, turning the base into an impregnable sarcophagus. Our scientists couldn't forecast the consequences of the wormway's collapse. The wave's nature was still classified research. I remembered a geek from our army school tell me that if they tried to shut the wormway down, it could cause a major catastrophe. Apparently, our continuum would collapse turning the entire Solar System into a new black hole...

"So Mark, what is it-" Wladas started.

Lightning flashed between the antennas. A deafening clap ripped through the air. I covered my ears and ducked. Many of the people fell onto the pier covering their heads.

The sailors seemed to be quite used to the local thunder and lightning. They'd finally managed to place the container onto the landing ramp. The crane operator prodded a lever unhooking the wire cables that held the container in place under the boom of the crane. Slowly, it slid down the slipway toward a square opening in the Fort's wall.

The corporal watching the crew from the bridge

turned on his jetpack and shot skyward. He made a steep arc through the air heading for the gate we'd just left. Three guards waited there for him. The corporal landed and motioned them to begin. All three turned their backs to the gate and trained their weapons on us. A harsh voice spouted from concealed loudspeakers,

"Prisoners! You have broken the Earth's laws and are banished for good! There is no going back! There is no forgiveness! From now on, you're deportees!"

His voice grew louder and more powerful. Now it echoed over the island, deafening and hair-raising, bringing one to his knees. "The Earth's laws end here! Within the limits of the prison world, your life span is your own responsibility!"

As he spoke, the Feds were retreating into the gate, their weapons still pointed at us. The loudspeakers concluded in a lower voice,

"The jumpgate base and the island are Earth's territory. All prisoners have two minutes to clear it. In case of noncompliance, the Fort will engage its weapons systems."

With this last word, the armored gateway closed concealing the Feds. The square opening in the Fort's wall opposite the ferry shut, and the slipway retracted. The sailors rushed to cast off; the operator lowered the crane and began covering the hoist with tarps.

The fat bald guy - who seemed to be the captain - hurried inside the cockpit and emerged a few seconds later wearing a lifejacket. He raised a polished megaphone and shouted,

"Need a special invitation? In the cage, quickly! By the left, single file, quick march!"

Several round embrasures opened in the Fort's wall. I

rushed toward the gangway, Wladas and the miner wheezing close behind. The rest of the deportees also jostled toward the ferry. The pier resounded with their howling.

"You idiots!" the captain yelled. "In single file!"

The crane operator, having covered the hoist, sprang to a low concrete stand nearby, jerked the lid open and produced a machine gun: an ancient German MG with its holed barrel shroud and wide-mouthed flash suppressor. The crane operator flung a leather strap over his head and hung the weapon at his thigh. He placed the gun barrel onto the railing, straightened the ammunition belt and drew the bolt.

"Halt!" the captain yelled from the bridge.

Lightning flashed. Another clap of thunder tore through my ears. I stopped in front of the gangway.

"Form ranks!" he commanded. "At the double!"

All over the pier, people started pushing and swearing.

"Do it, Georgie," the captain said without lowering the megaphone.

The machine gun rattled, sending a semicircle of hissing bullets ripping through the air overhead. Somebody screamed and collapsed onto the pier. Some rushed back to the shore, others froze. The thick dark barrels of weapon systems emerged from the round embrasures in the walls. The characteristic flattened ends of the barrels blackened with soot told me what they were. Flame throwers.

"Listen here!" the captain shouted. "You have ten seconds to fall in. The last ones will get a bullet. Ten, nine-"

He gave the crane operator's shoulder a shove pointing to an inmate who, despite the orders, had bolted along the pier back toward the base gate. The gun barrel traced the escapee and cut him down in one long spurt.

"Start moving on my command," the captain said matter-of-factly. "Three, two, one! Toward the cage, at the double!"

I took the gangway in three long bounds and dived into the cage's opening.

"Step it up!" the captain hollered. "And don't you dare puke on my deck!"

I strode to the bow side of the gate and rested my hands on the bars watching a fair-haired sailor cast off. In one practiced motion, he released the dock line from a bollard, threw the line into the water and turned round showing a young freckled face.

"Hey, Oakum!" the captain yelled in a strained, breaking voice. "Quit shirking! To the engine room, now!"

The youth chose not to walk back past the cage, apparently for fear of someone pushing him into the water or grabbing him through the bars. He unlatched a hatch under his feet and before I could call him, jumped down into the opening. The hatch closed with a clang and I looked up.

The whole scene must have taken a minute and a half. The barrels of the flame throwers moved forward all at once aiming at the pier. Most of the deportees had already boarded the ferry. The rest faltered on the pier, anxiously waiting their turn. Inside the cage, Wladas elbowed through the crowd toward me. He nodded at the murky gray mist thickening high above the island. Slowly, it formed an enormous conical thunder cloud.

"What's going on?"

"A hurricane, probably," I nodded at the antennas.

"The blast wave. Has to be, for sure. The jump takes too much energy disrupting the status quo and causing perturbations. The residual effect of transporting us to Pangea."

Wladas nodded. During jumps, the antennas worked like lightning rods redirecting surplus energy into the Pangean atmosphere. But the atmosphere had its own ways of dealing with this phenomenon.

Looked like our army school geek had been right about the future catastrophe, albeit a local one.

When the last deportee had entered the cage, the sailors hooked up the gangway with barge poles and dragged it onto the bridge. More sliding bars blocked the exit onto the deck. The cloud over the base thickened, heavy as lead.

"Full speed astern!" the captain barked.

The deck shook and the ferry wallowed as it moved between the pier and the Fort wall. The antennas emitted bolts of lightning, bathing everything in their colored blaze. The sky rumbled.

A guard boat came into view abeam: a squat vessel with square deck houses. It headed for the Elephant Ridge: a much shallower area than here, flooded with daylight, its horizon dotted with trawlers' sails...

The Elephant Ridge? Was I supposed to know that? Or was it Information defusing in my head again? I was a bit fed up with its nonsense. I'd get to the mainland first, and then I'd try and give it all a good think.

The anxious deportees argued and quibbled. Some squatted down, others stood holding onto the bars. I headed toward a tight bulkhead at the back part of the cage and stood under it. Wladas forced his way through behind me.

Soon the ferry caught up with the guards' boat and followed in its wake. Lightning flashed over the island although not as often. Still, the sky remained dark.

The guards' boat started to turn, the ferry mimicking its maneuver. On the bridge, an alarm wailed, and another one answered from the guards' boat. The deck swayed sending me sprawling onto Wladas. We collapsed. Everybody screamed. The ferry kept turning without slowing down.

When it turned its stern toward the island, a tornado swirled over the antennas, its funnel flashing occasional bolts of lightning. The leaden sky was pressing down on it as if trying to flatten it and crush it into the Fort. The thunder clapped and crackled; then sunrays ripped the top of the funnel and pounced through the thick darkness illuminating the pier and the Fort's gray walls. A tall rumbling wave concealed it from view.

It rolled on quickly, but I managed to take a deep breath and cover my face. The deck lurched. Water poured through the cage bars.

CHAPTER THREE

QUESTIONS

COLORED circles flashed before my closed eyelids. My lungs burned, about to explode. I pushed with my elbows struggling to force myself free from a stranger gripping my back.

I couldn't. I could barely tell top from bottom as I kept hitting and kicking. Pointless. The bulk of the water around me absorbed the impact.

My fingers brushed the bars. I grabbed at them, pushing myself up, and started climbing up toward the light, hoping that the inmate who clung to me would loosen his grip once we were out of the water.

When we surfaced, his fingers at my throat slackened. I took a swing and elbowed his temple. His nails scratched the skin on my neck as he went underwater.

Every second could be my last, the thought pulsated in my head. I climbed further up, higher, as far from the water as possible.

Once I'd climbed about six foot up, I forced my hand between the bars and gripped them tightly, pressing my side to the grate. No one was going to pull me away from it. I'd make a quick job of anyone who tried.

Turned out, I wasn't the only clever one. About a dozen more people, Wladas included, hung along the perimeter of the cage clinging to the bars. The deck was now to our left and the ceiling to our right. The ferry had to be lying on its side... sinking.

Below in the water, people struggled and screamed, calling for help and drowning each other.

I looked around. I had to get out of there. The ferry was about to become a mass grave.

"Over here! Help!" voices came from my right.

I turned my head to the bars. The guard boat rocked on the waves nearby, heading for the island. The deck was empty.

"Hey!"

"Come here!"

"Help!"

Our screams followed the boat. Apparently, no one was going to help us. They weren't interested.

Someone tugged my ankle. A gentle pull - not an attempt to grab my foot and drag me down. Someone was trying to get my attention. I looked down, prepared to kick a wet face, but reconsidered. Hanging below me was a Chinese. He looked like the one who'd just lost his buddy in the airlock. He pointed down, nodding.

What the hell?

"Why down?" I asked.

The Chinese started climbing down.

"Where are you-"

"Mark!" Wladas called.

I turned my head.

"Jump!"

— 31 —

The guard boat slowed down, the feathered waves in its wake settling. The turret on the stern turned its twin guns toward the sinking ferry.

I let go of the bars and kicked myself away and down.

What's better, the hydrodynamic shock or being showered with shrapnel? It depended on the gunners' aim, and I had a funny feeling they were about to target the emerging part of the ferry. Otherwise, the Chinese wouldn't have-

The bang came from the ferry's bow. It felt as if someone had put me into a barrel filled with water, covered the lid and started pounding it with a sledge hammer.

I surfaced, mouth wide open, trying not to scream from the earache. I nearly hit the Chinese when he grabbed my shoulder and pulled me in the direction of what seemed to be a gap in the grating. The explosion had bent the torn and twisted bars inward. On the foredeck, water gushed in amid billowing smoke and fire.

" Wladas!" I snorted and shook off the Asian's hand. "Where are you?"

The Asian pushed away a dead body drifting toward us and dived down. Lots of bodies around. And blood. The water was dark with it.

"Wladas!"

"I'm here-" the neurotech choked.

I made a stroke toward the gap and looked up. The bars drew closer. The ferry was about to go down hook, line and sinker.

If we wanted to stay alive, we had to get out as quickly as possible.

"I'm here! He-help!"

Wladas' head disappeared under water within a meter

from the gap. A disheveled burly man held him down and grabbed at the bars, pushing himself up. The Asian resurfaced nearby and grabbed his feet. Before the burly man had time to react, the Asian climbed his shoulders and locked his hands under the man's chin. Then he kicked hard at the man's shoulders, straightening his legs like a deadlifter.

Vertebrae crunched, and the dead man collapsed on top of me. I recoiled. The Asian dived into the gap, and Wladas showed his head again.

"Out!" I gasped. "Quick!"

I looked back. A few more men swam toward us, including the miner who'd fathered the cloned triplets.

By the time I looked back, the neurotech had already escaped. The gap was now halfway in the water, sinking. Or should I say, the entire ferry was sinking. Quite rapidly, too.

I took a deep breath and dived in, praying that no one else would catch up with me and grab my foot hoping to survive. Either that, or I could go face first onto a jagged bar. Or just miss the opening.

In front of me, the gap's uneven outline came into view, its bent broken bars barely visible. I stretched out my arms, put my legs together and slid, dolphin-like, through the opening. I surfaced and tried to get as far from the ferry as I could before the vortex pulled me under.

My heart pounded. With every third stroke, I made a quick gasp and kept going. I took another stroke and my hand bounced off inflatable rubber. I didn't have time to slow down. Face up, I'd collided with the orange side of the safety raft.

"Where d'you think you're going?" I heard overhead.

"He looks strong enough. Georgie, Oakum, get him out. Put him with the rest. And let's pick up the others."

I raised my arms. They grabbed my elbows and pulled me out.

The raft was a six-seater. The bald fatso, a.k.a. the ferry captain, sat on top of a waterproof personal survival kit. He was in his fifties, a round red face, a smooth suntanned skull, and bushy gray eyebrows. His shoulder sported a tattoo: an anchor with a towline wrapped around it and a spike-headed combat dolphin below. Military geneticists had developed those dolphins in order to destroy underwater saboteurs. From what I'd heard, the spikes on their heads were sharp and strong, and also venomous.

On either side of the captain sat the young sailor and the crane operator with his machine gun.

The crane operator, dark-haired with gray temples, looked older than the captain. His thin face, wrinkled and wizened, was covered with three days' worth of stubble. By the confident way he held the machine gun you could tell he'd been in a scrape or two.

I looked at the young sailor. His strawberry hair was tufted together making it stick out like... like oakum. That's how he must have gotten his nickname.

The youngster handed me a short paddle that looked more like a trenching spade.

"Take it and row," the captain said.

"Give me a chance," I leaned against the bulwark catching my breath.

"Georgie," the captain said.

The crane operator pointed the gun at me.

"You fucking clone's ass," he grinned showing gapped yellow teeth, "Shut your mouth and row!"

I grabbed a paddle and straddled the rubber float. The ferry boat was gone. Jetsam floated on the surface. Amid the growing oil slicks, two bodies rocked in the waves. The murky mist over the jumpgate base had dissolved, and the bright white sun blazed in the clear sky overhead. The silhouette of the guard boat was barely discernible against the steel-and-concrete island.

"Why did they shoot at us from the boat?" I asked.

"Just row!" the crane operator said in a coarse three-packs-a-day voice. "The Feds have their own orders."

"Where do you want me to row?"

"Over there," Oakum pointed behind my back.

I turned around. Wladas and the Chinese were rocking on the waves a few meters away. Neither of them spoke. I didn't like it. The neurotech lay on his back, arms wide apart, staring into the sky.

I sat down with my back to the machine gun, lowered the paddle into the water and pulled violently. Oakum on the other side countered, trying to make sure the raft didn't turn. We soon reached the two heads bobbing in the water. I glanced over my shoulder. Several large bubbles billowed up: all that remained from the ferry boat. A few more bodies resurfaced.

Wladas was pale - unconscious, by the looks of it. With the boy's help I dragged him on board. The Chinese climbed in with ease.

"Is he alive?" the captain asked as I bent over the neurotech. "I don't need no stiffs here."

Wladas coughed. I turned his head to one side and water spasmodically gushed out of his mouth.

"You're in luck," the crane operator grinned. "If it wasn't for..."

His stare met with mine, and the gun's barrel pointed

at my chest.

"Now," the captain said. "Don't even think of rioting. I'd rather have a chat with you before we reach the shore. I don't care about your names or sentences. But if you can tell me what's going on back on Earth... Having said that, any of you got sea legs?"

I shook my head and glanced at the Chinese. He sat straight, hands on his knees, smiling and looking much like a votive statue.

"What's wrong with him?" Georgie pointed his gun at him. "What's there to smile at, Chink?"

"He doesn't understand you," I said.

" He will when I shoot him!"

"Shut up, Georgie," the captain shrugged. "Give me a chance to talk to the people."

He sat up as if nothing had happened and went on.

"Any mechanics among you? My engineer's dead. I need someone to replace him."

Once again I shook my head. The Chinese kept on smiling.

"Shame," the captain scratched his tattooed shoulder and squinted at the boy. "I'm afraid, it'll have to be Oakum."

The kid's eyes lit up. He spread his shoulders and stuck his chin out.

I didn't like the way he spoke. Asking about the Earth and new engineers so matter-of-factly as if nobody had just died during the sinking. Okay, they were only deportees, but they were still human. Lots of them, turning into fish food even as we spoke. He didn't seem to care. Death must have become mundane here on Pangea, to the point where no one cared about the dead.

"Quit glaring," the captain lowered his hands. "Think

about those who've survived. About yourself and your future. You can't bring the dead back to life."

"You can't," Georgie butted in.

"Ferries sink all the time," the captain went on, like an old grunt telling war stories to rookies. "Last year, one just disappeared. Like that," he clapped his hands. "A bolt of lightning, and it was gone. Had to be Pangean devils."

Wladas finally caught his breath. He lay on his side wheezing and clutching at his throat. The Chinese sat with his back straight, smiling.

"So! No new Civil war out there, apparently?" the captain asked.

"Apparently not," I picked up the paddle and straddled the float.

"How about Siberia?" the crane operator perked up. "They haven't sold it to those slant-eyed clones, have they?"

"In your dreams."

"Good," Georgie grinned. "They've pissed away the rest."

"How many times have I told you?" the captain jumped up. "What do you want with that radioactive waste pit? Siberia! It won't change just because you ask!"

The crane operator sulked. Clutching his gun, he looked at the Chinese. His knuckles turned white.

"Georgie is a Siberian, see," the captain said. "A Baikal conflict volunteer. So he's one of our old-timers."

A Baikal conflict veteran. I see. I hadn't even been born when this Georgie was fighting for Siberia's independence against the Chinese clone settlers, razing their Irkutsk settlements to the ground. No one knew for sure but apparently, Siberian independence was the real cause behind the Civil war in Russia. A year after, the newly-formed Federal Security Agency had started mopping up. It took them several years to properly establish the new totalitarian regime. That had been their hay day - purges and arrests - right up until the Coup of the Seven Generals.

"Okay," the captain slapped his hips and turned pointing to the direction of the mainland. "Course north west, fifteen degrees starboard from Elephant Ridge."

"Leave them, Grunt," Georgie spoke. "Just look at them: they wouldn't tell north west from a shit sandwich. And that slanted-eye monkey don't speak no Russian."

The captain sighed. "In other words, row till you hit the shore. Oakum! You on lookout, make sure we don't lose the current. Keep an eye on the wind, too. Give your paddle to the Asian. Let him work for his rescue. Georgie, keep a bead on them-"

"Depend upon it!"

"... it would be safer for us all," the captain concluded.

The kid passed his paddle over to the Chinese and sat in front next to the captain. I nodded to the Asian. We made a couple of strokes adjusting to each other and paddled away. Luckily, the wind was at our backs otherwise we'd have to drift and no amount of paddling would have helped, not with all this windage. Now I understood why they'd rescued us: they'd needed someone to paddle. I glanced back again. The island and the Fort receded slowly but surely, and I couldn't see the debris any more.

"Permission to speak," the captain clutched his hands on his belly and reached out his legs. "Rookies have lots of questions."

Georgie snorted. I looked at Wladas. He sniffled with his head dropped onto his chest. The dumping and the shock had been too much for him.

"Why didn't they rescue us?" I pointed my paddle at the Elephant Ridge with its beam trawlers. "Couldn't they come and help?"

"Trawlers have no business in the Fort area," the captain said. "They'd be sunk straight away. And during these vortex incidents," he raised his eyes to the sky, "the Fort closes the channel and tells them to leave at full steam."

"How big is the base water area, then?"

"About five miles south from the Elephant Ridge. Right up to Cape Fang."

He pointed over Georgie's head to the east where a crooked black cliff hung over the shore. Far beyond it, mountain tops barely showed through a gray mist: that was the beginning of the mountain range that encircled the continent's east coast. The swamps had to lie by the northern foothills.

"The only way to get to the base is by ferry boat," the captain waved his hand, "and only when they're expecting a new shipment of convicts. We take carula on board, then wait for the go-ahead from the Fort commander and approach the base. Then we unload, ship the men on board and go back."

I'd barely heard his last words as the Information clicked on again in my head,

Herba Cearula, or blue seaweed, commonly known as carula, grows exclusively in the New Pang area. It is the only source of biocyne.

Biocyne? I thought, thus activating a new page:

Biocyne is a biologically active substance produced by the seaweed species herba caerula. It facilitates DNA breakage repair resulting in improved environmental tolerance and longevity...

"Quit gawking and row!" the captain shouted.

The Information finally shut up allowing me to paddle with renewed vigor. I glanced at the unconscious Wladas and the silent Chinese. What was going on here? Nothing but riddles. First the chain of accidents at the jumpgate, then this Chinese who looked as if he was keeping an eye on me. Now this complex informational software in my own head, and when had they ever had time to install it? I could only think of one instant when they could have done so: after the tribunal when army surgeons had removed my combat implants. They'd had to put me to sleep. But if the surgeon had installed the software, he couldn't have done it on his own accord, could he? He couldn't have cared less about me. Which meant he'd been forced into it - why else would he risk facing a court martial?

But what kind of force was it? Who'd care about a soldier and a murderer on his way to life in exile? And had the Chinese been sent here by the same force? And how about the jumpgate accidents, had they been arranged, as well, in order to distract the Fort operators and slacken their vigilance? True that they hadn't looked too deep into my mental scans - not deep enough to discover the unauthorized software, anyway.

My head was spinning. The Chinese, Information, jumpgate accidents... biocyne.

"What's carula?" I asked.

"Just some slimy shit," Georgie muttered. "Stinks to high heaven."

I looked at the captain. "Why do you send it to the Fort?"

He shrugged. "God knows. They process it, like, to

use as a food supplement. To help with overpopulation. According to them, we deliver food shipments."

"How often?"

"How can I say..."

"Regularly enough," Georgie grumbled.

"Exactly," the captain nodded. "We send, like, one shipment a month."

"How do you harvest it?"

"It's cultured. Once it blossoms, divers go down and filter the muck... Why would you want to know?"

I didn't say anything.

"Shitty job," Georgie winced.

"Not nice, no," the captain said. "But it's McLean and his people who deal with that. Virtually no Russians on his farms. And I shouldn't think of becoming a diver. They're dog meat, no one cares if they live or die. Worse than clones."

I stared in front of me. I'd just realized that the Information's data was classified. Here on Pangea no one seemed to know anything about biocyne. The deportees seem to think that the Earth needed the blue seaweed as a handy nutrient to add to cheap synthetic food they sold to the poor. Even on Earth, few knew about biocyne's precious properties. It was used to make medications to reverse aging, affordable to a select few like our President and corporate top brass. Had the common people learned that the authorities manipulated them in more than one way, achieving immortality while the deteriorating environment cut the average lifespan further with every year...

That was all well and good, but the average soldier like myself wasn't supposed to know these things. The Information had told me... no. It had only repeated something I'd known for a long time. This was no Information software - the installation seemed to help surface suppressed memories.

I got out of synch again, rowing slower as I got lost in thought. It looked like I was caught in a weird and disturbing situation.

I glanced at Georgie and the captain,

"I understand the Earth needs the seaweed. But what's in it for the settlers?"

"All our machinery," he explained, "is exchanged for carula. All the generators, spare parts, guns and ammunition... It's old: nothing digital, no pulse guns or computerized lathes. Even the gun cartridges are analog."

"And the fuel? There're no mineral resources here, are there?"

"There aren't," the captain grinned. "But we do have the Tanker."

Information butted in again. The Tanker is the oil riggers' base. It includes the supertanker Samotlor, an oil rig, a supply vessel and the icebreaking tug Svyatoslav Norg which were teleported to the Continent as a result of Boris Neumann's bomb test disaster.

"Heard about the Samotlor disaster?" the captain said. "You must have, it was all over the news. A whole convoy disappeared on its way from the Arctic oil rigs."

"I see," I mumbled.

"The tanker was full to the brim," the captain perked up, gesturing away. "When Neumann first discovered Pangea forty years back, we kept finding all sorts of shit caught in the jump. Raiders make good money out of it, seeking and selling their goodies on the New Pang market."

The crane operator nodded.

"Our Georgie here was with the raiders for quite a while. He used to work with Neumann himself before Earth pulled the plug on his research," the captain raised his bushy eyebrows wrinkling a sunburnt forehead. "You don't know what I'm talking about, do you? Neumann is the old egghead who went missing two years ago, but not before he talked the whole of New Pang senseless with his swamp stories and Continent mysteries. He'd researched all of Pangea by then, from top to bottom, and he had a good team to help him, too. But then-"

A wave hit the board. The raft jerked, showering me with briny froth.

"The wind's changing," Oakum said.

"Easy all," the captain ordered. For a few seconds he sat still watching the sea. Then he elbowed Georgie,

"Not good. There's a storm brewing from the Fang. It'll be here soon. The shore is a stone's throw away, but if we try to land, the waves will beat us to fuck on the rocks."

The crane operator didn't answer. From out of the corner of his eye he watched the Chinese who didn't avert his gaze from the cape.

I could see the Asian's anxiety, too. Did he understand Russian or was he just second-guessing our risks? I'd have loved to have known that.

The raft rocked harder, spattering Wladas with froth. He perked up.

"What's up?" Blinking, he turned his head and tried to sit up. "What's going on?"

No one answered. The Chinese turned to Georgie, feigned a smile and froze again.

The captain sized us up, gloomy, munched on his lip and said,

"Now, guys. It's better if you jump overboard. Off you go."

Georgie tensed up and grasped his gun tight. The young sailor bit his lip, looking scared.

"Don't move, Oakum! I'm talking to the deportees. We need to increase windage. This way at least some of us survive. You hear me? Jump!"

"Did you hear?" Georgie raised his machine gun, its butt hard against his shoulder. "Out, now!"

A shadow moved out of my field of vision. It looked as if the Chinese had simply turned, but Georgie emitted a stifled scream and dropped the machine gun. I reached out, grabbed the gun by its holed barrel shroud and pointed it at them. The Chinese was already undoing the slackened crane operator's pants belt while holding the sharp end of the paddle to the captain's throat.

"Hey," I called him, "what's your name... Enough for the time being."

The Chinese released the belt and grabbed it with his teeth. He pushed the belt's end through the buckle to make a noose and lifted his face.

"What's your name?" I asked staring into his expressionless slanted eyes. "Do you speak a word of Russian or not?"

He answered with a volley of gobbledygook stressing the word Wong.

"Wong. Is this your name?"

He picked up the noose and turned away.

"Wong. Please don't," I poked him with the gun and commanded, "Sit back down."

Wong turned to me and shook his head, disapproving. Still, he sat down next to the captain, barging the boy aside.

"What now?" the captain kept squinting at the paddle in the Chinese's hands.

I began unloading the gun.

"We'll split into pairs. There are six of us so we can take turns rowing. You and Georgie, take the paddles."

Wladas stirred. He apparently didn't look forward to straddling the dangerous rubber float.

"Move it," I dropped the ammo belt onto the raft, removed the buttstock and the return spring and began to remove the bolt. "Hear me, Grunt? Bring Georgie round and get rowing."

"Oakum," the captain rubbed his neck, "get some water out of the survival kit."

The kid bit his lip again and stepped toward the captain, undecided.

"How do you expect him to do it?" I said. "You're the one sitting on the bag. Another thing. I suggest we drop these stupid monikers, or not? What's your name, sailor?"

"Jim," the boy said.

"That's not a Russian name," Wladas raised his eyebrows. "What did they send you here for?"

"He's one of the locals," the captain rose and started undoing the survival bag. "Born here. What are your names?"

Wladas and I exchanged glances. Over the last thirty years or more, Russia had signed quite a few international agreements allowing other countries to get rid of their undesirables by sending scores of them to Pangea. About a decade ago, an epidemic had wiped out a large part of the Continent's population, but by now a new generation had replaced it: young men and women who had grown up in their prison world without once setting foot on Earth.

"I'm Mark," I said.

"Wladas," the neurotech added.

The captain had produced a flat water container, unscrewed the top and took a large swig.

"I'm Trophym," he wiped his mouth with his forearm. "Trophym Pavlovich Kuznetsov. But I'd rather you call me Grunt. I'm used to it."

"Georgie needs water," I reminded as I put the disassembled machine gun aside. I showed the bolt to the captain.

"I'll keep it for the time being. Now get on with it!"

I put the bolt into my breast pocket and glanced at Georgie as the captain splashed some water into his face. Apparently, Wong had overdone it. The crane operator didn't look as if he would recover any time soon. I ordered the Chinese to join the captain and row and told the others to be ready to replace them.

At first we didn't do too badly. According to Grunt, we'd reach the inshore current at any time which could take us to the shore before the storm.

But the wind grew stronger, the waves bigger, and the swell heavier. Finally, I told the rowers to ship their oars for fear of one of them ending up overboard.

"How far to the shore?" I asked panting.

"Less than a mile," Grunt stood up looking to the east. There, the blackened sea hung over the blurred horizon. The white sun behind our backs turned crimson as it set, its light covering the rocky Cape Fang with blood-red spots.

"It'll smash us against the rocks," Georgie pointed out.

"How much time do we have?" I opened the survival kit and looked inside.

A torn blanket, two flat water containers, some

purification tablets, a signaling mirror... but no sign of a first aid kit. I lifted the blanket and pulled out a sheathed machete by its leather strap.

"A bit more than an hour," the captain answered. "Provided we don't get flipped over."

I tied the leather strap around my waist and turned back to the bag. I handed Wladas and Jim a water flask each. Then I discovered a plastic container with a pair of field glasses inside, their ribbed case peeling with age.

I was just going to train them on the rocks and the thunder clouds above them when Wong exclaimed and pointed his paddle toward the north. I focused the glasses.

A truck drove along the shore.

CHAPTER FOUR

THE RAIDERS

THE GLASSES turned out to be only four-power but enough to make out a rusty truck and some people in it.

It looked as if the driver was pushing it to its limits. A cloud of dust trailed behind the vehicle as it traced the cliff edge flashing its lights.

Someone in the truck launched a flare. Its blinding red light hit my eyes forcing me to lower the glasses.

"Are they here to get us?" Grunt leaned against the board.

A large wave hit the raft. The captain sprung back. Wong who straddled the float raised his paddle and nearly fell into the water. I grabbed his elbow and pulled him down.

"Keep your heads down," I told everyone. "Lean against the board."

I stumbled to the middle of the raft, knelt and, grabbing at Wladas, lifted the glasses again.

The truck braked and the people started jumping out.

I counted four. Two more got out of the cab.

"What are they doing?" Grunt yelled above the wind.

A bolt of lightning flashed over the Fang, zigzagging across the sky. The clap of thunder crushed in our ears. The approaching storm showered us with a mixture of rain and brine.

I waited for the next wave to pass and raised the glasses.

The men had by then put up a tripod in front of their truck. It looked like a stand for a heavy machine gun.

Grunt reached for the glasses. "Lemme have a look."

"Don't move," I said trying not to lose the truck. It wasn't easy in the rain and the swell. The lenses misted over.

"What are they doing?" Georgie shouted.

They'd already mounted a thick tube on the tripod. A non-recoil?

I handed the glasses to Wong and reached for the gun to assemble it. The bolt didn't want to go into the breech; the belt feed pin wouldn't go into its locator. I grazed my fingers on some lugs inside the breech frame but finally managed to drive the bolt back into its carriage. It clicked along the runners locking into place. Next: the spring, the stock, the ammo belt...

"Step aside!" I laid the gun onto the float.

The barrel went up and down as the raft jerked. No way I could take aim, especially considering the distance.

"Give me the fucking glasses!" Grunt yelled.

The Chinese turned to me. I nodded. The captain grabbed the glasses from him and stumbled, face down, onto the float.

"Oh fuck!" Grunt's voice reached me between the claps of thunder. "Dropped 'em!"

He slapped the float with both hands.

"I've dropped the fucking glasses!"

It was getting dark as we spoke. Squinting, I wiped the brine from my face. The men on the shore raised the barrel higher as they aimed. Another flare lit up in the hands of a man who reached out to place it on top of the barrel.

"What are they doing?" the captain shouted in my ear.

"Trying to set off some fireworks!" I said as I tried to train the sights of my gun on the tripod and the people next to it.

"It's a rescue rope!" Georgie yelled. "Don't shoot, you clone's ass! They're not trying to kill us!"

I turned to him.

"They're loading a harpoon," Georgie went on. "They've attached a flare to it so that we can see it!"

Their gun went off spewing the light high into the sky. It seemed as if it would get lost in the dark clouds, but the next moment, the bright dot reappeared and started to descend. The illuminated harpoon fell a couple dozen feet away from the raft.

"Shortfall!" Georgie groaned.

"All they're going to do is make a hole in the raft!" Wladas said. "What's in it for us, anyway?"

The crane operator turned to him,

"The harpoon has a container attached to it, a cylinder with harnesses for all of us. That's how raiders rescue prospectors from the quick sands."

The men on the shore didn't bother to retrieve the harpoon but cut it and loaded their gun with a new one. It took them some time to start a new flare - apparently, their observer was making a windage adjustment. The growing twilight had all but swallowed the shore when a splash of light pierced the blanketing rain illuminating the tripod on the cliff, the men and their truck nearby.

Another shot. We looked up. This time the harpoon didn't disappear into the clouds but followed a low trajectory and hit the waves just to the right of the raft.

"Come on, Jim!" I handed my gun to the Chinese and jumped overboard.

We had to find the harpoon while the flare was still burning. The waves carried me off but Jim, born by the sea, proved to be an excellent swimmer. He grabbed my hand and chopped the air pointing where to go. Holding onto each other, we swam toward the blurred spot of light.

I dreaded it would go out before we reached it, but that didn't happen. Jim grabbed the container and turned on his back, clutching it to his chest. I caught hold of the collar of his vest and pulled him along.

The raft rode high on a tall wave. Wong and Georgie worked their paddles trying to bring it as close to us as possible. The flare went out while the raft dived deep into an eddy. I struck out with my legs steering with my free arm.

"Mark, Oakum! You there?" Grunt's voice came from my right.

"Over here!" I yelled and got a mouthful of water.

Another wave rolled onto us. A paddle hit my shoulder. I stuck out my arm, but my fingers grabbed at nothing and we were dragged under the raft. I prayed the kid didn't let go of the container. For a moment, all sounds disappeared - no ocean, no waves and no thunder. Then the top of my head scraped the bottom of the raft, again and again. Once we resurfaced, I grabbed at the rope strung along the floats and yelled,

"Get us out!"

Strong hands grasped my shoulders and dragged me out of the water. I didn't let go of the collar of Jim's vest. In a few seconds, we flipped over the float and collapsed on the bottom of the raft.

Georgie took the container from Jim: a smooth thick cylinder welded to a long chrome harpoon with three locking rings and a winch rope fed through one of them. The crane operator unscrewed the cylinder top and produced rolled-up harnesses fitted with spring hooks. He tore off the strings and unfolded the slings like paper streamers. Then he looked up.

"What now?" I said when I saw the expression on his face.

"Only three!"

I snatched the container from the crane operator and gave it a shake. A signal cartridge rolled out.

"Have you used a harness before? Cut the rope off the floats and tie it together to make another harness. Jim - help him!"

I pulled out the machete, handed it to Georgie and started checking the package. When I undid one of the hooks and lay the straps out in front of me, they formed a primitive harness. Easier than a parachute. I pushed the container toward Wong,

"D'you know how to put it on?"

The raft lurched. Georgie screamed as his head plunged underwater. Jim grabbed his legs and pulled him back on board.

"Move it," I ordered.

The crane operator pitched Jim a length of rope and leaned overboard to cut some more. The Chinese picked up a strap, threw it across his back and clipped the hooks close.

"Wladas," I turned to him, "spread your arms wide."

The neurotech was pale, his lips shaking, panic in his eyes. I forced his elbows higher and threw the harness over his shoulders. The straps lashed across his shoulder blades. I fastened the hooks on his chest and pressed him to the float. "Stay put!"

He nodded looking past me at the waves. I grabbed the third strap and turned to Grunt, "Raise your hands!"

When he locked his fingers on his head, I fed the straps under his arms and clipped the hooks. I straightened a twisted shoulder strap, reached for the harpoon and attached Grunt to one of the three lock rings.

"Got the straps?" I turned to Jim.

"Here," he spread out two lengths of rope tied together to form a makeshift harness. Another one was already fitted across his chest. Next to him sat Georgie, the machete on his lap, finishing yet another harness.

"Hook me up," I leaned toward Jim and spread my arms wide. He did it in seconds and pulled at the knot testing it.

"All done!"

I took the machete and the signal cartridge and checked the others. Wong, Grunt and Wladas sat still, already hooked up to the chrome harpoon. The Chinese straightened the rescue rope that hung overboard.

"Georgie, hook yourself up to the captain. I'm with Wladas, Jim with-"

Wong grabbed the youngster's shoulders, pulled himself close and clasped the boy's chest knot with his own hook. I did the same with Wladas. Georgie and the captain took quite a while.

When they were finished, I raised my hand with the signal cartridge and unscrewed the base. The lanyard dropped into my hand. I pulled it.

A snap. Hissing, a splash of white light headed for the low clouds.

"Hold on!" I managed. The rescue rope jerked out of the water, drew tight and pulled the raft toward the shore.

The waves foamed, the thunderstorm raged overhead, bolts of lightning ripping through the dark. One or two hit the ocean piercing the water far from the raft which bobbed about on the waves. Every now and then its bottom slammed the water with a heart-stopping jolt before jumping up in the air again.

We approached the rocky shore at neck-breaking speed. As the raft jumped again, a bolt of lightning illuminated the reversing truck by the cliff and the men inside. The tripod was nowhere to be seen, and the rescue rope disappeared inside the truck.

The raft dived and Wladas screamed in my ear. For a moment, we soared over the waves - but already without our little vessel. I tried to draw my knees up to my chest. Too late. We hit the surface, jumped out and smashed back down again, drawn deep under water.

We could unhook ourselves at any moment. No need to panic. The steel rescue rope wouldn't have broken just like that. More likely, the truck driver had slowed down to make sure that the frantic jolting didn't break every bone in our bodies.

Gradually, we were forced out of the water and dragged along the slowly arching shore. The sound of the truck engine broke through the battering surf. The truck drove along the shore westward where the setting sun pierced through the thunderclouds painting the sea orange.

My muscles cramped with exertion. My body had turned into one smarting bruise. When I decided that the driver had apparently taken us on a scenic route around the Continent, the vehicle stopped. Here the shore was as steep as ever, but a strip of sandy ridge showed in the water between two cliffs.

Our rescuers were shouting something, but I couldn't understand a word. Another flare descended and hit the sand illuminating the ridge's outline with a panoply of sparks.

"Get out!" Georgie yelled, spitting out brine. "That way!"

He slapped the water pointing at the shore. The rescue rope drew tight but not as tight as before. I looked up. Three men by the cliff edge were heaving the rope in, pulling us closer to the shore where the surf was weaker.

We dangled on the rope like dead fish unable to wriggle off their hooks. If we didn't get up and walk, the surf would smash us against the cliffs, too close to each other for comfort.

"Hold-" I choked on a mouthful of brine, coughed and croaked, "Hold hands!"

The men on the cliff pulled the rope harder.

"We're coming out!"

They pulled the rescue rope hard, dragging us out of the water. Then the line slackened. The shore loomed close as they let go of the rope and we all collapsed on the sand.

My hands refused to move as I unclasped myself from Wladas. I turned over onto my back and stared into the dark sky.

"Hey!" I heard from above. "Hello?"

Georgie swore and explained,

"These are McLean's men, may clones screw their asses."

"Which means?" I scrambled to my knees.

Wong sat cross-legged next to a squatting Jim. A bit further, the captain rubbed his eyes spitting out wet sand.

Wladas lay face down. I reached to check on him when he stirred and turned onto all fours, shaking his head.

"What was that about McLean's men?" I asked Georgie.

"They'll present us with a bill now," he answered enigmatically and forced himself onto his feet looking up. "That's why they dragged us out."

I rose, too. "Tell me. But be quick."

"Nothing to tell, really. This clone's ass McLean chartered us to take a seaweed shipment to the fort. Not for the record, you understand. That we did, but we also took a return shipment."

"Also for McLean?"

"Worse. It was for the riggers. And they'd already paid for the delivery. In gold. Now the ferry has sunk and all their equipment with it."

"In gold?" I stared at Georgie, not quite believing it. "I thought Pangea had no mineral resources of its own?"

"It hasn't," the captain spoke without taking his eyes off the cliffs. "The gold was jumped from the Earth. Remember the Arctic goldmines transport caught in the jump? Well, surprise surprise, it ended up here. Pointless trying to retrieve the gold as it would cost more to jump it back. So the locals use it to mint our money."

Grunt waved at where the Continent lay to the north. "It's a long irrelevant story," he glanced at Georgie. "But

---

to cut it short, McLean is not in a good mood. He's the one responsible for the delivery of the shipment to the riggers. Our cargo has gone down and we haven't. So he must have sent those there raiders."

"Some of the fishermen must have seen the ferry sink," the crane operator added. "He had plenty of time to get back to New Pang and tell McLean the story."

From the cliffs above, someone shouted in English ordering us to hook up to the rope two at a time.

"Yeah, I got the idea," I watched Wong attach Wladas to the rope. "You've got a lot of answers to find, first to McLean and then to the riggers. Grunt, you go with Wladas. Wong and Jim, second. We..." I glanced at the crane operator staring at the cliffs and the armed men overseeing our ascent, "Georgie and I will go last."

The Chinese motioned to Grunt who struggled onto his feet. Wong attached his hook to a lock ring and waved to the goons overhead.

"Heave up!" I shouted back and added in a low voice,

"Do they understand Russian?"

"Everybody does," Georgie grumbled. "Even in New Pang they speak it better than we do, and New Pang is McLean's stomping ground."

The rain stopped abruptly. Just a moment ago, billions of raindrops had been hitting the earth around us, and now they were all gone, their pattering subsiding, the roar of the surf behind growing closer and louder.

I raised my head to look back at the ocean. The storm clouds dispersed and melted as I watched. I could already make out the outline of the jumpgate base, its wall bristling with square radio telescope dishes. I had a sick feeling I'd seen it all before from this particular angle, as if watching my own life from the sidelines.

"New Pang is the city on the west coast, right?" I asked.

"It is," Georgie spat onto the sand watching Grunt and Wladas being hoisted up the cliff slope.

"How about an Old Pang? Logically, there should be-"

"No such thing. Not much worth mentioning, rather. Just some ruins."

Georgie squatted, stuck a finger into the sand and drew the Continent's outline and a double-ended arrow pointing north and south. He looked up at me.

"Where are we now?" I squatted next to him.

Georgie drew a horizontal line across the picture. "Equator," he explained and pointed at the south west corner. "We're here."

Something snapped in my head again, and the map of Continent Anomalous lit up before my eyes overlapping the crane operator's clumsy drawing. His finger moved north east.

"Nothing but mountains further up," he said. "This is swamp," he drew an ellipse, made a hole in the sand next to it and said, "And this is the City of Forecomers."

"What city?"

"No one really knows," we rose and he started shaking the sand off his hands. "Just a name for some poor devils that used to inhabit Pangea before us ages ago. So they built those structures to live in. We've tried to settle there... didn't work."

"What, nobody there at all now?"

"Only some farmers but they're much further south, closer to the river. They wouldn't go near the ruins."

"Because of the swamps," I suggested comparing Information's facts. But he didn't hear me, glancing upward and shifting his feet.

"What can we do about McLean's men?" I asked as Jim and Wong hooked themselves up and started ascending. "What weaponry might they have?"

"Shotguns and handguns, that's for sure," Georgie grumbled. "Let me think... Sometimes they carry heavy carbines and machine guns but that's normally when they go to the plains. Good for fighting off tigers."

"Come on, then," I drew the machete and walked toward the foot of the cliff foot where the rope dangled.

"You surely don't mean you're gonna fight them?"

"I might," I caught the end of the rope, "unless you have any other suggestions."

Georgie approached and clipped his hook to the rope without saying a word.

"They wouldn't start with strangers, right?" I said. "They can tell by our clothes we're new so they'll leave us till last."

He nodded.

"As for you," I hooked myself up to the rope hearing some heavy-duty bumping and swearing overhead, "they'll probably deal with you first before taking you to McLean."

"Deal with us! Beat us to pulp, more like. They've already started, can't you hear? So what do you suggest?"

"Haul us up!" I shouted and added in a low voice. "Don't do anything without my signal."

When we were about ten feet away from the surface, I heard a female voice overhead. Georgie swore under his breath.

"Who is it?" I whispered.

"Kathy. She's French," he stared at the three human shapes looming on the cliff edge. "She's a real bitch from hell, this one. Killed three clones with her bare hands once."

The raiders grabbed our shoulders, jerked us close to the edge and dragged us up. The men took my machete and shoved me toward Wladas and the Chinese who stood aside. Then they knocked Georgie in the teeth sending him flying to the ground to join Jim and the captain. A burly African stooped over Grunt spitting curses in his smashed-up face, his bloodshot eyes glistening, his long strong fingers squeezing the captain's chin. He had to be the squad's leader.

Three other raiders surrounded the ferry crew watching their chief. One swarthy with a scar across his cheek and angry vivid eyes. The second one stood sideways from me offering a glimpse of his straight nose and oily hair done up in a ponytail that is so handy to grab at in a fight. Opposite them stood the squat Kathy, her hair cropped close.

I approximated their combat potential as four and a half, knocking off half a score for not taking us seriously, which they should. I squinted at the truck. Inside, a red-haired raider fiddled with the tripod, oblivious to the world. The driver, grim and broad-faced, chilled out in the cab with his feet on the running board and one hand on the door, puffing on a cig. Six men in total, counting the female. Six of us... having said that, Wladas didn't count as much.

Apart from the driver, all the raiders had pump-action shotguns. All wore faded tank tops over combat pants with holsters and ammo belts, and muddy combat boots. Raindrops glistened on their bronzed bulging muscles, including Kathy who stared at the ferry crew grinning and playing with my machete.

"Wong," I whispered praying he understood Russian,

"I'll take the leader and the girl. The two on the left are yours."

Wladas groaned. The Chinese didn't move. I had no idea whether he'd heard me.

"We'll knock them out and deal with the rest. Wladas, you stay aside. Don't get involved. Just wait." I nodded to Wong, and he darted off.

Simultaneously, Georgie kicked the approaching Kathy in the leg but then collapsed, knocked down by the African. That gave me enough time to bash the leader across his kidneys and follow up by a knee in his groin. Kathy moved toward me raising my machete but doubled up, stopped with a well-aimed kick in the guts. The blade fell from her hand. Georgie behind her kicked her in the ass and jumped on top of her, forcing her onto the ground and pounding her ribs.

By then Wong had knocked the swarthy raider down with two short blows, avoided the other one's punches and slid behind his back, grabbing his ponytail and aiming his elbow at the small of the raider's back. The man screamed while the Chinese rushed to the truck.

The vehicle reminded me of an antique Studebaker with its rusty corrugated cab, three axles and high trailer sides. The Chinese did it by the book. First thing, he forced out the driver choking on his cigarette. Then he jumped into the truck. The red-haired raider raised his gun and wailed as his elbow joints were snapped. Immediately, Wong got hold of the gun.

I leaned over the African, snatched his shotgun, then undid his ammo belt and threw it over my shoulder. He wheezed trying to move and I had to pistol-whip him to calm him down again.

"Georgie, let the girl go! Pick up their guns. Jim - tie

them down," I turned round. "Wladas, help Grunt up. Then get into the truck, both of you. Move it!"

I jumped onto the running board and checked the cab and the truck. Wong sat on a truck bench smiling, the gun butt resting against his thigh, his foot pressing between the red-haired raider's shoulder blades.

Jim squatted next to Kathy, now free from Georgie's grasp, and started tying her hands behind her back.

"Where did you get the rope, man?" I jumped down.

"In the cab," he drew the ends tight with a square knot and moved over to the African.

Georgie removed the raiders' guns and holsters and threw them into the truck to Grunt and Wladas. Then he started searching the raiders' pockets wiping blood off his smashed-up lips. I wanted to stop him but reconsidered. One of McLean's men could have had a knife or a blowpipe. If they wriggled free and used them...

I glanced at their combat boots, then to my own disposable footwear.

"Wong? Come here!" I started removing my shoes. When the Chinese approached, I motioned him toward Kathy, "You two are about the same size."

The smile never leaving his lips, the Chinese straddled the French girl's back and started removing her clothes. Already conscious, she cussed in English, rolling her eyes and calling us cretins and motherfuckers. She must have thought we wanted to rape her as she struggled under Wong's weight. I failed to notice him punch her as the girl jerked and quieted down.

By then the African had come around again and showered us with all sorts of Russian expletives. It sounded strange coming from a foreigner. The red-haired raider groaned in the truck.

"Do shut them up, will ya?" I said as I stripped two more raiders to equip Wladas and myself. By then, Jim had strapped and gagged the rest. He unearthed an ancient first-aid kit from the depths of the cab clinking bottles and vials in the truck as he tended to Grunt's sores and scratches.

Opposite them on the bench Wladas sat in his prison clothes.

"What're you waiting for?" I asked him.

He startled and began pulling on some pants. I turned to Georgie who was rummaging through our trophies in the back of the truck.

"What have we got left?"

"Three twelve-gauge semi auto Remingtons with loads of ammo," he pointed at the guns and the ammo belts confiscated from the raiders. "Three eight-round Colts and a non-recoil mounting," Georgie nodded at the tripod on the cliff by the cab. The Chinese had already climbed the roof of the cab and surveyed the area through a pair of the raiders' field glasses. We had to go before it got dark.

"Have you found the gun itself?"

"Sure," he patted an under-seat box to his left. "The gun's here and the shells in the box opposite."

"Now. We'll leave the raiders here and go to town. How far is it?"

"About thirty miles," Georgie winced and felt the growing bruise on his swollen cheekbone.

"That far?"

He shrugged. "We'll have to follow the coastline. Can't make it any shorter because of the rocks. It's quite a detour."

"Get in the cab with me. You can show me the way."

We closed the truck's back flap. Soon the vehicle rolled along the cliff drop leaving the tied-up raiders behind.

* * *

The night closed in fast. The stars crowded the sky clustering into strange constellations. To the left of the drop, the black ocean loomed, jagged rocks gaping under the headlights. Waves smashed against the boulders and dissipated in clouds of silvery dust and foam.

"It's been two hours," I glanced at a large alarm clock welded to the dashboard. "How much further is it?"

"Not far," Georgie to my right mumbled, half asleep.

I could use a few Zs myself. All the stress and exhaustion started to show. Had I still had my implants installed, I'd have thought nothing of it. They could keep you awake for seventy-two hours.

"You shouldn't have left them the knife," Georgie grumbled.

"Do change the record."

The crane operator rubbed his face, patted his cheeks and winced at his injuries.

"Why should I? It would have been better to have used the gun on them. Now Kathy and Fumba will bend over backward to hunt us down."

Apparently, Fumba was the African's name. According to Georgie, he used to be a clones' slave driver at an opium plantation back in Africa until he headed a revolt against the local authorities and consequently was deported to Pangea.

The track in front of us inched uphill. I dropped it into second. The truck roared and struggled to climb the steep slope.

"In order to hunt us down," I spoke, "they need to get back to town first."

"Did it ever occur to you that McLean will look for them?"

"His best team?" I pushed the gas pedal to the floor. The engine growled good and loud, pebbles hammering our undercarriage. "It did. But not now. Not for another day."

"McLean will go apeshit. He cares for his men. Then there's the truck and the guns. I suggest we split."

I shrugged. "As you wish."

The Studebaker cleared the ridge. Far below lay a bay flooded with light. I stopped, opened the door and stepped onto the running board.

"Nearly there," Georgie got out his side.

Grunt's voice called from the truck, "See the beacon?"

He pointed west to a single black cliff in the sea. On its summit stood a spiraling pillar, thin and incredibly tall. Its end throbbed with a bright white light.

"What's the source of the light?" Wladas said.

Wong jumped on top of the cab and raised his field glasses. We kept looking at the beacon. This was no human work. The shape was like nothing on Earth.

"Did the Forecomers build it?" I asked.

The next moment, I nearly fell off the running board and grabbed at the open door, squatting, my eyes shut. My head exploded. I could see New Pang's filthy side streets, sewage ditches running along the squat slums made of planks and clay brick... Then I saw clearly a two-story building, its first floor high with slotted shutters; the second floor small with tiny windows glazed with a kind of cloudy film. Music and voices came from inside. A shop sign hung above the door - I knew that it pictured an open seashell with a flame inside. A lopsided inscription read-

I couldn't remember what it read. I knew the house was a hotel, probably the biggest in the whole town.

But how the hell did I know it? Had I been in New Pang before?

Had I been on Pangea?

The thought knocked me senseless. Impossible. I couldn't have known the place from before.

Now I knew it. I had to get to town. Straight to the hotel, immediately.

I glanced at Georgie, stood up and got back into the cab. I slumped in my seat clutching at the steering wheel. My hands shook. My decision to go to the hotel kept growing, as if the sight of the nightlit city had triggered a preinstalled code, very much like that Information software.

Preinstalled by whom? Who had downloaded the Information program and my memory of this place?

"Where d'you think we can stay?" I asked Georgie, by then back in his seat. "Any hotels in New Pang?

Grunt heard my question and popped his head through the door.

"There're a couple but we can't afford them. Rita's, for one..."

"Who's Rita?"

"The owner of the Seashell."

The red letters on the shop sign flashed before my eyes. That was it. I had to get inside this Seashell place. So apparently, my visions made sense. I didn't take my eyes off the cluster of far-away windows glowing on top of the cliff. At a distance, the houses looked clean and tidy. Wish that they were... I knew the place. The Filthy Slums, the hotbed of a recent plague epidemic that had ravaged New Pang taking out two-thirds of its population.

Now it was my own memory, not Information. The city had no sewage system, and the locals poured their waste into ditches that traced the slopes opening into the ocean. On a calm day the stench in the bay made one reach for a gas mask.

"What do you use for money? Can you show me?"

Grunt exchanged glances with Georgie who searched his pockets and placed a coin under the windshield, dull and yellow with a large 5 on it.

"Five rubles," he explained. "Riggers mint'em, fucking gangsters. They own whatever gold there is. Never mind. This should be enough for a night," he shook his head. "Then you should run before McLean finds you."

The ease with which he'd parted with the coin could be explained by the fact that he'd expropriated it from the raiders. Surely he'd found more in their pockets.

"Mark, what's he saying?" Wladas climbed over the side of the truck jumping off.

"Our friends from the barge will go their way. We'll go ours," I hung out of the cab. "Wladas, Wong, it's up to you. You can go with them if you wish."

The Chinese glanced at me and went on studying the shore through his field glasses.

Grunt and Jim slung the guns across their backs and prepared to jump down.

"Well, Mark," the captain leaned across the side of the truck and stuck out his hand. "Nice meeting you, man," I shook his hand and he jumped down.

"We'll go by the river," Grunt adjusted the holster on his belt. "We've got no business in the city tonight, that's for sure."

"Wladas?" I said. "What have you decided?"

He looked aside. I nodded to the sailors and shut the cab door.

"If you really need to go to that hotel," Georgie spoke, "take a right from the fork under the hill and keep driving. Make sure you keep your back to the beacon. When you enter Broadway - that's the biggest street in town - go three blocks and look out for a two-story house to your left. You'll see the shop sign."

He opened the cab door.

"Well, nice meeting you." He wanted to add something but reconsidered and slunk off.

I sat up glancing into the side mirror as Wladas climbed back into the truck. I started up, shifted into third, gunned the engine and rolled downhill toward a nightlit New Pang.

CHAPTER FIVE
THE TRIGGER CODE

THE TRUCK rattled down a dark lane and rolled out onto an intersection with its back to the bay and the beacon. The streets were dug up in places. Lengths of water pipes heaped up along trenches snaking past sandstone walls and squat houses.

It looked as if the town had embarked on some large-scale renovations - most likely, building a water pipeline. I was forced to take a detour to bypass more dugouts and finally reached the main street after ten more minutes of driving around, guided by the beacon.

I glanced into the back window. Wong and Wladas sat on the bench on the truck's right-hand side keeping an eye on the road.

The truck droned past the houses. The Broadway lamplights emitted the same white glow as the beacon. Could be some gas or special liquid but it could also be the mixture of some weird local tree saps or something discovered by local tinkerers. I vaguely remembered something about the rainforest stretching between New

Pang's eastern borders and the desert: I thought I'd heard of one or two local plants suitable for that purpose. But my memory refused to help, and Information wouldn't oblige, eighet.

As Georgie had said, Broadway was indeed broad and paved with stone, sloping gently upward away from the sea, and wide enough for three trucks like ours to pass each other leaving enough space for pedestrians. No trenches there.

I steered toward a two-story house at the end of the block, with brightly lit windows and a red sign over the front door. I drove past it and stopped in front of the next house, then reconsidered and backed up, parking the truck in a tiny side street by the wall of the Sea Pearl. I killed the engine and heard a bunch of drunken voices bellowing the old Russian anthem - something about the unbreakable union of freeborn republics. I got out and with a quick "Come on, then" headed for the front door.

I couldn't have cared less about the drinkers. All I wanted was to get inside. One hand already on the door handle, I looked up at the bright letters of the hotel sign. My eyes stung; I blinked. Something went off in my head again - it felt as if the memory chip, removed before the trial, woke up and started testing neuro chains. I almost expected to see a 3D model of my nervous system. Then the illusion faded. The hollering inside grew louder coming from the bar in the right wing of the first floor. I pushed the door and walked along a hallway leading to a brightly lit room. No vacant tables; faces blurred behind blue clouds of tobacco smoke. I walked past. The other two followed me in silence.

At the end of the hallway I discovered two doors and a staircase. One door, scratched and padlocked, seemed to open into a utility room. I walked past it and reached for the next door - fancy and carved with a chest-high sea shell design. Wong took the steps to the next floor, bent over the rails and nodded. Wladas in the hallway shifted his feet, nervous. He had no weapon: the Chinese upstairs had both guns, one across his back and the other training everywhere. I had the spare handgun. I pushed the door and walked in.

I had no idea why I did so. It must have been a knee-jerk reaction. There was a lamplit desk by the back wall; to its right, rows of shelves housed large clay pitchers, their mouths tied with pieces of clean muslin and sealed with seal-wax. Had to be the establishment's stock of liquor. On top of the shelves stood figurines made of stone, wood and even glass.

A ladder leaned against the shelves. On it stood a tall woman in a floor-length dress: her black hair in a bun, her face in the shadows.

"What do you want?" she said in a low voice hoarse with agitation. "I've paid up already. McLean promised me that-"

She reached for a fat figurine which looked much like a piggy bank and turned to the light. "I thought we'd discussed everything. He did promise that-" She froze, breathless. Her large dark eyes glinted with fear on a broad face.

I closed the door behind me, walked to the desk and looked around. To my left was a bare wall. A derelict strong box stood behind the door opposite a wooden cabinet. Next to it, window curtains were open a crack.

I walked around the desk to the window and looked out. The Studebaker stood at arm's reach. She must have seen it and mistaken us for McLean's raiders. So now she went up the ladder to get her piggy bank...

The woman stood on the ladder, figurine in hand, staring at me without blinking.

"I need a room for three," I said in a low voice. "For one night."

I took out the fiver and dropped it onto the desk. The woman's face relaxed. She looked away, blinking, and very nearly fell down the ladder. I caught her, one arm under hers and the other round her waist, and helped her to her feet.

She recoiled, then pulled herself up. Clenching the figurine she squeezed herself between me and the desk, rearranging the front of her dress. She sat up onto a stool and raised an already businesslike face.

She had to be just over forty. Puffy eyelids, crowfeet, her eyes tired and disillusioned. It was as if she wanted to get rid of me but couldn't, so she put on a stern face waiting for me to speak.

"So what about that room?" I said.

She studied me, her hands on the desk.

"And?" I was losing patience. I was hungry and sleepy, in reverse order. "I can take my custom elsewhere!"

A thought struck me. This woman didn't have to be the owner. She was no Rita.

"A ruble per head," she finally said. "Dinner in the room?"

I nodded. She opened a drawer and brushed the coin into it in a practiced motion.

"Dinner is two rubles," she handed me a room key with a white ball on the key ring.

The white ball - which had to symbolize a pearl - bore a large number 3 and felt like a piece of plastic.

"Go up to the top floor. Ask-" she shook her head

and glanced in the window. "No. I'll take you there."

She took the key and rose from the desk. I stepped aside letting her pass. Once she turned her back to me, I said,

"Rita."

"Yes?" she turned cocking a brow.

"Let's go, then," I stepped aside and opened the door for her.

She paused, then walked out into the hallway. She glanced at the Chinese bristling with guns, acknowledged Wladas' tired smile with a nod and walked upstairs.

On the top floor, a narrow hallway led to both sides from the stairs. The weak odor of beeswax and herbs hung in the air. Some sort of fluffy mat covered the floor dampening our footsteps. The woman turned right and walked past the row of doors to a dimly-lit counter at the back.

"Claudie," she called out as she walked. "You can't be sleeping, surely? How many times do I need to tell you..."

A cute sleepy face showed from behind the counter. A girl jumped up, her expression clouding with fear, and started mumbling apologies.

"How on earth can you sleep with all that racket downstairs?"

I could see the owner wasn't angry, just keeping up appearances in front of a client. The anthem-bawling voices ceased. I could catch a few words.

"We've got new guests. Is the water tank full in room three?"

"Yes, Madame," Claudie tucked in a few loose hairs away from her face, rearranged her homespun frock and looked up at the owner. "Uncle Vanya filled it today as soon as the room was vacated. It's cleaned and the sheets have been changed," the girl said in her melodious high-pitched voice it as she glanced at us with a smile.

"Oh well," the owner turned and handed me the key. "Make yourself at home."

Her hand on the key lingered. "Get them their dinner now."

"Yes, Madame," the girl jumped up and hurried to the stairs.

Rita gave us another studious look and walked away without saying a word. I waited for her steps to die away, then unlocked the door.

The room had three beds lined up against one wall, each with a bedside cabinet. Above one of the beds, the filmy pane of a tiny window let in the weak glow of a streetlight. To the right of the door, one corner was partitioned off with a plastic curtain. I pulled it aside: it was a shower, or rather a rusty water tank under the ceiling, with a bent shower head and a faucet. Plus a few slivers of soap on a shelf, three white towels on a rack and a drainage grate on the floor.

"And what do they do when they need to take a-" Wladas started and stopped when I turned round. "No more questions," he waved me off. "Outdoor plumbing, I suppose. I'll hold it."

"You sure you can?"

He shrugged and mumbled it could wait till morning, then stretched out on the bed under the window.

Wong pulled off his shotgun and sat on the bed to the left of the door. He inspected the bedside cabinet, took off what looked suspiciously like an old-fashioned oil lamp and started studying it. I had a look around. The walls were lined with laminate panels. The same kind of fluffy matting covered the floor. You could barely hear what was going on downstairs.

Someone knocked. The Chinese placed the lamp back and took up his gun. Wladas sat up. I lay one hand on the gun under my belt and opened the door.

"Dinner," the voice chanted on the doorstep. The drunken patrons downstairs started a new song.

The girl walked in holding a tray with two pitchers, three mugs and three platefuls of food.

"Why are you sitting here in the dark?" she looked around.

"Actually..." Wladas rose. Claudie shoved the tray at him and crouched by Wong's bed with her back to me. The Chinese watched as she fiddled with the lamp on the cabinet. In a second, something clinked. The room filled with a soft white glow.

Wong passed me a meaningful look and gave the girl a wink.

"Thanks a lot, Claudie," I nodded at the door. "I hope for some peace and quiet till morning."

"Depend upon it," the girl left the room. In the hallway, she turned around and added, "If you need anything, I'll be at my desk."

"And if you're not?"

"Ask Uncle Vanya."

"Which is who?"

"He's got a beard like this big. He fills in for me."

"Will do," I locked the door and walked to the last vacant bed. Wladas kept standing, tray in hand, staring at the lamp.

"What're you standing here for?" I leaned the shotgun against the backrest, shoved the pistol under the pillow and started unlacing my boots. "Time for some grub, a shower and some shut-eye."

"Time to be making some plans," Wladas placed the tray onto his bedside table and brought two of the plates to Wong and me. "We need to decide what to do next. Don't you think?"

"Let's eat first," I reached to my plate for a greenish fruit that looked a lot like an unripe plum. "That's not too bad," I mumbled munching it whole. "Tastes nice."

Wong nodded, smiling, and attacked his dinner.

I placed the plate on top of the cabinet, kicked my boots off, peeled off the tank top and my pants, threw the belt and the holster onto the bed and headed for the shower. I needed to have a think. Lots of things to discuss, many of which my new friends had no business knowing.

The warm shower left a metallic taste in my mouth. I lifted my face to the weak jet thinking of everything that had happened at the jump base, of the Information in my head, of the silent Chinese and my strange urge to head for the Sea Pearl.

Now why would I come here? Why the hurry? I shook my head, ran a hand against my outgrown crew cut, picked up a sliver of soap and started to rub my neck, chest and stomach washing off all the sweat and brine.

Rita's stare, her hesitation... she seemed to question my actions.

I rinsed off the soap and closed the tap. Wiped my face with one of the towels on the hooks. I lingered staring at the shower curtain before me. Wladas was a chartered neurotech. He had to understand military mnemotechnics as well as I did guns. He had to know all about the latest research developments. About brain-installed wetware. Wouldn't be a bad thing asking him. But how would I begin?

I wrapped the towel around my hips and headed back to my bed.

"Is it edible?"

Wladas took a large swig from the pitcher,

"You could say that! Consider yourself lucky we didn't demolish your plate."

The Chinese removed his clothes and walked into the shower.

"Here," Wladas went on, "try their fruit juice. Or energy drink, whatever." He filled a mug and reached it out to me without getting up, "Have a taste. It's a bit tart but really clears one's head. Great stuff."

I lifted the mug catching a whiff of oranges and took a large swig. I concentrated. My belly lurched and started rumbling, and that was that.

"So," Wladas nodded at the mug, "how does it feel?"

I took another swig, returned the mug to the cabinet and shrugged.

"Good enough." With that, I attacked my plate.

The shower curtain rustled and the water started gurgling. Wong whistled a cheerful quiet tune. If I needed to speak to Wladas, I had to do it now while the Chinese couldn't hear.

"Feeling better?" I asked him munching on a handful of bilberry-type fruit.

"Actually..." the neurotech paused, "no, I'm all right."

He turned to the window, then sat up. "No. I'm not all right. I mean, I don't know what to think. Too many things have happened." Wladas groped the air in front of him. "My head is a mess. But overall, I'm fine. I really am."

I lifted my face and shoveled the remaining berries into my mouth. "I need to ask you a few questions," I said with a full mouth and washed the food down with my drink. "You might find them a bit out of the ordinary."

"In our situation, any question would sound out of the ordinary. We're-"

I raised my hand forcing him to stop. "Wait till I ask."

The Chinese stopped whistling and said something quick. Then he started up the tune again.

Wladas and I looked at his wet brown feet beneath the shower curtain.

"He's weird," the neurotech said.

"It's not about him I want to ask you," I turned to Wladas. "What do you know about memory implants? And downloadable wetware? Only the latest research, please. Come on, I'm listening."

Wladas placed his elbows onto his knees and locked his fingers.

"Go ahead, spill. What's the purpose of such implants and the possible size of downloadable files? Can you give me the figures?"

His complexion darkened, eyes glistened with agitation. He didn't look at ease with my questions. "Why would you need them?"

I raised my hand again. "Just answer my question, okay? I mean the Feds' research where they decided to use chemicals instead of memory chips."

"Urban legends," Wladas unlocked his fingers and shook his head. "To download a file into a brain, you need a memory chip. You know that as well as I do."

I nodded. "I do. But imagine an information file installed into one's brain via a memory chip. Then they remove the chip. Is it possible?"

"Well, theoretically..." Wladas looked up at the ceiling, thinking. "Everything's possible. But," he shook his head again, "but that's theory. The Feds haven't made much headway on the army in this respect. I do know they experimented with chemicals. But experimentation is one thing, and getting results is something totally-"

"Who did you work for? The Feds or the army? What did you do back on Earth? Tell me."

Wladas sighed and stared at the floor. I looked at the shower curtain. Soapy water ran down Wong's legs. He'd nearly finished washing while I hadn't gotten anywhere with my questions.

"I used to be deputy head of one of the General Staff's laboratories," Wladas spoke in a hollow voice, staring blankly. Blood had left his face. "I served in Sector B."

He looked up at me. I raised my eyebrows.

"You should know it controls the ground forces," Wladas looked down again.

Holy shit. I was talking to a man privy to the country's top classified crap. People like him were the backbone of our defense. What idiot was responsible for sending him down here? Sector B, for chrissakes... I had another look at the neurotech. He was still staring into the distance, his sallow face frozen. Not good. Our conversation had taken a bad turn.

The faucet screeched. The shower curtain rustled. Wong walked back to his bed, lay the shotgun across his lap and began to dismantle it.

"So you were responsible for the top brass' brains," I ventured. "Why are you here, then?"

Wladas took a deep breath, rubbed his face and let the air out. "I..." he scratched his hollow cheek with a thumb, "I was found guilty of grave negligence. The investigation confirmed multimillion ruble losses that had undermined our defense..."

"Which is what?" I interrupted him. "Can you tell me in two words?"

"Just a bad supplier I signed up. Should have read the fine print. So - here I am."

I was itching to ask him about the size of his cut. I was more than sure that the said supplier had then paid a nice amount into some shady overseas bank account - either Wladas', or his chief's. But I refrained from commenting. We all had our skeletons in the closet, otherwise we wouldn't have ended up here in the first place. But now we had to decide what to do next.

"I digress," I yawned and rubbed my eyes. I felt as if I hadn't slept for three nights at least. "How would you introduce information into one's memory so that the file unpacks at a particular moment?"

Wladas lifted a glazed stare. He wasn't good at switching subjects.

"Well, provided you have a memory chip installed..." he frowned and moved his lips. "What am I talking about? Once the chip's introduced into the brain, you set the timer. The file unpacks at the set time."

"And without a chip? Can you think of anything?"

Wong clicked the firing pin, looked into the barrel, blew into it and looked again against the lamp light.

"Well," Wladas cocked his head rubbing his chin, "there's this memory layering technique. Simply put, they program the information carrier through the chip, then introduce the trigger code. Later, when the carrier perceives the trigger code, the file unpacks in his brain."

I felt lightning-struck. But of course. I remembered the jumpgate corridor on the Base when I'd very nearly picked a fight with the now-drowned miner. I'd looked at the ceiling, and...

"Does the code have a particular shape? How is it introduced?"

"Through visual perception, or alternatively, certain memory areas can be activated by a vocal command. That's when the carrier reacts to a particular trigger word or phrase. Visually, it can be any kind of image, like a snapshot or an object of some sort."

Oh well. I closed my eyes trying to tie everything together. First, my brain had reacted to the Fort's colors on the jumpgate ceiling. That's when the Information had first come on. Then it had to be the biocyne facts - yes, that's right, it had happened when Grunt had spoken about carula, and I had reacted by remembering the trigger word, biocyne. What else? Yes, the map of the Continent, it showed up twice. Most likely, similar objects or their recognizable characteristics triggered the installed images. First it had happened when I'd seen the ocean and the Pangean coastline. The second time the map had been conjured up by Georgie's sketching the Continent's outline in the sand.

Okay, that much I now understood. Images and words activated certain memories installed in my brain. And still I must have overlooked something. There was more to it, but what?

A cartridge popped down the barrel. I instinctively forced my eyes open. Wong put aside his shotgun and reached for the other indifferently. Wladas, pitcher in hand, gave me an expectant look. I yawned and rubbed my temples. My head felt heavy. I couldn't keep my eyes open.

"And what if-" I paused, trying to locate a fleeting thought. A very important one which stayed restless at the fringes of my mind exhausted by today's events and the data overload. "What if..."

Wait. My mind scan. Had the mind scan operator detected the slightest deviation in my identity from the one in their database, they would have detained me on the spot. Most likely, they'd have sent me back to Earth for further investigation. True, the mind scan had glitched. They'd had to do it twice. But at the end of the day, it had worked.

"Wladas? And what if, say, the carrier is subjected to such identity-altering memory layering against his will? Say, if they could put him to sleep or something? Can the mind scan show he's been tampered with?"

The neurotech's grin had just a touch of condescension.

"Mind scans detect any deviation from the existing pattern. You can't fool a machine. That's why the Feds have dropped biometrics. They have no need for them anymore," Wladas grabbed the pitcher and finished the fruit drink. "Actually... Your questions are a bit off, don't you think? We wanted to discuss what to do next. And you-"

"Wait," I raised a warning finger. "And what if somebody tampers with mind scan settings..."

"Impossible," he shook his head. "You might just as well suggest paying off the entire mind scan staff. You just can't. The equipment is too complex. Every module has its own operator, plus three more doing the scan and the duty shift supervising their work."

"I see," I let the air out of my lungs. The tiredness was getting the best of me. I lay down and closed my eyes.

"Mind telling me why you need to know all this? All these mnemotech inquiries. What're you up to? Mark?"

Valdas' voice grew far and low. I wanted to look at

him but couldn't open my eyelids. I couldn't even move my hand.

"It's n-nothing," I managed. "To- morrow... we'll see... where to go... Wong-"

I heard a rustle. I sensed the Chinese coming near me.

"Try to get... some rest. Tonight we're safe..."

Hundreds of bright dots appeared before my shut eyes. My mind collapsed into a void and rushed toward a brilliant kaleidoscope of shapes and stripes. The last thing I saw was the hotel sign. The glowing lettering loomed close and took over my brain. The light grew unbearably bright before it went out.

I had no idea what was going on but suddenly I knew that from that moment on, everything was different. A strange voice boomed in my head, painfully familiar. Its sound calmed me down drowning me in a vortex of memories. I gave in to the flow and sank in, willingly and yieldingly.

CHAPTER SIX
NEW IDENTITY

"M ARK?" came from afar. "Mark..."
I forced my eyes open. A haze filled my vision.
"Mark!" a voice spoke clear next to me. "D'you hear me? Wake up!" Wladas' anxious voice cut through the mental fog.

Only then did I realize he was shaking me awake.

"Get up, Private! Now! Come on..."

I sat up and shook my head, trying to rid of the haze. For a moment I squeezed my eyes shut. When I reopened them, the blurred outlines around me started to take both shape and color. Wladas stood by the bed looking into my face. Behind his back, Wong's silhouette loomed by the half-open door. He was fully dressed, shotgun at the ready.

A strange disturbing sound came either through the door or through the window. I couldn't work out what was going on and what time it was.

I turned my head. Sunlight poured through the

window. I'd slept all night. The sound came from the street. Now I knew it: someone was banging at the hotel door with a gun butt yelling to be let in.

"What..." I licked my dry lips. My throat felt like a blocked drain as if the night before I'd made my way through a bottle of vodka. The downstairs banging echoed in my head. "What's going on?"

"Mark, it's those people in the street," Wladas stepped over to his bed and took a peek out of the window. "I think they're looking for us."

Wong stood by the door, cool as a rail. One shotgun was slung behind his back. The other aimed at the floor, his finger on the trigger, the lower part of the butt touching his shoulder: a practiced stance that betrayed a professional. This wasn't his first mission.

A mission! My mission... The Chinese was my partner and my cover man. I was Mark Posner, an FSA major, sent to Pangea on a confidential mission. I had to locate the researcher, Boris Neumann, and bring him back to Earth with me. I took my orders from the Federal Agency director alone. Seeing as Wong and I were now in the hotel, our penetration of the Base must have gone like clockwork: the visual triggers must have unpacked in the right progression and now the night's sleep had undone the temporary modifications done to my identity.

But the man, what's his name... Wladas, yes. What's he got to do with us?

"Mark? What do we do?" Wladas stepped toward me. "They'll break the door down in a minute."

"Wait," I waved him off.

The gesture brought my headache back. My temples throbbed. Blood flushed my face, and I felt queasy. I winced, rubbed my temples, reached under the pillow for my gun and started to dress.

The hammering of gun butts shook the whole building. I stepped over to the window swaying. Wladas grabbed my elbow and shoved me a mug.

"This should help. Try it."

My fingers shook. I upended the mug and reached to the window, setting one knee against the bed. A large backyard was bounded by a sandstone wall. A huge tank sat in the far corner - apparently, holding drinking water. Some pipework ran from the tank to the house. Next to it, a man with a shotgun guarded a water pump. Judging by his clothes, he was one of McLean's men. Two more waited by the side gate. On the other side of the wall, a Willis stood in the street - an ancient army jeep, a driver waiting in its seat. In the truck a gunner sat next to a machine gun mounted in its cradle. He leaned forward, his hairy arms crossed on the extension, puffing on a roll-up and squinting at the sun. All five men stared into the yard and did nothing. But those on Broadway kept yelling demanding to be let in. How many raiders were there?

I turned and sunk onto the bed. My head had stopped spinning but was still pounding.

"Mark," Wladas placed his hand on my shoulder. "Stop jumping up and down. Let me examine you."

He squatted and showed me his open hands. Our eyes met.

"May I? It's only to take your pulse and check for a papillary response."

'Go ahead, then."

He pulled back my eyelids, one after the other.

"Got vertigo?"

"Almost gone."

"I want you to look up and follow my finger," Wladas

started moving his index finger in front of my nose while holding my pulse. I could hear him counting to twenty. Then he stood up. "Papillary reflex almost normal, with a slightly quickened pulse. You show all the symptoms of memory release. So you were right about the chemicals, then."

It sounded like a statement.

"It's classified," I finally remembered his name and our conversation from the night before. The Feds had warned me about possible chemical withdrawals. They'd just started tampering with identity-modifying injections and I knew they could cause temporary amnesia and memory overlap. Side effects were not fully known. I had volunteered, as the situation had demanded. We needed an experienced operative to infiltrate Pangea and we couldn't sit and wait for Federal neurotechs to finish their field trials. The Agency director himself suggested my cover as an ex-army convict. He had summoned me into his office and spent three hours letting me in on the kind of secrets only a limited few would know. That's why I accepted his offer. I had no way back.

"You're going to kill me now?" Wladas gave me a grim look. "You're here on a mission," he glanced at Wong. "You both are."

"Wong? He's only a cover man," I answered. This Wladas wasn't stupid. It had taken him no time at all to put two and two together.

"I..." he leaned forward. "You... you two are going back to Earth, right? I have a family, I... I will cooperate, I'll do what you ask me to. If only you'll take me along. I won't let you down, promise. I..."

"Do shut up," I got off the bed, checked the shotgun and slung it over my shoulder.

In view of the new developments, Wladas could be useful. My withdrawal could last another twenty-four hours or even more. Besides... I looked at Wong. He could be the best fighter in the world with his six-unit combat potential. But he wouldn't be much use against cyber troopers. We needed every pair of fists available.

I turned to Wladas. The mission made provision for engaging some of the deportees in our operations, without revealing any details.

"Wong? How much time do we have?"

The Chinese took his hand from the gun and raised two fingers. A couple of minutes. Enough to rearrange my plans.

"Keep an eye on the yard," I told Wladas.

I gave it some thought and decided against entrusting him with any weapons. I couldn't verify what he'd said about his supposed family and homesickness. Thoughts were crowding my mind. Rita, the hotel owner. She must have ratted on us to McLean. I needed to see him anyway, but had planned to do it the same night and under different circumstances. Firstly, I had to meet my contact. McLean was a big fish, a player in the great game between Pangea and the Federal Security Agency. Or should I say, between the Feds and General Varlamov, the ex rebel. He'd been in charge of the Fort at the time of the coup and had had time to disappear with a handful of his supporters. The Feds had sent a squad of our best men to bring Varlamov back. None of them had returned. The general had lain low somewhere in the mountains. According to our sources, he'd used Professor Neumann for his own interests, but what those interests were, we had no idea. About two dozen men had followed Varlamov, three of which were cyber troopers. You wouldn't want to meddle with those guys. Their bodies were crammed full of combat implants, their skeletons reinforced with Teflon, titanium and bypass resistors, their neural chains modified, their brains shortwired to those of tactical autonomous combatants.

Cyber troopers were radio-controlled and supervised by the general himself. Nasty boys, worse than Pangean tigers, unless you're a cyber yourself. Or unless you happen to have a clever neurotech at hand. He'd still need special radio equipment to connect himself to their brains in order to scorch their neural chains or at least disrupt their communications. But that would be asking for too much, wouldn't it?

The racket downstairs stopped. Wong raised his shotgun and walked out into the hallway. So. My mission was to find Professor Neumann. The Chinese was the muscle man protecting the information carrier. The carrier being myself. Apart from me, the only other person who knew of the mission was the FSA director. He had supervised my identity modification personally, afraid of eventual leaks in his own office where General Varlamov could keep a mole or two. I was forbidden to engage in action unless in dire need, leaving all the dirty work to Wong. I winced. My head was splitting.

"The raiders seem to be on the move," Wladas said without taking his eyes from the window. "The driver has got out. They've picked up their guns. They're getting ready."

"Wong," I told the Chinese, "we're going out. Don't shoot."

I needed to see McLean because he was the unofficial baron of New Pang and had agreed to help the FSA. He had his informers everywhere on the Continent feeding him intelligence on the confederation of settlers who'd fled the coast during the pandemic. McLean had been the only one - apart from the clones - who'd at the time ignored the invitation to join the confederation of loggers, farmers and oil riggers. He didn't give a shit about the confederation and its laws. All he cared about was turning the city into an empire of his own. And as for the clones...

The room swam. I tried hard to remember something about the clone settlers in the mountains at the Continent's eastern edge. I couldn't. My heart pounded as I remembered the army school - an unwanted, non-existent memory, part of my cover story. I forced clone thoughts away and tried to relax and think of something else.

Wong stole down the hallway and disappeared past the wall.

"Follow him," I glanced over the room and walked out behind him.

We were the only people in the hallway. I could hear Rita's angry voice downstairs, playing a pretend game. She must have grassed us up to Tex (which was was McLean's cover name according to the Information that had just gone off in my head again) and now she was doing a decent job of sounding innocent. Now my contact would lie low, and I'd have to play it by ear when I met McLean. The worst thing was, I had no idea what exactly McLean knew about Professor Neumann.

I rummaged through my memory for the basic facts. Neumann, who'd moved to Pangea over thirty years ago, wanted to get to the truth behind the Continent's anomalies. The place hadn't yet been a prison at that time. The government had funded his research until it became clear they couldn't expect a quick return for their money.

And when rioting had gained momentum followed by the Coup of the Seven Generals, they became too busy to continue financing. Six of the conspirators had been shot; the seventh, General Varlamov, had escaped. Two years later our Continent informers became active sending contradictory messages. The FSA analysts had come to the conclusion that the insurgent general had more on his agenda than just taking control of Pangea. It looked like he'd gotten hold of something capable of changing the course of world history. Neumann had helped him, apparently. The FSA then decided to use McLean by warning him about the planned attack on New Pang. Varlamov and his clones had to-

I stumbled and grabbed at the wall. Wladas turned to support me.

Once again, my thoughts turned to jelly. The clones seemed to be the stumbling block. It was probably better not to concentrate on them for a while. The FSA specialists had warned me of the possibility of a glitch when memories merged blocking certain areas. The contact might help but now I had to forget about him too, at least for a while.

The Chinese walked down a flight of stairs. The voices subsided. I heard a rustle, followed by the clacking of gun bolts.

"Wong," I called out. "Step back."

He didn't seem to hear me. He squinted, his index finger squeezing the trigger.

"Don't," I ordered. "Come back here. Now!"

His eyes glistened. He started moving back up the steps. Another step. And another. Only then did he lower the gun.

"Wait here," I took the shotgun from my shoulder,

handed it to Wong and walked downstairs.

Bright light hit my eyes. The sun hung over the roofs opposite. Four long shadows stretched from the front door down the hallway. I had to avoid confrontation at any cost: that would mean the end of the mission. I had no idea how many men surrounded the hotel nor how many were already inside. Neither what weapons they used.

"Please don't shoot! I have a proposal for Mr. McLean!" I spread my arms wide. "Who can I talk to?"

A burly gorilla-like raider stepped forward blocking the light. Behind him in the hallway three men clutched their guns. Beside them, a scared Rita clung to the wall, a raider grasping her arm.

"Let the woman go. We're coming out. Wong, Wladas, come down!"

The gorilla approached, removed my handgun from my holster, turned me face to the wall and pulled the Colt from behind my belt.

"Well, well, well," a voice spoke from the front door. "What do we have here? Or should I say, who do we have?"

A man in a brown Stetson entered the hallway, broad-shouldered and taller than the gorilla raider. A deep scar crossed his furrowed long face. A black patch covered his left eye. His right eye, gray and unfriendly, shifted to my men descending the steps.

"Your Russian is good, McLean," I said.

The gorilla gave me a shove in the back and swore under his breath, then headed toward Wong and Wladas. McLean waited while his man searched them and removed their guns. Then he walked over to me, pushed his Stetson back and whispered in my ear,

"Actually, I half-expected you yesterday, mister..."

"Mark," I turned to him.

"Your skin is too white," he looked away at my men and whispered again, "Haven't been in the sun lately. How did you expect to-"

"I'm Mark Posner," I spoke in a firm voice. "Tell your men to let the woman go and leave the building. We don't need to attract attention."

McLean pivoted toward his men and barked a command. As they cleared out, he rearranged his hat again and said,

"Please, Mr. Posner," he made a welcoming gesture. "After you."

Was he always such a poser? Or was he just nervous? I walked past Rita and turned my head to the open bar door. Claudie and a hunched old man with a beard sat at the table - probably, the Uncle Vanya that Claudie had mentioned last night. Next to her stood another man, unshaven and squat. For some reason, I decided he had to be French with his black hair, a square chin and black eyes glistening over a Gallic nose. He reminded me of someone. Who could that be? Obeying McLean's command, the man started for the door.

I glanced over my shoulder. Tex walked behind me. My men followed, overseen by the gorilla raider bristling with guns. Frenchie trailed behind. Idiots. McLean was a cretin. Wong and I could disarm them at our leisure, and then the conversation would take a very different turn. Their buddies outside wouldn't even know what had hit them. Shame we had to keep up appearances otherwise I'd be only too happy to give Tex the third degree.

We walked out onto the street. It was crowded with people, armed and unfriendly. On both sides of the hotel, the road was blocked with truckfuls of people, their machine guns pointing in our direction. Engines purred; heated air curled over truck hoods. The truck we'd hijacked from Famba's men the night before had already been driven into the shade at the house opposite.

I stopped a few feet past the front door squinting at the sun. It was bright and too white.

"These are my boys, Mr. Posner," I heard behind my back. "They'd love to know what happened to Famba, Kathy, Muller, Kurt, Baxter and Red Johnny."

"They'll live," I turned to McLean. "Nobody's hurt. Might be here by midday."

"Fine," Tex rearranged his hat and slipped on an enormous pair of sunshades. "We'll wait till midday. In the meantime, Mr. Posner, be my guest. We'll talk about your proposal."

Now I could get a good look at him. Well-tanned, he wore a brown coat with a pale shirt and a dusty pair of cowboy boots over oilcloth pants. The only thing missing was a pair of spurs. McLean lay his hand onto the silver buckle of his wide leather belt. The hem of his coat swung to one side revealing a narrow holster with the handle of what looked like an expensive and seriously rare handgun.

How could it have got here on Pangea?

"I can see you're a connoisseur," McLean noticed my interest. He took out the gun, pushed the trigger guard with his middle finger, broke the long nickel-plated barrel and shook out a rifle cartridge. "Have a look."

He snapped the barrel shut and handed me the unloaded gun handle first.

"Go ahead, don't be shy."

I inspected the gun. It looked very much like a

Contender, but... you could tell it was a homespun job. The cocking mechanism was too tight and the weight distribution a bit off. The handle also needed some work as it lay a bit awkward in hand. Still, it must fit Tex' broad claws.

"Local job?" I looked up.

McLean nodded, took the gun and walked to one of the trucks. Someone shoved me in the shoulder advising me to move my ass and get into the truck. I looked back. Wong was smiling as he walked with his hands folded peacefully, apparently oblivious of the others. Wladas' eyes shifted. He was pale, his head and T-shirt soaking wet with sweat.

Once we got into the truck, McLean leaned sideways against the back of the cab waiting for everyone to settle on the benches. My men took their places opposite me, Gorilla and Frenchie at our sides. One of the gunners raised and locked the tailgate. The other turned his back to us and pointed his gun forward.

McLean slapped the cab roof, "Off we go!" He stretched his arm toward the bay far beyond.

"I thought you might want to do a bit of sightseeing, Mr. Posner. Unless you'd rather I call you..."

"Mark is good enough," I rose and stood up holding onto the tailgate.

The truck moved down Broadway. The city lay before us. Its size and ambition surprised me, considering this was here on Pangea unknown to man until thirty years ago, with next to no technology. Houses cascaded toward the ocean, their roofs orange to our left and blue to our right. Further by the bay, the roofs were red and green. It really helped to find one's way amid the city blocks. On every roof stood a cumbersome rainwater vessel of some description. All the houses' walls were rendered with white clay.

Deportees hadn't wasted their time here.

"Enjoy what you see," McLean said, pleased. "We'll take you across the city to the other side of the bay. We're going to show you the port and the seaweed farms - everything we've done in these past years! Very soon New Pang will have its own plumbing. Can you imagine? I'm building it. And I have no intention of leaving it to anyone!"

Tex shoved a cigar between his teeth. His fist crunched. His face darkened, his jaws moved. What a strange reaction. Shame I couldn't see his eyes. It looked as if he was scared shitless even as he spoke so he tried to replace fear with anger.

"How long will it take?" I asked.

Out of his inner pocket, McLean produced a gold-plated timepiece on a chain and flipped the lid open. "A half-hour. Why, are you in a hurry?"

I shook my head. "Not me, no."

Good. Enough time to think. I glanced back. Hotel guests and passersby had started gathering by the hotel. One of them could be my contact. Rita stood by the front door, together with Claudie and Uncle Vanya. The latter hugged Claudie's shoulders, his head cocked to one side, urging her. The girl sniffled and wiped her eyes with a handkerchief. The owner watched us leave. Some of the guests tried to ask her questions, curious about the details. Rita didn't notice them. She stood there watching the trucks disappear along Broadway.

CHAPTER SEVEN

COMRADES IN MISERY

" A CIGAR? A drink?" McLean snapped his
fingers at the steward busy by the serving table
near the verandah door. Then he turned away
while staring at the ocean.

The harbor spread below the cliffs that housed the
baron of New Pang. He lit up, sat back in a wicker
armchair by a rattan screen and rested his feet on a stool
carved from a whole piece of wood.

The steward - a mute crew-cut man of about thirty -
placed two full tumblers onto a tray, added a cigar and a
lighter and brought the tray to me.

I motioned the cigar away, took the tumbler and tasted
the amber drink. Jesus, this man had real Bourbon!

"So, what do you think?" McLean said without taking
his eyes from the ocean. "You don't get whiskey like this
on Earth any more. It's the cao fruit I get from loggers.
With its juice we make excellent whiskey like this one,
feed the pulp to the cattle and use the dried rind as
fertilizer. Lots of interesting plants Pangea has to offer,

Mr. Posner.

I nodded. He sat half-turned toward me. The steward took him the other tumbler and returned to his post at the serving table by the exit. He moved a massive stone ashtray aside, lined up the bottles, placed the cigar back into its box and shut the lid closed.

"To welcome company," McLean toasted me with his glass and leaned back sipping his whiskey.

I took another swig and glanced into the room behind the rattan screen. Two men sat there on a bench: Frenchie and the gorilla who'd confiscated my guns. Wladas and Wong were kept in the yard downstairs, guarded by a few raiders. The house had three levels: the second one served as the entry, opening into the yard. A rough spiral staircase led downstairs from the verandah. The first level was built into the cliff, supported by wide beams that stuck out far above the water. A net was stretched under the beams - just in case.

From the net to the water had to be fifty feet or so. Worth a try. I leaned against the log railings and tried to estimate the depth. I could barely see the bottom. No rocks on the surface. Easy to get out onto the shore, too: all I had to do was swim to the left, along the cliff toward the pier that separated the port from the seaweed farms. Further from the pier, several abandoned jetties stretched into the sea.

The shore bustled with people carrying heavy bails on their backs to a pontoon wharf behind the jetties. Two motor boats and a few junks rocked there, moored along the wall. Further on, fishermen dried their nets stretched wide on poles. An ancient barge lay stranded on the shore sunbathing its black tarred side. Shells covered its bottom below the water line, and a good dozen locals were busy scrubbing it clean.

"My boats will be back in two hours," McLean said. "I'll have to go there and inspect the catch. One needs to keep an eye on these people."

I got the message.

"It won't take long," I finished my whiskey and stood with my back to the ocean.

My head still swam after the memory release. Every now and then colored circles flashed before my eyes. Probably, drinking wasn't such a good idea. I concentrated on my heart, still beating fast like I'd just finished a cross country run. McLean glanced at me from under his hat and puffed on his cigar waiting for me to go on.

I really didn't want to speak first but I had no other option.

"Are you going to help us?" On my way there, I'd decided I'd put my cards on the table. Pointless trying to keep secrets from him. Tex knew about me and the FSA. I'd already dropped a few hints about General Varlamov; now I needed to know everything New Pangers knew about him.

McLean's eye, gray and cold, stopped blinking. His face froze. Then he laughed out loud, his mouth wide open, his head dropped back. The steward watched the scene, indifferent, his hands folded at waist level.

"Wow," McLean wiped a tear and grinned one last time. "Your FSA bosses must be really up their own asses. Did you really think I would work for you?"

The smile disappeared from his face. Hatred glowed in his eye. His voice became icy.

"We deliver carula, and what do we get in return? More and more dead meat: sick and useless men unable to survive here." McLean sat up and clenched his cigar until it broke sending sparks flying onto his pants. He didn't notice. He leaned forward and gave me a poke. "And now you want me to help you? Who do you all think I am?"

His whiskey splashing his boots, Tex rose and threw the glass over the railing. He was heaving. I glanced at the doorway. Frenchie and the gorilla already stood there, gloomy-faced, clenching their guns.

"Oh no, Mr. Posner, I don't think so! First, I want you to tell me everything you know. Carula, mainly. Also, I want to know why your agency wants Neumann after all these years. Leave your Varlamov story for some other idiots. You give me the accurate information. Then I'll decide where to go from there."

So! Apparently, I couldn't count on McLean's help. I had to find Neumann all by myself. When our analysts had developed this scenario they predicted the odds of a negative outcome as negligible. They reasoned that McLean was tied down by Earth suppliers and confederate obligations. They claimed he'd been informed of the repercussions following his refusal to cooperate. But apparently, McLean was no coward. He even tried to put the situation to good account by using me.

Potential information leak, the Information butted in. Mission compromised. I froze. How on earth had the software analyzed McLean's words? What's its algorithm? Did the thing read my thoughts?

Was it a warning or a system error? It could be a false identity overlap as it had already happened with clones back in the hotel? Up until now, all my actions fell within the programmed algorithm, bar the failed meeting with the contact.

Threat identified, a voice resounded in my head. Third degree alert. Carrier to leave New Pang immediately. Failing to do so will result in annihilation.

Oh great. I squeezed my eyes shut and pressed the spot above the bridge of my nose. It prickled and stung a bit. Rationalizing hadn't done me any favors. The invisible helper was at the point of scorching my brains.

The FSA director was a real jerk. He should have let me know that the information program could force me to act against my will. So it looked like they kept me on a long leash, giving me little freedom of choice.

The pain in my forehead grew leaving me no illusions. It felt as if a white-hot rod was forcing its way through my skull.

Third degree alert. The procedure of memory capsule formatting commenced. Its termination will activate automatic liquidation.

"In how much time?" I asked without thinking.

Information answered, Four minutes twenty-two seconds.

Looked like I had to hit the road whether I liked it or not.

"Agreed," I stepped toward the door. "Let's go downstairs."

"Why?" McLean raised a surprised face. The gorilla blocked my way.

"One of my men is a chartered medical specialist," I struggled to preserve a calm expression. "He can explain this carula stuff."

McLean rose in his chair and looked back. "Butch!"

"Yes, boss?" Gorilla squeezed himself sideways through the doorway and stopped next to the steward shifting glances between me and the booze on the serving table.

"Go down into the yard. Take four more boys and bring me the prisoners."

"What's their business here, boss?"

McLean slapped the armrest. The chair squeaked. "On your way!"

Gorilla staggered across the room, panting and stomping his feet, and disappeared down the staircase.

I used my glass to point at the bottle. While the steward was pouring me another whiskey, the stairs filled with voices and stomping feet. Wong entered the room first, followed by Wladas, Butch and the bald-headed raider. Two more took the stairs and stood guard on both sides of it. My men walked out onto the verandah.

"I told you to take four men," McLean glared at Butch. "Idiot!" he turned red in the face.

Butch sighed, licked his lips and shrugged. "But boss-"

"Shut the fuck up!" McLean jumped up.

Wladas by the serving table flinched. Wong pretended he was scratching his neck as he glanced at the raiders by the stairs and shifted sideways between gorilla and the bald raider. Now Frenchie couldn't see him from his room.

Third degree alert, the Information wailed. Carrier to leave New Pang immediately!

"I'm losing patience, Mr. Posner," McLean returned to his seat and nodded at Wong and Wladas. "Which one is your medic?"

The stinging in my head turned into drilling. A cramp clutched my cheek. My spine shuddered. My brain might boil at any moment now. Time to beat our retreat.

I was about to step toward the doorway when I noticed three familiar figures down on the pontoon wharf. A wizened fat man in pale shorts climbed over the fence and jumped into a moored motor boat. His skinny friend threw him a barge pole and followed. My last doubts disappeared when I saw Jim, disheveled as usual, climbing the fence after them. He cast the boat off, threw the rope's end to his bosses, stepped onto the prow and kicked away from the jetty. Georgie wielded the barge pole turning the boat around.

"Wong," I threw my drink into Butch's face, punched him in his Adam's apple and jumped toward the guards by the stairs.

I had to admit they had excellent reaction times. Still, they forgot they stood in a fenced-off area. As soon as they raised their carbines, I used both my hands to punch them in the chest. One went ass over tits down the stairs. The other let go of his gun, grabbed my shoulder and pulled me down with him.

I'd lost precious moments. I had to dig my wrist into his chin to free myself from his grasp. Only then could I push him down the steps.

Punches resounded behind me, followed by a slap. Wladas cried out. I turned and nearly collapsed. My head was swimming and I had to lower myself onto one knee. McLean slumped in his chair. He hadn't had a chance to draw his gun. Butch and the bald raider lay on the floor a few feet away from the senseless Frenchie in his room. Wong froze in the doorway, pleased with his work. The steward was pointing his compact pistol at him.

How could I forget the steward? That was a beginner's mistake. Apparently, Wong wasn't without error: the steward would shoot him before the Chinese had a chance to wring his neck. If only Wladas...

Wladas raised his hand and smashed a whiskey bottle

over the steward's head. Glass flew everywhere. The mute steward collapsed in the doorway. Wong stepped over him, gave the neurotech the thumbs-up and ran to the steps.

"Jump," I croaked and got up.

The Information finally shut up. My forehead stopped stinging and I could breathe again. I looked down. The raider lay in the safety net below.

"Wladas, jump, quick!" I straddled the railing and looked at him.

The neurotech stared at the collapsed steward in the hallway, his head covered in blood.

"Wong!" I gasped. "Help him."

McLean stirred in his chair. An enormous bump ripened on his Stetsonless head. Judging by the size of it, Wong had hit him with the ashtray.

He tried to get up and reach for the gun. But the Chinese on his way to Wladas restored the status quo with a deft hand chop.

"Jump," I nodded at the pier. "When you surface, go for the jetties. Ask those in the motor boat to take you on board."

Wong grabbed Wladas' hand. He jumped over the railing and stood on the edge. Turning to Wladas, he grabbed him under the other arm, squatted, then sprang back to his feet and flipped Wladas over his head like a wrestler on the tatami. At the last moment he kicked himself away from the verandah, tucked up and somersaulted down the cliff.

Wladas hit the water. Next to him, Wong opened up and entered head first. In two seconds, he resurfaced, grabbed the struggling neurotech by the scruff of his neck and swam toward the jetties.

I heard a noise on the spiral staircase. Someone was calling for help. Instead of jumping after Wong, I returned to the verandah. I grabbed a few bottles off the serving table and smashed one against the wall, then hurled another toward the stairs but missed as it fell between the banisters.

I swore and grabbed another bottle and the lighter off the tray. I ran to the stairs pouring the whiskey onto the steps and the floor around. Then I smashed the bottle against the banister and flicked the lighter setting the verandah on fire.

The raider in the net underneath stirred and raised his head. I hurled the burning lighter into the room. It hit the spilt whiskey on the wall. A blue flame licked the wood as it spread toward the bench and ran across the floor before climbing the rattan screen.

"Fire!" I shouted, then took in a chestful of air and yelled, "Fire!"

I climbed the railing, kicked free from it, crossed my arms on my chest and entered the water feet first.

By then, Wong and Wladas had climbed out onto a jetty and were running toward the pier, waving their hands to the sailors in the motor boat.

I looked up. Smoke belched from the verandah. Stevedores stopped with bails on their backs and pointed at McLean's estate. No one looked at the pier.

I couldn't see the motor boat for the jetties around. I decided to take my chances by not swimming ashore. Georgie and Grunt would surely try to use the commotion to leave the harbor unnoticed, and my men would tell them where to look for me. I swam to the seaweed farm.

The water was murky and thick with a noticeable

stench. A few times my body brushed something soft and slimy - most likely, the seaweed rippling just under the surface.

When I had swum far enough away from the cliff, I turned to a jetty one side of which faced the ocean. The engine of the approaching boat roared as it sped up.

Then my hand hit an obstacle. I stopped and waded up to my chest. A fishing net was stretched under water next to the jetty, its floats rocking on the waves. A few feet further, I saw another one; and a yet another.

Shit. The last thing I needed was to get stuck there in full view.

The engine approached. The boat must have passed the pier and headed for the seaweed farm at full speed. I climbed over the floats trying not to get caught in the net. Why did they need all these nets here? I moved toward the next one. The engine started to die away, and its wake reached the jetty causing the floats to move and push me up. My hand got stuck in the net. I moved back and immediately regretted it as my feet got caught up. My head was still out of the water but now I couldn't go anywhere, spread-eagled between the nets.

I heard voices. Wong and Georgie came onto the jetty, Wong pointing at me.

"Jim! Get the pole!" Georgie shouted.

He caught the pole thrown from the boat and grabbed its other end, crouching.

"Hold it!" Georgie shouted as the sharp tip nearly pierced my shoulder.

Wong went down on one knee and held the pole tight as I clasped my end. They pulled it, and I cried out in pain as something snapped in my trapped foot.

"Don't! My foot!"

The Chinese and the crane operator leaned forward together.

"What the fuck's keeping you!" Grunt's voice came from the boat.

Georgie waved him off. He pulled out a knife, balanced it in his hand and hurled it to me. I nearly missed it, catching it by the blade. My cut-up fingers stung but I managed to get hold of it with my other hand that was caught in the net. I cut through the mesh until I'd freed it. Only then did I check the cuts. Blood ran down my hand to the wrist. Why did it hurt so much? It stung worse than that damn software in my brains. Could be the salt in the water, but still.

I wriggled myself around and cut through the net by my feet. Now I could move again.

"The pole!" I reached out toward the jetty and grabbed the pole's sharp end. "Pull it!"

Georgie and Wong stood up pulling the pole like a fishing rod. They raised me out of the water and lowered me onto the jetty.

"Come on!" Grunt shouted. "Move it!"

Wong helped me onto my feet. With his assistance, I jumped into the boat. Jim sat astern next to Wladas.

"Welcome aboard," Grunt eased the throttle forward and lowered his hands onto the steering wheel.

The engine spat a jet of water from its cooling box. A wake began to foam on both sides of the boat.

"Hold on tight," Grunt took a tight turn around the jetty and headed for the cliff.

"Why there?" I slumped into the seat behind him and winced. The palm of my injured hand was burning. I could barely move my fingers. For a moment, I had the impression that the blood vessels under my skin glowed red.

"Shut the fuck up," Grunt said without looking at me. "I'm the boss here."

We were approaching the cliff leaving the seaweed farms to our right. Next to it, McLean's house on the cliff emitted clouds of rancid smoke. The ocean spread away to our left.

"Where do you think-" I didn't finish.

Right in front, I noticed a narrow ravine. From the shore, it could easily have been mistaken for a wide crack in the cliff. Still, it was a passage opening into a large grotto.

The moment we entered it, Grunt shut the motor down to near idle, its purring echoing from the tall domed walls in front. Jim and Georgie moved to the fore and started paddling with their hands, each on his own side, to prevent the boat from scraping the stones all around.

"Where now?" I asked when the boat grated against a rocky ledge turning a corner. "I can't see jack shit. We'll hole her!"

Grunt turned and gave me a meaningful look.

"Kill the engine," Georgie said.

I looked forward nursing the wounded hand at my chest. Daylight streamed from around the bend, lacy shadows dancing on the surface.

"Oakum, take some soundings," Grunt handed him the pole. "Georgie, take care of the motor."

Instead of doing what he'd been told, Jim opened a hatch on the prow and produced a lamp similar to the one we'd seen in the hotel the night before. He turned a knob on its base, filling the cave with a soft white glow.

"What if they sent someone after us?" I peered into the darkness, listening.

"Shut up," Grunt dropped.

He took the lamp from Jim and lifted it overhead while Jim lowered the pole into the water pushing the boat deeper into the cave. In a low voice he reported the approximate depth. Georgie got Wladas to help him dismantle the motor. When they secured it in a horizontal position, the crane operator sat down next to me.

"Show me your hand," he said.

He grabbed my forearm and turned the wounded hand to the light.

"What is it?" Grunt asked.

"Not fucking good," Georgie wrinkled his nose. "He cut it real deep."

"What are you talking about?" I looked up at him. My hand was so numb I didn't feel my fingers anymore. "Is it dangerous?"

"Carula," Grunt answered. "It secretes a strong toxin. If it gets into the bloodstream..."

Jim reported the depth again, and the captain told him to steer starboard in order to avoid a shallow patch. We sailed around a cluster of rocks protruding from the water. Past them, the cave split into two, one side overhanging so low the boat couldn't take it.

"Just say it," I demanded. "What's this toxin stuff about?"

Georgie spat into the water and wiped his lips.

"You cut your hand and let the toxin in. It's some sort of slime the plant secretes when it's in bloom. Heavy shit," he looked me in the eye. "If you don't get a serum injection pretty quickly, you're toast."

I opened my mouth to answer but Georgie hurried to add, "Serum isn't the answer really, as you can still get gangrene from the wound. We might have to amputate the hand once the serum works. Or even the whole arm."

"Go ahead," I rose. "Inject the serum. What are you waiting for?"

He shook his head. "We don't have it. Only McLean does."

"What kind of toxin is it?" Wladas asked. "Do you know its formula? If we..."

Georgie smirked. "Why do you think I know? Carula is an alien plant local to this Continent. These life forms here may look as if they're nothing different, but the thing is, they are different. That's why..."

"Quiet!" Grunt ordered.

Jim reported the depth again. The captain responded with a "Keep her steady!" and leaned forward with the lamp. Georgie returned to his place at the stern. I waited a while, then sunk onto the bench and lifted my hand to my eyes. The palm had swollen. The cut itself had turned black and almost stopped bleeding. My fingers had turned blue.

I heard a hum coming from above. Grunt turned to us. "Georgie, get the guns ready."

"You think," the crane operator stepped over the bench and pulled two handguns from under his belt, "the raiders are already by the waterfall?"

"Could be. If they saw us leave and semaphored the patrol..."

"Nah," Georgie clutched one gun under his arm and got busy with the other. He unclipped the magazine, snapped it back in and put a round up the breech. "The patrol's on the plain. They'll never make it. Too much road to cover."

He handed Wong a gun. "Take it. You sure know a gun from a clone's ass. Am I right?"

His smile unchanged, the Chinese took the handgun.

"When we clear the cave, look eastward," Georgie started to explain. "Once you see the waterfalls, fire away."

Depends on the distance to the potential target, I thought mechanically and had another look at my swollen hand.

"Georgie? You think you have a small axe?" I looked up at the captain. "Or something like a hatchet - sharp and heavy?"

"Forget it, Mark," Grunt knew straight away why I wanted it. He laid his hand on my shoulder and looked me straight in the eye. "Even if you chop your hand off, the toxin's already in your bloodstream. We need to get you to the loggers. They might help."

His tone was weird, as if he sent a message to the others. I paused and asked, "So what's the plan?"

"That's better," Grunt nodded. "The current is about to take us out." He thumbed back at the cave's entrance. "New Pang is there. The river is in front of us. Its estuary is far north from the city. Not an easy place to get to because of all the rocks and sandbars. If we sail, it'll take us about two hours by sea to get to the loggers' camp. But up there, on the plateau," Grunt pointed up, "there's a crater. A big one. Filled to the rim with fresh water. McLean and his raiders guard the access to it because he's busy building a water pipeline. Builder my ass..."

"Wait a sec. How come there're waterfalls there?" The map of the Continent had been blinking before my eyes for some time by then, but I couldn't see a lake anywhere on it. "The river level is way below the plateau. How come there's fresh water up there?"

My temples stung as the map changed resolution and

New Pang grew on it, stretching its coast beyond my view. I recognized the harbor we'd just escaped from. To its north, a cluster of cliffs jutted out into the ocean. A blue circle appeared on the plateau, too neat and round to be a natural crater. Past the cliffs, a thin ribbon snaked northward to the horizon edged in green. It had to be the river he'd spoken of.

"It is," Grunt grinned. "The lake water had washed its way through the cliffs into the ocean."

"Why doesn't the lake shrink, then?"

"No one knows, that's the whole thing. Could be some underground streams. Could be the Forecomers' work. The crater has to be artificial. Neumann proved that it had nothing to do with the river." Grunt shrugged it off and looked up. "No point talking about it now. All we need is for the waterfalls to be raider-free."

"They would have to make a detour around the lake," I realized. "It's quite a distance."

"It is," Georgie said. "He's not stupid," he nodded at me, "and he's still standing."

"True," the captain rose looking in front of him and scratching the tattoo on his shoulder. "That's why we'll go north. They can't catch up with us if we take the river course. There're no roads nor bridges nearby."

"There were other boats in the harbor," Wladas said. "And a motor boat by the pier. If they..."

"They won't make it," Grunt answered. "The tide is coming in. As for their motor boat, Oakum took care of that."

The cave in front of us seemed to widen, its walls sloping to the water. The current carried us to the opening, barely wide enough for the boat. I could see the ocean and the narrow brown strip of the coastline.

"How about the trawlers?" I asked as I sat back down. I started to shiver, cold sweat covering my face. "The fishermen McLean was talking about. If they head straight for the estuary, they..."

"Nah," Georgie drawled. "They're too far to semaphore anyone."

"Why semaphore?" I wiped the sweat from my forehead. "Why won't they use a radio?"

"Not enough radio transmitters here, that's why. McLean has two, and another one at-"

"Do shut up," Grunt butted in. "Come sit down, Oakum. Georgie, start the motor up."

The crane operator gave Wladas a shove with a "gimme a hand, will ya?", then got busy with the motor undoing the braces to lower the propeller into the water. Wong raised his gun and sat on the stern.

"How's your hand?" Grunt asked in a low voice. He glanced at the others and added, "How are you, in general?"

I cringed. He nodded. "Hold on for a bit. A couple hours. I'm sure the loggers will know how to help you."

Jim fastened his pole to the hooks along the side of the boat and sat next to the captain.

"Why did you help us?" I said.

The captain and Georgie exchanged glances.

"Just a gut feeling," Grunt said.

"Why didn't you leave last night?" I broke into a bout of coughing but didn't let him answer. "Just... ahem! just don't tell me that that was a gut feeling, too."

"Well," Grunt bit his lips. "Well, we had to see how the ground lay first. When the trawlers left we decided to borrow the boat. Can't you see we left the shotguns behind to make it look innocuous?"

"Yeah," Georgie mumbled next to him. "We're now, like, comrades in misery."

He spat into his hands, pulled a handgun from behind his belt and said,

"I'm ready. Fire her up."

Grunt gunned the throttle. The motor coughed alive and idled.

"Duck in," the captain looked over the boat one last time. "Off we go, then."

He grabbed the steering wheel with one hand and gave gas with the other.

I felt much worse, gasping for air.

"One last question," I managed. Mustering my strength, I leaned forward feeling I was about to faint. "Why should the loggers help us? Grunt..."

CHAPTER EIGHT
KING OF THE FOREST

DARKNESS. Light. Voices and screams came from afar. Darkness again - heavy, swampy and soundless. My head felt hollow, my mind failing to escape. A grenade exploded - no, that's a slap on my cheek, followed by more pain. A flash of light. A familiar voice called my name, repeating, "Mark, wake up! Open your eyes! Mark!" It died away... never to come back...

Reality can surprise you sometimes. It may hurt worse than a nightmare.

I took a deep breath and opened my eyes. It was pitch black. Where was I? Why was it so dark? I lay on something hard, a piece of tarp covering my head and body. It stank of diesel and motor oil.

I pulled the tarp off my face, propped myself up on one elbow and squinted into the dark.

A hut. That's where I was. A sagging old brush hut with a dirt floor. Twilight came through the silent doorway.

No, not quite silent. I could hear muted voices and

smell campfire smoke. Something else, too... like the rustling of trees...

I forced myself up and stepped into the doorway. It stood amid a woodland unlike anything I'd ever seen before. Treetops thick and heavy, their trunks warped, interlacing, growing every which way, their leaves rustling weakly.

Where the fuck was I?

The Information in my head ignored the question. I stood there musing until I remembered Grunt's words. Something about going to the loggers who could help me... For a moment, I was overwhelmed by the kaleidoscope of events, places, conversations, fights and chases. I staggered grabbing at the wall and remembered everything that had happened.

Another whiff of campfire brought the smells of food and drink. A booming voice was answered by what sounded very much like Grunt's. Wladas spoke next. Plates clinked. Then the place fell silent.

Things were getting better. There were people nearby, and that included Wladas. I sat down trying to control my breathing. The campfire had to be somewhere in the forest nearby... But of course! The rainforest. Where else would you find loggers?

But why was I here and not with them? Why had Wong left me? He couldn't have done so because... because he...

I vaguely remembered Grunt's story about the toxic carula plant. I'd asked him for a serum injection which they didn't have. I remembered I'd wanted to chop off my hand.

I stared at the tarpaulin. I'd been as good as dead. Grunt had known it, and so had Georgie. They'd chosen not to tell me. They must have left me here for dead. So they'd covered me with this tarp planning on coming back to bury my body. In the meantime, they were having a wake?

Looked like it.

But I wasn't dead. I was alive and kicking!

I walked out of the hut and followed the smoke trail. A bird crowed and another replied. Not necessarily a bird - it could have been a Pangean monkey for all I knew, warning its troop about the intruder.

What had they done to me? They had probably tried to save me and failed. Or they'd thought they'd failed. No matter. I had to decide on my next step. Should I come out to the campfire or should I listen to their conversation first?

The night fell fast. I stood still wondering if I should come out at all. What if Wladas had told everyone about who I really was? That could change everything. In that case, it wasn't a funeral party but a feast celebrating the successful liquidation of an FSA operative. Then Wong was dead, too: they must have killed him first realizing he didn't know much. As my cover man, he'd have tried to defend me, so it seemed logical to have killed him first. Then they would have tried to bring me back to life and force the FSA's plans out of me. But it hadn't worked because I'd kicked the bucket... or they'd thought I had, and that had been the end of it. Wasn't I right?

I had to be.

I nodded. The only solution it left me with was to try to get back to New Pang, find my contact and start everything all over again. Which I couldn't really do because I didn't know the city, had no money and risked bumping into McLean's men at every street corner, which was much worse than simply going solo. I still had to make it back to town in one piece. No, that wasn't the way to find Neumann and get us back to Earth.

I heard Wladas' voice in the thicket: he was rambling on, barely coherent. A fast tirade in Chinese interrupted him, followed by a grim "yeah right" and a burst of hooting laughter.

"Leave him alone, Wong," the booming voice said. "He's drunk as a skunk."

Wong? I hurried along. So Wong was alive and with Wladas! Looked like I didn't have to go solo, after all.

I saw a narrow passageway cut through the trees, their trunks scarred with fresh gashes. After a few more steps, I came out into an opening. My friends all sat around the campfire. Wladas faced me, swaying, trying to fill a mug from a flask. Jim sat by the fire stirring a pot of soup. Behind him on a log sat Grunt and Georgie, red-faced from either drink or the heat. Or it could have been be the twilight and the flames lending their hue to their expressions. Wong walked over to them and was about to sit down nearby when he saw me. He froze studying me intently.

Excellent! All present and correct. Plus a stranger who sat on a block of wood sideways to me. A burly guy with a beard, wearing a dirty-gray shirt, a pair of leather pants and short wrinkled boots.

Wladas noticed me. His face paled. He backed toward the fire, stumbled and fell flat on the ground. The others turned their heads toward me. Jim dropped his spoon into the pot. Georgie cleared his throat. Grunt stared at me, unblinking, while the bearded giant rose, his head reaching the clouds, and lay his hand on the hatchet behind his belt.

He was a good seven foot tall, blond with a red beard on a freckled face. Slowly, his lips stretched into a smile. Who did he remind me of?

"Er," Grunt raised his hand, his fat finger pointing at me. He exchanged glances with Georgie who mentioned clones under his breath. Jim swallowed and tried to fish the spoon out of the boiling soup. Wong came to me and motioned me to another block of wood next to the stranger's.

"Hi there," I nodded to Jim as I sat down. "Everything okay? Not too scared of me?"

The boy gave me a weak smile, then looked at the stranger and went on stirring the soup as if it made him feel better. The others didn't speak.

"Swenson," the giant boomed and sat down next to me. "Lars Swenson's the name. I'm the boss here."

He held out his hand, wide and calloused.

"Mark Posner," I gave him a firm handshake and looked over my friends. "Cat's got your tongues? Nothing to say about my resurrection?"

Lars slapped my shoulder as if he'd known me for years and said with a grin,

"I imagined you different. My nephew told me a bit about you..." he studied my face. "You are different. Definitely."

His voice was as strong as the rest of him.

"Your nephew?" I raised my eyebrows.

Lars took my injured hand and turned it palm up to the light.

"Look, it's healed," he sounded surprised. "And you seem to be alive, too. I would never have believed it myself. You're one lucky man!"

He looked up at me.

"Oh yeah," he waved his hand at the fire. "That Jim over there is my nephew."

I glanced at Jim. Now the likeness was apparent. Both had the same-shaped eyes and faces, but their noses were different, and so was their hair color - the boy's was lighter - but both were covered with freckles. Grunt and Georgie stirred and helped Wladas still hugging his drink back onto his feet. Several bowls and mugs stood on a piece of tarp next to a couple of enormous flasks. Wong moved into the shadows and squatted.

"Jim is your nephew," I repeated. "And what does that make you?"

Lars sized me up and slapped my shoulder.

"Do you always take the bull by the horns?" he reached to the tarp. "Wipe your face with this," he passed me a wet cloth. "Have a drink and a quick bite. We can speak as we eat. No hurry, but you need to understand a few things."

I ran the cloth over my face and hands, sniffed it and cringed.

"Smells funny."

"It's cao juice," Lars said. "An organic insect repellant. Perfect to keep midges away. Come on, rub it in before they feast on you," he grew serious. "Tuck in."

Jim took the pot off the fire and filled a bowl for me. It smelled good. Lars produced a spoon from the side of his boot.

"Do us the honors, Private."

Private. Oh well. I wiped my face with the cloth and reached for the spoon slowly, watching Wladas. Had he been discreet enough? More than likely. Wong wouldn't have let him speak out of turn. And in any case, I'd have gotten a very different kind of welcome then.

I began to eat. My new friend picked up one of the flasks while Wladas held out two mugs. Lars handed one to me, filled to the brim.

"To your return from the dead."

The drink left me speechless. Warmth poured down into my stomach where the brew exploded in a ball of liquid fire clearing my head. McLean's bourbon couldn't hold a candle to it. A chocolate aftertaste clung to the sides of my mouth.

They must have polished off the other flask while I'd been lying "dead" in the hut.

Lars squinted at me smacking his lips. He tilted his head and poured the drink into his huge mouth.

"Well," he said wiping his beard, "looks like we need a change of plans. You being alive and all that."

"We need?" I asked dipping into my bowl.

"Exactly. Now listen. Jim and this buddy of yours here," Lars nodded at the yawning Wladas, "they told me how you scorched McLean's digs."

"Shit happens," I attacked my food.

"That'll teach him," Lars nodded staring into the fire. "He's been going a bit too far just lately." He turned to me and added obscurely, "McLean and us, we're supposed to cooperate, but he seems to have put his eye on our little business. He wants us to dance to his tune. To which I say, fuck him!" He gave the finger to the twilight enveloping the woods.

For a Scandinavian, he had an excellent command of Russian. Too good, even. He spoke like a native. I put the spoon down and glanced up at him.

"Sorry, buddy, I forgot you didn't know us," he said. "We're loggers. I'm the foreman. We camp five miles away. Do a bit of logging, then drive the trunks down river to New Pang. We supply them with whatever edible fruit there is here, and send them fresh meat. Wind boar is plentiful around here. Hyena pelts, too...

Edible fruit. Wild boar. What did it all mean?

Lars glanced down at his pants. He sat down by the fire, licked his finger and rubbed at a dirty spot on his pant leg. "Everyone needs clothes, but there isn't much here to make them with," he shrugged. "The woods give us all we need, apart from oil, machinery and ammo."

I pushed the bowl away and took a large swig from the mug.

"And McLean, he controls all the Fort deliveries. Plus the fishing boats. Plus the port," Lars gave Georgie and Grunt an angry look, "And now he's the only one with a ferry boat. No problem, we can always build another one. But it'll take time..."

"Listen, King," Grunt shrugged. "It wasn't our fault, really. No good crying over spilt milk..."

Lars spat and didn't finish. I was itching to find out who he really was and why Grunt called him King. Instead, I asked,

"Why are you telling me all this?"

I was racking my brains for any scrap of information about Lars Swenson. But it didn't look as if the Feds had supplied me with any.

"I'll tell you in a minute. You eat," he shifted on the log stretching out his legs. "Where was I?"

"McLean," I said. "He wants a larger piece of the cake. Don't know why yet."

"Exactly," Lars looked at Jim who was busy raking the coals to bake a large, tasty-looking fish packed in clay and ashes. "McLean is just a gangster who played his cards right. Has anyone told you about the pandemic?"

I nodded.

"Thing was," Lars Swenson glanced into his empty mug, "with that pandemic, that's when it all started. A lot of people fled New Pang then. McLean did the right thing, I have to admit. He organized those still in town and made them believe they'd survive the pestilence. He ruled the city with an iron fist, though. No mercy for the infected. He burned them. Burned them alive, imagine. Locked them in their homes and..."

He fiddled with his empty mug. "Naturally, we gave shelter to the fugitives. We stopped working and set up a quarantine camp. And once the pandemic was over, McLean declared himself the lord of New Pang. Never mind all those who'd built the city - loggers, farmers, oil riggers, free raiders... even clones had added their two cents' worth of labor. Lots of people had invested in it, so no wonder many wanted to go back. But once they did come back," he raised a warning finger, "McLean waited a bit and lay down the law. He charged them three times the old price for everything: their houses that weren't his to begin with, the right of passage, the jetties... This was when we founded the Confederation. All Continent settlers signed a friendly agreement. We had to meet McLean halfway in certain things so he demanded compensation for fire prevention and street cleaning. His men did shift shit from our streets, you have to give them that. Now he's building a water pipeline. Highly commendable."

He paused. "You see, the thing is, McLean wants to bite off more than he can chew. Now he taxes everyone he can lay his hands on. He wants to control our estuary gate where we charge a toll for the riggers' oil tanks and farmers' food barges on their way to New Pang."

He must have misunderstood my stare because he added, "What do you want? They won't transport it by land. Gas stocks won't last forever so everyone's trying to go easy on them."

"Yeah," I twiddled with my spoon. "I still can't see why you're telling me all this."

"Eh," Lars froze open-mouthed. He shook his head and added, "Never mind. Get on with your food."

I finished off their soup in no time, wiped the spoon with the edge of the tarp and gave it back to the logger.

"It was good," I said to Jim, "thanks a lot."

He nodded.

Lars put the spoon back in his boot. "Ready to go on?"

"If you tell me why."

The logger frowned and scratched his cheek. "I want you to help us."

"How exactly?" I hadn't expected him to say that. "I've got nothing. I only arrived here yesterday. I nearly died!"

He felt my shoulder, squeezing the muscle. "Nothing hurts?"

I shook my head.

"Feel okay?"

"I think so."

"Then you owe me one," He let go of my arm. "What're you looking at? We spent two vials of serum to set you right. Any idea how much that costs?"

"I see," I nodded. "So what's your problem?"

Lars looked over the men by the fire.

"I... what was I saying?"

"The pandemic," I offered.

"Right. So everything seemed to be fine. The disease was gone," he sighed. "I'm sure we'd have found a way to

POINT APOCALYPSE

arrange it all with McLean, but... Things got a bit rough on the Continent."

"As if they were ever easy," Georgie murmured.

Lars shot him an angry glance. "Two years ago, there was quite a bit of commotion in the Fort. You tell me - you being in the Army and all that - what do you know about the generals' coup? Eh?"

Now we'd come to the interesting bit. I shrugged. "All I know is that one of the generals escaped to Pangea with his men."

"He did, he did," Lars reached under his collar and scratched his hairy chest. "They sent some troops after him. There was some action on the coast. The Fort reported that the defectors had been eliminated. We didn't even know about the coup then. We learned about it later from new arrivals. Things subsided after that but," he frowned as if searching for words. "How can I explain..."

"Just spit it out," I said. "It's not as if we're pressed for time."

"Okay. Here's the lay of the land. On one side, there's us, plus the oil riggers and the farmers. On the other side, there's McLean. We have more guns but he controls the city where our families live."

"Which is how he can blackmail you," I butted in. "Your women and children."

"You're thinking in the right direction. But he won't live long after that, and he knows it. He won't have the guts to take our families hostage. He doesn't have enough men. The moment isn't right."

"So what's the problem, then?"

"It's the clones," he paused. "Not even..."

"The clones. They don't mix much with humans, do

— 125 —

they?"

"They don't. They moved east a long time ago. Everyone treats them like dirt, anyway. We've lost all contact with them."

"Why east?"

"They were sent there to drain the swamps. I don't care, let them stay there. Less mouths to feed," he sighed and went on. "But some time ago, they paid a visit to the farmers and you know what they did?" he shook his head, unbelieving. "They must have been famished out of their minds. They sent a messenger to tell the farmers they had a week to vacate their lands or the clones would destroy the crops and burn their farms. The farmers turned to the oil riggers for help, seeing as they were camped nearby. The riggers sent a party to..."

"Wait a sec. Where are their farms?"

"In the north. South from the swamps."

"I told you, didn't I?" said Georgie. "Remember the diagram?"

"I do," I nodded. "It's next to the City of Forecomers." I rested my elbows on my knees and turned to Lars. "I still don't quite understand the situation, though. Why are the farms so important?"

"Without them, we're dead meat. We'd starve."

"We wouldn't," Georgie cringed. "We-" He shrunk under Lars' stare and looked to Grunt for support. But Grunt turned away pretending he was studying the tattoo on his shoulder.

"Oh yes we would," Lars barked. "McLean's hauls aren't enough for everyone. Also, some fish here is not good for you."

He turned to me to explain that not all Pangean foods were edible. Some didn't agree with Earth-based life leading to toxicity and death. That's why Neumann had brought with him some animals, plant seeds and equipment. And some top-of-the-range biologists. And when they'd looked into Pangea's wildlife, they discovered that all the Earth's organisms they had introduced were mutating. Different species changed at different speeds, but they did mutate, and that included man. According to Neumann's research, first traces of mutation in humans took ten generations to manifest themselves. We wouldn't live to see it.

"Our fruit and meat is barely enough for us alone," Lars glanced at Georgie who was shrinking with the logger's every word. "So who is there left? The farmers, of course. There's only one place on the Continent suitable for growing Earthly crops. You know that as well as I do."

Georgie looked as if he wanted the earth to swallow him up. Lars drove another nail into his coffin,

"Looks like we gonna starve if the clones stick to their word."

You could cut the silence with a knife. I raised my head and watched the sparks escaping from the fire. A quiet buzzing attracted my attention. I checked the dark gray sky above, turned and noticed a swarm of midges hovering around Wladas' head. He slept where he sat, nose down in his lap, oblivious to the world.

"Don't you think?" Lars glared at Georgie.

Georgie mumbled something. I said, "Let's get back to the point. How can the clones stick to their word, as you say? Are they really so numerous and well-armed?"

"I like the way you think," Lars slapped his cheek and squashed a midge between his fingers. "No, they aren't numerous at all. But they're not alone. They serve as a smoke screen for someone."

"Who is?-"

He lowered his voice. "Cyber troopers."

Georgie and Grunt exchanged surprised glances. Wong stood up; Jim froze for a moment, reaching for the baked fish. Wladas alone didn't budge, sniffling in his sleep.

"They have to be," Lars buried his mug in his broad hands. "They killed the riggers' volunteers who were marching to join forces with the farmers."

"If they killed them, how did you find out about it?" I glanced at Wong who was all ears.

"The cybers let one rigger go. He told us about it. So I think," Lars paused, "the Fort gave us the wrong information to begin with. The traitors weren't eliminated. They're somewhere here, on the Continent. They've been lying low for a while, and now they seem to 've started to stir. But it all looks a bit too complex. What do they want from us? We're not their enemies, surely they understand that?"

I glanced at Wong, and he gave me a barely perceptible nod. The only person on Pangea capable of controlling cyber troopers was General Varlamov himself. And if so...

"It was just a demonstration," I sat up. "To show you what you were up against."

If the general had taken action, it meant I had little to no time. But the only person who knew of his future plans was Neumann.

"You're a soldier yourself," Lars poked me with his finger. "Can you tell us how to stop those cyber motherfuckers? If we can stop them at all?"

Okay. Now I knew what they needed me for. Lars

Swenson was afraid - not so much for himself but for the city and his family in it. Ditto for McLean - that's what he'd meant when he said he wouldn't surrender New Pang to anyone. It was fear. They're all afraid, each in their own way, of the force that comes from the east. And they were right to be afraid. The best thing they could do was to unite, but it didn't work like that. McLean kept his own counsel, so he wouldn't risk everything for the loggers' sake as they hated him, anyway... So apparently, the general was using Pangean clan war in his own interests. He manipulated the clones while in fact targeting the farmers. But why? What did they have there on their lands?

The Information chirruped in my head. The map of the Continent gleamed into view flashing numbers: settlement population, surface area, weapon inventory, etc. It looked like the riggers in their camp deep in the Continent could, in theory, stand up to Varlamov's soldiers. As for the farmers...

"We can stop them," I said quickly, estimating the advantages of our conversation. Now I could ask Lars for some food, guns and a car. Neumann had to be where the soldiers were. "If we disrupt their communications, we'll disable their control center."

Lars seemed to have expected to hear something like that.

"You think you could do that?" he gave me an intent look.

"Well," I pretended I was thinking, "risking my ass to-"

"Remember," the logger boomed, "you owe us one. Help us and we'll give you whatever you want. A house in New Pang, the best food, an interest-free loan for your future business. A car and house staff..."

"Enough," I raised my hand. "What guarantees do I have?"

"The word of the King of the Patch," Lars rose from his log and offered a broad hand.

Georgie and Grunt started nodding to me. Jim bit his lip, starry-eyed.

I lived up to their expectations. "Okay," I rose and shook King's hand. "I will need men though, and also..."

"You have it."

For a few moments, we looked each other in the eye.

"So," I started carefully, trying not to overdo it. I had to admit I was going a bit too far. But Lars had already turned to the sailors ordering them to return to the camp to prepare the raiders' gear and weapons, and then to go back to the river check the boat's motor and tank her up.

Grunt and Georgie rose in silence and headed for the trees. Jim stayed behind to serve up the baked fish. He placed two plates in front of us and left, too.

"I think I did the right thing about the boat, don't you think?" Lars said passing me a plate. He shook Wladas awake and told him to fill our mugs. "Much quicker by river."

I gave it some thought and nodded. "I'd also like a bit of money to buy a car. You think I can get a good one from the riggers?"

"You might. Money I can give you, and ammo, but as for men..." he faltered.

"I'll take Grunt, Georgie and Jim," I spoke. "They're out of a job, anyway. It'll take you some time to build another ferry. Georgie used to be a raider once, so he knows the area well. Grunt is a genius with boats. Jim is young and strong. Plus Wladas and Wong, of course," I shoved a spoonful of fish into my mouth and added, "They and I, we're literally in one boat. We're comrades in misery."

Wladas, still sleepy and clueless, blinked and nearly spilled his mug. He grabbed it just in time and closed the flask. Lars stared at the fire, pensive.

"Okay," he finally said. "You should sail off at dawn but make it look as if you're going back to New Pang. Grunt will take her along the bayous to bypass the tollgate. This way, no one will know you're going into the Continent. Full steam ahead once you pass the tollgate. The straits are wide enough there."

Lars turned to Wladas, reconsidered and looked back at me. "No one will know your true objectives. Not even my men."

"Understood."

"On the river, you'd better listen to what Grunt says. But in action, you're the one with the orders. Also... If you get hold of the cybers' weapons, we can always use them."

He took his mug from Wladas and took a big gulp before attacking his fish.

"You know what you were saying about all those plants," I set my plate aside. "You said not all food here in Pangea was edible. Does it mean that people used to get poisoned? Still do?"

"Sure," he mumbled with a full mouth. "McLean's divers snuff it all the time."

Wong came to the fire, picked up his share and sat opposite us. Wladas, finally awake, stood up and started to massage a stiff back.

"Has anyone survived?" I asked after a moment's thought. "I mean, I have."

"No!" Lars exclaimed. "That's the whole thing! You're the first! The serum only helps if injected directly after the infection. Do it a minute later, and your chances drop by half. After two minutes," he shook his head, "you're fish bait."

I looked at my hand. The cut was almost gone. Curiouser and curiouser.

The night covered the rainforest. The fire crackled sending sparks flying into the air buzzing with midges. From time to time, something rustled in the thickets or a bird crowed in a tree.

When Lars finished his fish and got up, I said,

"Take you, for instance. How come you know Russian so well? You've got a Scandinavian name."

Lars glanced at me sideways. "My mother was an Inkeri from the North West of Russia. I left her when I was twenty and moved to my father in Sweden. Started earning good money felling wood. Three years later I returned to get her and..."

"And what?" I looked up at him.

"She was denied clearance. So I went and roughed up the Consul real good. Then they nailed me."

"Was it a long time ago?"

"Quite," he turned and walked away saying, "You'd better sleep in the hut. There's a thunderstorm brewing."

His large silhouette disappeared among the trees. We heard, "Don't worry about the wildlife. My men will watch over you. They'll wake you up in good time."

PART TWO

CHAPTER ONE

THE RIVER

THE THUNDERSTORM came at midnight. Amid blinding light, claps of thunder rattled the hut. The roof did little to stop the downpour and rainwater was soon running down the ceiling. I rolled myself up in the tarp trying to sleep, but the noise kept me awake.

The rain stopped. The air grew sultry. It clung to your throat preventing you from breathing, thick with sweat and the liquor breath emitted by Grunt and Georgie who snored away next to me. Neither them nor Wladas seemed to be affected by the thunderstorm.

Finally, I gave up and got out. I curled up outside by the hut door and dozed off for an hour or two until Jim arrived to wake us up.

A few minutes later, we all walked down a trail toward the river. The rainforest was waking up filling the path with animal noises and bird calls. The dawn shone through the leafy branches. My head was buzzing with the lack of sleep and I kept reaching for the water flask packed by Jim. One time I lost my footing and nearly stepped into a young termite mound. Georgie pushed me away just in time and twirled his finger around his temple. According to him, they were not deadly but would guarantee an itch from hell for the best part of next week.

We took a narrow trail to the river, following in each other's steps. Jim, Grunt and Wong had gone in front. I stopped and raised my wounded hand to my eyes. It was warm, and the pain pulsating in my forearm was quite bearable.

"You okay?" Wladas asked.

"Yeah," I splashed some water onto the wound and clenched my fist a couple times watching the reddened scar. Then I looked up.

Two enormous steel structures loomed over the river bed. They reminded me of the Maunsell fort towers used in the Second World War for anti-aircraft protection. Quite a few of them still stood in British shores. But these had no trace of rust, their meter-thick supports smooth and intact. The armored forts were solid without a single rivet or seam. A hanging walkway connected the two - definitely man's work, but the towers themselves had to be Forecomers' creations. A tall rod stuck out of one of the forts, exactly the same as the one I'd seen near New Pang. The top of it pulsated with a bright white light bathing the river and its banks in its soft glow.

Jim headed for a long log jetty. There, Lars Swenson waited for us by a moored motor boat. Several armed men stood nearby guarding a stack of crates. A sentry looked down from the walkway above.

Wong headed for the river. Grunt followed. Wladas, Georgie and myself stayed put. The neurotech rubbed his eyes, took a deep breath and hiccupped. The hangover was getting the better of him. I gave him the flask and turned to stop Georgie who tried to bypass us on the narrow trail.

"What's this, another beacon?"

"Yeah," he wanted to walk past but I motioned him to stand still.

"What's its purpose?"

"Dunno."

"What does it run on? If I understand correctly, it never goes out."

Georgie shrugged. "They went on two years ago. Just before the generals' coup. Neumann had been busy with them for a long time and he couldn't do it. They just lit up on their own." He looked up at Swenson gesturing to us to hurry up. "Come on now. Time to hit the road."

We walked to the river.

"They lit up, you said? How many are there?" I asked. "How many beacons in total on the Continent?"

"Four," Georgie pointed east. "There's one in the desert, and another one in the mountains."

"And what's there inside?" Wladas asked catching up with us. He handed the flask back to me. "Any machinery?"

"No one knows," Georgie answered. "You can't get inside. You can neither blow or cut them open. No idea what's in there."

"So it can't be steel," the neurotech said yawning.

"Maybe not."

We stopped by the jetty where the others were already waiting. Lars paused studying us.

"Everything all right? Did you sleep well?"

"Not bad," I glanced at the yawning Wladas who shook his head and rubbed his sunken stubbly cheeks.

Lars grew serious. "Let's get to the point, then."

By the looks of him, you wouldn't say he'd been drinking alongside the rest. His voice was strong, his breathing level. A strong guy.

"You," he pointed at each of the seamen, "check the boat, the kits, the bags, everything you packed last night. Grunt, you report to me once you've finished. Mark - the money," Lars handed me a fabric tube with what felt like coins inside. "This should be enough for a car and some juice."

"How much here?" I weighed the tube in my hand.

"Three hundred. Two hundred can get you a good truck with enough gas for a round trip."

Wladas coughed in his fist. We looked up at him.

"Tell Jim to show him the first-aid kit," I offered noticing the sign of the red cross on one of the bags. "Wladas is a doctor but Jim has grown up here on Pangea. Let him explain all about the local lotions and potions."

"Good idea." Lars called Jim and repeated my words to him. "Want to check the guns?"

I shook my head. "Just load everything on board. Wong will check them later."

"Oh well," Lars waved to his men who began carrying the crates to the boat. "There're some carbines, explosives and a machine gun. Everything's been oiled and is ready to fire. I've checked the guns myself."

"How about a few knives and handguns?" I raised my wounded hand and traced the cut with my finger. The stinging had subsided a bit.

"Knives..." Lars knitted his eyebrows and mumbled, "How the fuck could I forget them?"

He spat out a quick command. His two remaining men walked onto the jetty following those who carried the crates.

"You'll have knives in a moment. But handguns are a problem," Lars made a helpless gesture. "You have three Colts you took off McLean's raiders. He's the one with handguns. In the forest, you need something more powerful... something you can trust."

"I see. Let's go, then," I clenched my fist and scratched at the cut. The pain was nearly gone. "You think I could get some from the riggers?"

Lars gave it a thought and nodded. "Make sure they don't sell you bullshit. Plenty of garage guns around. Mainly in New Pang though."

"Got it. And what about communications? Something like a radio transmitter?"

"I'm not a commissary," he chuckled. "Communications are a problem. Whatever equipment there is is all under lock and key. Better not ask them about it. They might misinterpret you."

I didn't ask him why. Electronic equipment had to be worth its weight in gold here.

Lars lowered his voice and added,

"Once you're at the riggers, ask to see Fritz Havlow. He's technically Russian, from the Volga Germans. He used to be a tanker engineer so you can't fool him when it comes to machines. He'll get you whatever you want. The commune leaders listen to him so they'll sell you a car or a truck, full tank, no questions."

"How will I know him?"

"You can't miss him. Red hair, eyebrows, goatee. Constantly chews tobacco."

"I'll remember."

"Just don't show him the money before you agree on the price."

"Will do."

"And don't forget what I told you about the cybers' weapons. Try to bring them here, okay?"

We walked out onto the jetty. Grunt gave me an armful of knives collected from among the loggers. Wong jumped into the boat and I followed him. With Georgie's help, I checked the bags' contents, inspected the knives - they were sharp and handled well - and asked Wladas if they'd clued him in on the local medications. Hearing his affirmative, I turned to the river bank. Grunt and Lars seemed to be talking, or rather, Grunt was listening to the logger's instructions. "I'll have to warn them about it," I heard. Lars Swenson slapped Grunt's shoulder and told him to get under way.

Warn them... Who was he going to warn and about what? My hand stung. I glanced down at it, winced and looked back up.

Lars waved us goodbye and strode away. Georgie yanked on a lever. The motor coughed and started burbling. Jim grabbed an oar and shoved off from the jetty. Grunt turned the steering wheel and guided the boat between the jetty and the beacon. There he put on speed and headed southward toward New Pang.

I plumped down on the bench. The river curved in front of us, its banks covered by the rainforest. As the day broke, the trees and shrubbery merged into a thick mass of brown and green. The words that Swenson had said to Grunt kept worrying me. But I brushed the thought aside. First things first. The guns.

Wong opened the crates. He checked and handed out the carbines. Then he sat next to me and began assembling the machine gun. The carbines were the M14 army type, with wooden stocks, detachable twenty-round magazines and diopter sights. Not the best choice for jungle warfare, but indispensable on open terrain such as a desert.

The captain and Jim sat in front, Georgie and Wladas at the stern.

Soon the jetty and the loggers' tollgate disappeared around the bend. My hand didn't hurt any more. The redness was now gone, and the pale scar had all but disappeared. The boat glided along the water. Grunt had put his foot down, and the wind lashed at our faces bringing tears to our eyes so I was forced to sit with my head down to one side.

We loaded the magazines and shared out the remaining shells. Then we distributed the bags for the hike ahead. We had a lot to carry: a backpack each with three days' worth of rations and raiders' gear, including a pneumatic crossbow complete with a harpoon and a cylinder containing a flare and harnesses for three people. There was also a decent pair of naval glasses in a case. Each of us had a waist bag with two flask holders for water and some local moonshine, well known for its excellent antiseptic properties.

When we finished sorting out the bags, I opened the crate with explosives. The motor's high-pitched whining had changed to a drone as Grunt dropped the revs and took his hand off the gas. The boat slowed down.

I stood up. Jim began shipping the oars into the oarlocks. Grunt raised his arm pointing at a barely noticeable bayou to our right.

"Now we must keep quiet," he said. "Not a sound until I give you the all-clear. Understood?"

I nodded and looked over my shoulder at the opposite bank. Georgie was busy securing the motor. Wladas slept cuddling the first-aid bag. The Chinese had moved to the prow and sat there cross-legged holding his gun in front of him.

"How much more do we have to row?" I whispered in Grunt's ear.

"Not too far," he answered. "A couple kilometers at most. We'll take turns rowing."

He glanced at me and explained,

"They can't see us from the gate: the forest's too tall. But river drivers may hear us. Their camp is not far from here."

"I see."

The loggers had seen us leave for New Pang. The only person who knew our real destination was Lars Swenson. But if he didn't want his men to know, what had he tried to warn someone against?

Jim touched my shoulder and motioned me to sit down. He took Wong's vacated place on the bench. I sat next to him, placed the carbine in my lap and spat on my hands before taking up the oar.

* * *

We passed through the bayou keeping nice and quiet until we came out into the open. Grunt let out a sigh of relief. Georgie grinned and began restarting the motor. Wladas had slept through the whole thing. I'd decided against asking him to help and gestured to the others to leave him well alone. Hungover, untrained and unaccustomed to long journeys, he needed his rest.

The boat motor whirred to life, and Grunt steered her slowly down river. He sat at the wheel staring in front of him. Jim crouched next to him; Wong and myself took the middle bench. Wladas and Georgie stayed at the stern.

Jim lifted a bag into his lap and started taking out food.

I asked Georgie how long it would take us to reach the riggers. Tomorrow morning we'd arrive at their camp, he said.

"Will we have to sail at night?" I asked.

"No," Grunt answered. "We need some rest. We'll get to the desert and drop anchor. Then at dawn we'll head for their camp."

"Why can't we go there now?" I took a packet of food from Jim. "We can spend the night at their camp."

"We can't," Georgie shook his head. He asked Wladas to hold his food packet and leaned overboard to tweak the motor.

"Why?" I chewed on a slice of dried meat - or fish, judging by the taste, all life salted out of it. "Why do we need to stop for the night?"

"Because by midday, the sun will scorch your ass, river or no river. You'll beg for some shadow. You'll even beg for a tree," he nodded at the thinning rainforest lining the right bank. To our left, it still stood thick and strong but Grunt went on, "We'll get to the desert by midday. There we'll wait up until the heat subsides and play a bit of catch-up. Once it starts getting dark, we'll stop again.

"But why can't we move at night?" I lost it and raised my voice. "What's there to be afraid of?"

"Humpbacks," Georgie spoke. "They hunt at night."

"What's that?" Wladas turned to him, his food untouched.

"It's a fish. A predator," Georgie bared his teeth and spread his arms wide. I thought he showed us the fish's size, but he added, "It's got teeth this big! It'll make quick work of a boat. This clone's ass will swallow you without even knowing it."

Wladas' eyes opened wide.

"You eat," Georgie reached for the slice in Wladas' hand, broke some off and volleyed it into his own mouth. "Cheer up. No humpbacks here. They usually hunt by waterholes and on sandbanks. They'll take out an antelope, but not a tiger. Only when it's stupid enough to get into the water."

His words reminded me of the food in my own lap. I finished off the meat and opened the flask. "This fish, what's it like? Compared to terrestrial species."

"Fuck knows," Georgie picked his teeth with a crooked fingernail, took the flask from me, spat and took a large swig. "It looks a bit like a haddock but waaaay bigger. And they have a large hump instead of a dorsal fin. That's why we call them humpbacks. It's flat-shaped like a shark so it can run aground easily. Its scales are brown and so thick that a bullet won't touch it. Neumann used to say they're a deve... lopmental species on their way to evolving into reptiles."

"We won't live to see the day," I said and turned away.

The Information wasn't too forthcoming with more data on humpbacks. Most likely, the file only included a few key modules relevant to the mission. I didn't like it. Too many unpredictable situations. Too much ad libbing.

The sun was getting hotter by the minute. The morning freshness was all but gone. We could speed up of course, but what was the point? We were about to stop for the day, anyway. Pointless wasting gas.

Grunt kept the vessel steady as she crept forward hugging the middle of the river. I stared in front listening to the motor and watching the right bank, almost bare by now: trees few and far between, the thickets interspersed with bald patches revealing the hills beyond.

Twice the boat had to skirt shallows coming close to the bank. Georgie pointed out an antelope: a strange-looking animal, a bit bigger than a sheep, covered in thick curly hair. Its horns were about a meter long, sharp and slightly curved; his tail, short with a fat tuft of hair at its end.

When the antelope sheep heard the boat, it disappeared into the thicket. Amid much bleating and rustling, the branches parted as a few more animals emerged. They ran along the bank leaving the boat behind. The leader pranced in front, shaking his head. A few moments later, the small flock reentered the thicket and disappeared. I glanced at the sky and wiped the sweat off my face. The heat nearly melted me. I leaned overboard, scooped a handful of water and sprinkled my face.

Wladas did the same. Georgie grinned, immune to the local heat after years on Pangea. Wong stirred in his seat. He pulled off his tank top, wrung it like a towel and lowered it in the water, then put it back on without wringing the water out.

"Aha," Wladas quickly pulled off his.

Geogie chuckled. Grunt glanced at us over his shoulder. "Round the bend there's a good place to stop. We'll camp there."

Once the boat reached the bend, we saw the flat right bank. There, the antelopes were waiting, their heads hung low. I recognized them by the large dark spot on their leader's flank.

The boat being still at a safe distance from the bank, the antelopes apparently didn't consider us a threat. The leader walked into the water and shook his horns at us, indignant at our intrusion of the flock's usual watering hole.

"Just look at him," Georgie rose and raised his carbine. "That's one hell of a dinner," he said slowly taking aim.

He didn't shoot. The animals raised their heads, alerted to the sound of a truck engine from the bank.

A truck? Was it possible? Who owned it?

The next moment the water in front of the flock leader parted with a slap. A dark lithe shape lashed out of the depths toward the antelope. A murky blue-black fish eye glinted in the sun. The fish's teeth snapped the animal's neck and the antelope collapsed in the water raising a wave.

The water seethed. Here and there, more humpbacks were arriving trying to grab the animals' legs. But the antelopes had already darted away, wild with fear, leaving their unlucky leader behind.

Grunt cursed and stepped on the gas. Jim dropped his oar and barely made it back to his seat. Georgie cried out and very nearly fell overboard. Wladas grabbed his hand at the last moment.

"Didn't you say they hunted at night?" I didn't take my eyes off the shallows foaming red. The leader's head appeared for an instant, agonizing fear glistening in his eyes. Then the waters closed in above him.

"Hold on tight!" Grunt ordered.

I turned to him. We were heading for more shallows. There, a humped back ploughed through the water toward the boat.

Out of instinct, we opened fire, carbine bullets creating splashes of water all around the powerful fish.

"Hold on tight!" Grunt repeated.

It finally dawned on me that he knew best. I dropped

the gun and grasped the side of the vessel. The boat took a sharp turn, its prow aiming at the fish. The next moment, the hump disappeared. A flipper-like tail rose and fell as the fish escaped into the depths. Grunt jerked the boat the other way to avoid the shallows and slid between them and the bank.

"Raise the motor!" the captain shouted. "Do it! We'll fuck the propeller!"

Wladas hugged the motor cap and struggled to lift it out of the water. Georgie grazed his fingers raw as he undid the screws. I couldn't help them, and neither could Wong.

The keel scraped the sand bank throwing us face down. The motor stood up horizontally on its own, the screw still spinning sloshing water all around. The boat literally jumped across the shallows and landed in deeper water.

"Lower the motor!" Grunt yelled.

Georgie and Wladas slammed the motor down against the backboard. The boat jerked and glided forward.

We grabbed the carbines from the floor and looked back. The predator had chosen not to chase us.

Grunt cursed out loud, wiped his bald head glistening with sweat and steered the boat toward the opposite bank. We tied up.

"I know," Grunt turned to Georgie. "Isn't it spawning season soon? The fucking fish is out of its mind then, hunting day and night. But I thought we had another week before it started?"

"Has to be climate change," Georgie mumbled.

We dragged the boat halfway out of the water and tied the mooring line to a tree. Then we stretched a canopy between some tree branches, and Jim started setting up camp. Wladas volunteered to help him. Wong stayed on the bank watching the river through his field glasses. I called out to Georgie and Grunt,

"Did you hear that engine? Just before the humpbacks attacked. The deer seemed to cock their heads to the sound."

Grunt shook his head. "I was watching the river."

Georgie nodded. "I did."

"Are there trucks here?" I asked.

"Could be raiders," Georgie suggested, then added in reply to my silent question, "Not necessarily McLean's men. There's a penal settlement a few miles upriver. A shepherd and his wife live there. They raise ostriches and goats and keep a whole gang of free workers. They take turns selling their wares in New Pang while the other half raid the area looking for artifacts. Could be them."

I looked at Wong with his field glasses. "All right then. Let's have lunch and some rest. Grunt? Any more humpbacks ahead?"

He scratched at the tattoo on his shoulder. "Dunno. Could be a couple more places where we might find them."

"You think you can bypass them?"

"We'll have to."

There was no fear in his eyes. Wladas, on the contrary, kept casting scared glances in our direction as he helped Jim.

"So let's do it this way," I said to Grunt. "When we sail off, I'll sit in front with you. Georgie in the back with Jim, Wong and Wladas in the middle."

"Deal," Grunt nodded.

CHAPTER TWO
GOD LOVES THE INFANTRY

W E TRAVELED to the night camp without further incident. This time we decided to moor the boat on the right bank: the rainforest to our left had given way to an expanse of brown and yellow. The desert. The river washed its southern edge: sand dunes lay to our portside while to our right rose a hill range covered by wilted grass, brushwood and occasional tufts of low gnarly trees.

Grunt steered on, the motor almost idling as he looked for a place to tie up. Under the high crumbling bank, lumps of eroded soil showed above the water line. The captain explained that the riggers' water-jet barge created a strong wake that undercut the bank.

The warm setting sun caressed the skin. The heat subsided; the water started giving off a light chill. I looked up at the cloudless sky hoping for a calm night.

I turned to Grunt. "You think it's gonna rain?"

He didn't answer. Georgie spoke instead, "Don't think so. Not after yesterday's downpour. The thing to worry about here is sandstorms. Not "worry" worry, you know. Not yet. Another ten miles to the east, that's where the desert really starts and that's where you should keep your eyes peeled."

"There we are," Grunt stretched out his arm. "We'll land over there."

He pointed at a large mound of soil by the water's edge, an uprooted shrub still clinging to it. The place was good. Here, a hollow ran down the slope, once grown over but now bare and muddy, easy to climb up the foothill for a bit of recce and to post a lookout for the night. Alternatively, you could walk further away from the river - a good preventive measure considering that the other hills were higher than this one.

A truck appeared on a distant incline. We froze. We couldn't hear the engine: from where we were, it seemed as if the truck rolled out onto the hilltop by itself and then headed down, soundless.

"Wong, the glasses!" I reached out for them without taking my eyes from the hills.

Finally I heard the sound of an engine. The wretched hills worked like highway noise barriers. Now we'd missed the truck!

It was quite a long way away still so nothing said they'd seen us. Before I could raise the field glasses to my eyes, the truck had rolled down the slope and disappeared behind the range. We stared at where a cloud of dust was now settling. The truck didn't reappear.

"It's weird," I lowered the glasses and looked over the bank and the river below. "It looks as if it's been following us."

"Coincidence," Georgie half-asked.

"Grunt," I raised the glasses again, "What was it you

spoke to Lars about just before we left?"

The captain mumbled something. He didn't sound happy.

"Spit it out," I grabbed his shoulder and turned him to face me. "Well?" I looked into his eyes.

He glanced away. Wong stood up on his bench. Georgie followed suit. Wladas and Jim didn't move and just stared at us from above, uncomprehending.

"What was this warning Lars was going to send? Who to? And how?"

Grunt looked back at me and opened his mouth to speak. Wong cried out, pointing at a harsh hissing sound approaching from the desert. As we heard a delayed sonic boom, a line of white smoke rose from behind a dune heading for the sky.

A missile!

"Step on it!" I pushed Grunt into the driver's seat.

The line kept rising, about to change its path. They must have fired it from a covered position. The missile technician had sent the rocket higher in order to get a better look at us through his camera.

The missile lingered in the air, then headed straight for us. The boat's prow jerked up as we sped away leaving a powerful wake. I tumbled into my seat. Reaching for the open bag underneath, I pulled out the harpoon and the welded-on container with the harnesses and the flare. I unscrewed the flare's top and tugged on the lanyard.

A bright flame erupted and headed toward the missile. My purpose was to temporarily blind the technician. He reacted just as I expected by exploding the missile.

I struck Grunt's hand on the steering wheel. The sky seemed to roar. The boat veered toward the bank and hit the lump of dirt that was our planned landing. I was thrown high into the air. Trying to tuck myself up, I covered my face with my elbows as I fell into the water and buried my hands in the deep silt clinging to it as hard as I could.

A wave of fire rolled over the surface spitting and spreading shrapnel all around. Followed by trails of bubbles, the boat's fragmented hull sunk next to me. My shoulder smarted. I pushed hard with both legs and resurfaced.

The remains of the boat lay on the bank, overturned and smoking. A large hole gaped in its hull. The missing motor had been torn from its mountings with part of the backboard. Jim, covered with mud, was struggling up the slippery slope trying to drag Wong into the hollow.

"Wong!" I turned round, up to my waist in the water. "Wladas? Grunt?"

The captain's body bobbed up next to me, a bloodied mess in place of his face. I recognized him by the tattoo on his shoulder.

"We're here!" Wladas shouted to my right. The neurotech, complete with the first-aid kit over his shoulder, waded along the water's edge toward the hollow. There, Georgie had finally scrambled to his feet and limped up the slope leaning on Jim. Behind them, Wong walked while tying a tourniquet around his arm. Blood was seeping from his slashed elbow down to his wrist and was dripping onto both the ground and the butt of his carbine.

The guns! We had no guns, no gear! So much for all our equipment! I got out of the water, glanced over the scratch on my shoulder, then checked the knife on my belt and the field glasses still dangling around my neck. Kneeling next to the smoking boat, I covered my eyes from the fumes and reached down the hole hoping to salvage a bag or a carbine. Almost immediately, toxic flames struck out snake-like from the hole. My eyes stung as the hull caught fire threatening to reach the tank. I caught a whiff of the gas leaking from under the boat.

Fuck it! I started climbing the hill. By the time I finally caught up with the rest, the boat exploded. We hit the ground, waited for a bit, then rose and continued our climb. Georgie and Jim lagged behind, so I stopped and helped them along.

"Where's Grunt?" Georgie croaked.

"Dead."

A high-pitched sound came from across the river: the electric motor of a sand buggy - a multipurpose combat vehicle controlled by a cyber trooper.

Which didn't necessarily mean he was alone in it.

"We've got to get the body out," Georgie shrugged Jim's hand off his shoulder.

"Up!" I pulled him along. "We've got to hide. You can't help Grunt now. Come on, Jim!"

Georgie nearly fell over as he tried to follow me with his eyes still on the river.

On the opposite bank, the squat combat vehicle appeared amid the dunes. Its long flattened body resembled tortoise shell with the underframe painted yellow. The buggy was shod with light-colored tires - not an easy thing to see on the sand. Armored cowls covered the front wheels. No windshield: instead, the cab was equipped with a monitor that collected information from cameras and combat modules. But it was little less than a backup system. Most likely, the buggy was controlled by a cyber trooper whose neural chains were hotwired to microprocessors and whose brain contained all the necessary software channeling every snippet of information from radars and sensors directly into his brain. A cyber trooper: half-man, half-robot, chock full of performance-enhancing implants.

"Who... who are they?" Georgie gasped. His filthy hair was clinging to his scalp, his face turning pale with pain and anger.

"Later," I looked up. Wong and Wladas had already disappeared over the hilltop. "I'll tell you later. They won't leave us alone. Now move it!"

The combat sand buggy rolled into the water and moved across the river purposefully, like a predator catching up with its prey. A narrow hatch slid aside on the roof. A twin pulse machine gun on a swivel mounting zoomed out and turned in our direction.

We went over the crest of the hill and froze a few paces below. Georgie gasped and fell on one knee holding his hip that had been gashed by a piece of shrapnel. Jim jerked his hands up as I reached for the knife handle on my waist. Then I let it go.

"Freeze! Put your guns down!" ordered a tall African at the base of the hill.

Famba and three more of his raiders - Kathy included - lined up in front of their truck pointing their guns at us. The grim broad-faced driver sat in his cab, hands on the steering wheel, nervously chewing on an extinguished roll-up. The red-haired raider sat in the truck next to his tripod staring at us over the sights of the gun pointed at the hilltop.

Wong lay unconscious, his face beaten to pulp. Next to him, Wladas also lay face down, hands on his head. His first-aid bag stood next to the grinning Kathy.

I remembered the other raiders' names from what

McLean had told me. Muller, Kurt, Baxter and Red Johnny - apparently, the one in the truck - looked at me expectantly.

"We need to hurry," I started.

"Shut up!" Famba barked. "Get down!"

"Idiots," Georgie leaned on my arm and mentioned clones under his breath.

Jim, too, started walking down. A thorny thicket behind the truck blocked our retreat. A grassy hill slope rose to our left. A small grove to our right could hide you from the human eye but not from cyber-controlled sand buggies with their thermal detectors. On top of that, we still had six of McLean's trigger-happy assholes to take care of. It didn't look good.

We had to come up with something pretty quick.

When we reached the foothill, Wong stirred on the ground, scrambling to all fours. He coughed out a clot of blood, rubbed his chest and gave me a subtle nod, his eyes fixed on the shrubs.

"Get down!" the swarthy scar-face shoved his gun barrel into Wong's neck and kicked his shoulder. Wong hurled himself down to the ground.

What had he tried to tell me? Why had he pointed at the shrubs? Wong was more than just a combat fighter: he was a tactician trained to assess complex situations and act on cue against the deadliest odds.

What was his plan?

"Where's the captain?" Kathy demanded. She turned to the raiders. "The fat bastard, you know, with no hair. Where is he?"

"None of your fucking business," Georgie ventured. "You bitch-"

Kathy stole toward him and punched him hard in the

stomach. The studs on her fingerless glove glistened as she rabbit-punched his neck.

"We have no time for this!" I turned to Famba and spouted, "We all need to go, now! If we don't-" I recoiled, barely avoiding a gun butt.

"Don't move!" the African's eyes became bloodshot. "Don't move, fuck you!"

The raider with the greasy ponytail stepped close and thrust his carbine into my cheek. I showed him my empty hands, listening for more sounds to come from behind the hill. There were none.

Now I knew why the raiders looked so calm. Even if they'd heard the faint echo of the explosions, they must have taken it for their own engine backfiring.

The raider took away my knife and the field glasses. Then he frisked me and found the fabric tube with the coins. He threw it to Famba who started toward me, clenching his strong bony fists.

"There, look!" Kathy pointed at the hilltop. She stepped over the collapsed Georgie and pushed Jim aside. The smoke from the burning boat was rising high above the hill. Suddenly, thick black clouds belched from behind it, as if a giant on the other side was blowing at the smoke trying to see what was going on in the hollow. The murky haze subsided revealing a combat sand buggy on top of the hill.

The heavy pulse gun on its roof shot up the foothill. Everyone ran for cover. Streaks of flame reached the truck piercing the hood and cutting through the cab like a white-hot wire slicing through Styrofoam. Red Johnny had just enough time to get off one shot sending a shaped charge right into the sand buggy's front end. Then both he and the swarthy scar-face were mown down by the machine gun.

An explosion flared on the hilltop. I jumped up. Now I knew why Wong had pointed at the shrubs. He was heading there now, dripping blood and dragging Wladas behind him.

I ducked and ran across the opening. Grabbing Georgie's hand, I nudged Jim and headed for the shrubs. Famba and his men ran to take cover in the trees. Big mistake.

The cab door opened and the driver fell out. His forearm torn off by the pulse charge. A large hole in his side was surrounded by a caked brown crust, both wounds scorched and almost bloodless. The driver collapsed onto his back. His glazed-over eyes stared skyward.

Something screeched and clapped inside the cab as its metal frame and engine parts disintegrated, parched by the thermite charges. The truck shuddered and sagged, falling apart. I growled struggling to keep my grip on Georgie, and crashed into the thicket just as the exploding gas tank thundered behind me.

A hot wave bounced off our spines propelling us forward. Flames licked the back of my head as I landed face down into the thorny brushwood. I scrambled onto all fours and crawled on dragging Georgie along with me; then I stopped realizing we shouldn't get too far from the burning truck so that the cyber trooper driving the buggy couldn't detect us with his thermal viewer. While the truck was still ablaze, we were better off staying put and choking on the toxic smoke, but at least we were indistinguishable from the fire spot on the buggy's monitor. Good job Wong had Wladas; now he had to get to Jim before the cyber trooper noticed the boy, in which case we were all toast.

Someone gasped and tried to suppress a cough. It might have been Jim struggling for breath. I shoved a few branches aside and met with Kathy's stare. She held a gun. I pressed a finger to my lips nodding at the smoking truck by the foothill. There, the buggy's electric motor whirred as it approached.

Georgie behind me stirred as he noticed Kathy. I had to hiss at him, restraining his arm. It wasn't a good moment to settle old scores.

After a few moments, the buggy's motor stopped. The combat vehicle came to a halt in the hollow where we couldn't see it through all the smoke. Still, I could hear one hatch slide open and then another. Then voices. The motor hummed again, and the buggy rolled out into the open. A trooper in full Centurion gear jumped off the armor, pulse gun in hand.

He raised his visor and looked around checking the area. His stare lingered at the bodies by the truck. He came closer and kicked one of them, then swung round staring at the grove of trees away from the hill.

The cyber driver peered out of the front hatch. He had a wide face with a squashed nose. Cables trailed out of his neck and the back of his head disappearing into the depths of the cab. If he strayed away from the regs and disconnected himself for a little walk, we could risk a surprise assault.

"Did you see him?" the driver leaned out of the hatch. The cables behind him drew taut but he didn't disconnect them, just cocked his head studying the cowl damaged by our shaped charge.

The trooper kept looking at the trees without answering. He could be a cyber, too, judging by his clouded stare. Most likely, he was busy downloading data from the buggy's microprocessor and restoring his files damaged by the impact.

"Didn't you hear?" the driver said. "It was him!"

"How can you be so sure, flat face?" the trooper's eyes cleared as he looked at his partner. "You went blind as shit when they hit your fat mug!"

A branch crunched amid the trees. The trooper shut his visor close and swung round raising his pulse gun. The driver disappeared inside and slid the hatches shut.

Kathy raised her gun aiming at the trooper. I laid my hand on the barrel and jerked it down, unable to tell her that the cybers knew of Famba and his men taking cover in the grove. Now the soldiers played cat and mouse with the raiders. With their armor and guns, they thought nothing of the raiders' carbines. Nothing short of a grenade launcher could harm them.

Kathy tried to pull her gun out of my grip, ready to spit abuse in my face. Georgie sniffed, exchanging glares between the cyber and the girl. Without me, these two could kill each other simply over the gun.

The hiding raiders were losing it. They opened fire. The pulse gun clattered on the buggy's roof, followed by the trooper's rifle. A raider's bullet hit him in the shoulder striking sparks off his armored vest. For a moment, the soldier stepped back but he didn't stop shooting. A scream was cut short behind the trees.

A few seconds later, it was over. The grove thinned out as trees burned. Famba walked out into the open - his clothes smoking, his hand clenching a gun, his eyes empty.

The trooper raised his rifle. The barrel spat fire. Famba jerked. Boiling blood splashed out of his chest and back. He dropped to his knees and lowered his head, staring at the wound. Then he raised a vacant face and tumbled to his side.

The trooper lowered his visor and turned to the shrubs. Kathy tensed up. I clasped the barrel of her gun. Georgie stopped breathing.

The smoke from the fires started to cover the hollow. The trooper started toward us. Then he pressed his fingers to his temple receiving a radio message. He stepped back, turned round and got back into the buggy.

The vehicle backed up. The electric gear box clicked as the driver revved up the engine and the buggy whizzed off toward the hilltop.

For about a minute we sat motionless. Then Kathy tried once again to tug her gun free but I wouldn't let her have it. I grabbed her arm, pulled the gun's stock and headbutted her in the face.

She raised her bleeding forehead. I grasped Georgie's elbow and pulled him out of the thicket toward the foothill.

"Wong! Wladas! Where are you?"

Kathy spat obscenities to my back. Georgie swore too but at least he didn't resist me but limped obediently behind.

Branches rustled. Wong and Wladas appeared from the brushwood followed by Jim.

All alive, even though Wong and Georgie were slightly worse for wear. I slung the carbine over my shoulder and told Wladas to find his first-aid kit and take care of the wounded. Then I called Jim and headed for the grove to collect all the raiders' weapons.

Georgie screamed my name. I looked round.

Kathy attacked me and even managed to punch me in

the face when Wong arrived and swept her off her feet. He clenched a pistol in one hand while the other dangled, lifeless, as he trained the gun on the girl and started pulling the trigger. His face showed no emotion.

"Wait!" I raised my hand. "Don't."

Wong glanced at me without lowering his aim.

I touched my swollen cheekbone feeling for any loose teeth, and spat blood. The girl knew what she was doing. Without taking any notice of Wong, Kathy showered me with expletives. I really wanted to slap her face but stopped myself as her last phrase superseded my anger and cleared my mind.

Wong and I exchanged glances. He put the gun down. I nodded to him to join the rest and held out my hand to Kathy.

She knocked it away and hissed, glaring at me, "Quit gawking, you idiot! I was just going to set you all free back there at the coast! But you needed to play Superman, didn't you? And now..."

"You," I squatted in front of her. "You knew about me. On the day when the ferry sunk. You are..."

"Exactly! I'm your contact, you fucking idiot. Now people have died because of you. Johnny's dead now..."

"Keep it quiet," I pressed my hand to her mouth. "If you have something to say, stick to the point. Emotions won't help."

I removed my hand. She gasped for air, her glare burning a hole right through me.

"Better now?" I checked the others out, giving orders. Jim went to collect the raiders' weapons left in the grove. Wladas had to get out some bandages and antiseptics and start helping the wounded.

Wong was already busy, his knife slicing through the

tourniquet on his arm. Georgie stared at us in amazement, forgetting the gash on his hip.

"So?" I looked down at Kathy.

She nodded and spoke in a quiet voice,

"When McLean realized the ferry was gone, I arranged it with him to be sent to the coast with the rest. I tried to tell you..."

"Doesn't matter," I shook my head. "We can't change it now. What was your objective?"

"To meet you and provide you with arms and transport."

"I see. Get up then. You can go with us."

I offered her my hand. After a moment's hesitation, she accepted it and rose.

We came back to the dead Famba to retrieve our money. While I was frisking him, Jim reappeared from behind the trees, two shotguns on his shoulder. I took one and told him to give the other one to Wong. Having shoved the fabric tube with the coins into my pocket, I slid Famba's handgun into my belt and hurried after Jim. Georgie tried to tell me something; I waved him away and took my field glasses back from Wong, then ordered him to go up to the hilltop.

"Try to be quick," I told Wladas and followed the Chinese. I needed to have a good look around. Kathy trailed behind.

The sun had nearly set flooding the desert with crimson. Humpbacks slowly circled the dark waters by the bank. They'd finished Grunt off and were looking for more edibles.

"Did you sleep with any of them?" I asked inspecting the desert through my field glasses.

"Why would you want to know? It's history."

I looked at her. Kathy was now her old self. Okay, her nose was swollen and she was growing two black eyes even as we spoke. Still, cold superiority shone in her glare. Even when Georgie and Grunt - may he rest in peace - had fished us out of the water, they hadn't given us this kind of eyeballing.

Apparently, McLean valued her enough despite her character. Still I wondered how she'd convinced him to send the truck to the coast to get us out. The FSA, too, must have prized her enough to assign her as my contact. What had they promised her? An amnesty and safe return to Earth? No deportee would dare dream of more. She'd followed me all the way to the desert - no small feat...

I didn't like it. When you lay yourself out for a cause straining every sinew, the cause had better be worth it. A mega cause, one you'd do anything to achieve, otherwise it wouldn't be worth her while tracking me down. She could have reported to the FSA that she'd lost me, end of story.

I lowered the glasses.

"I wonder why they left? The cyber troopers?" gingerly, she felt her broken nose. "They could easily have found and killed us all."

"They could have received new orders."

How old was she? Could be twenty-five or in her thirties, even. Fine crow's feet webbed her eyes, but she was fit and bronzed, her teeth white and straight. She definitely took good care of herself.

"Could they?" again she felt her nose and winced as she touched a raw scratch. "I don't understand it."

"They were cybers - cyber troopers. Their controller must have called them off. According to the Feds' data, Varlamov has three of them. Apparently, he needed them to do something else." I looked at the expanse of sand stretching to the horizon. "That's not what worries me. How did they know we would travel by boat?"

"That's easy," Kathy chuckled. "King radioed the riggers about you."

"King?" I turned to her. "That's Lars Swenson."

That's what he'd warned Grunt about just before we left. I should have checked. But why had he done it? Did he mistrust me? Possible. For him, I was an infantry sergeant who could easily take the side of the escaped conspirators. Then he'd lose the booty I'd promised him. Wonder what he needed the weapons for?

"What was the radio about?" I asked.

"Just your names. The thunderstorm started, so they couldn't read beyond that, just that you were heading for the riggers' base. If we were able to intercept the message, they," she nodded at the desert, "could have done it just as easily. They're not stupid. These cyber troopers might've had better reception, too, which could explain why they found you first."

I nodded. She went on, "Didn't it surprise you that the cybers recognized some of you?"

I tried to remember their conversation. At the time, their words hadn't rung any bells, but on second thoughts...

"You think we have a mole?"

She shrugged.

"All right then. Let's go."

Something rustled behind our backs. Sniffling and gasping for air, Georgie limped up the slope.

"What's with all this shooting the breeze?" he croaked eyeing Kathy angrily.

"Go fuck yourself," Kathy suggested.

"You bitch!" Georgie bared his knife. "I'll rip your guts out! I'll make you fuck clones!"

Wong, returning from the recce, caught up with him and twisted his arm, leading him down the slope like a cop with an arrestee. We followed.

Biting his lip, Jim watched us. Wladas touched his shoulder, "Help me to repack the bag, will you?"

"You fucking gook!" Georgie wriggled in Wong's grip. "If I... If you.."

Finally, Wong forced him onto the ground and strapped his hands with his belt.

"We need to find somewhere to spend the night," I said to Kathy. "Know someplace safe?"

"Yeah," she waved south. "Past those hills, there's a cave. We could go there."

"Fine. You'll show us."

I gave the others five minutes' grace to pack their stuff and freshen themselves up. After some consideration, I presented Wladas with the handgun and passed the shotgun to Jim. I kept Kathy's gun.

"Whatcha gonna do next?" she tried to conceal her disappointment at not being trusted with a weapon. "We'll stay there for the night, and then what? Back to New Pang?"

"No. That's wasting our time. We need to go eastward to the swamps. I need to have a word with the farmers." I tightened my belt, checked the sheathed knife at my side, attached the water flask next to it, blew at the field glass lenses and looked up at her. "Know where we could get a car? Georgie said something about an oasis seven miles away or so. According to him, it's some raiders' base or other."

"I know," Kathy said after a pause.

"You think they have some wheels?"

"Used to," she frowned.

"Is it a big detour from where we're going?"

She shook her head.

"All right, then. Tomorrow morning we start straight for the oasis. If we can't get a car, we'll have to follow the river until we find the riggers. They'll think of something car wise, I'm sure."

"Across the desert? Are you nuts?"

I sized her up and down grinning.

"God loves the infantry," I rearranged the gun on my shoulder. "If we can't get the wheels at the oasis, then we'll work something out with the riggers."

"Why can't we go there straight away?" Kathy stared at me, uncomprehending. "Wouldn't it be easier?"

"It wouldn't. First, we have casualties. Second, I've no idea who's waiting for us there. Could be Varlamov's cybers for all I know."

"I wouldn't bet on the raiders giving us a car," she interrupted. "They could be home or in New Pang, you can't tell. Besides, any vehicle here is worth its weight in gold. More."

"I've got gold," I patted my pants pocket. Before I could continue, she butted in again,

"They'll kill us and take the money."

I looked at her as I considered all the pros and cons. I had to agree with Kathy: our little group was badly armed and had two wounded men to boot. Now we were more than just comrades in misery: we were outlaws entering a trap. The girl was right: the moment the raiders saw the money, we were history. Lars Swenson knew it - that's why he told me to go see the riggers and Fritz Havlow first.

"Right," I said. "Imagine we arrive at the oasis and the raiders aren't there. What is there? A farm? Some livestock?"

Kathy thought about it.

"We could swap some ammo with the shepherd for his mules and a bit of food."

"That'll do," I turned to the rest. "Everybody ready?"

Georgie looked at me frowning. Wladas nodded. Jim apparently couldn't care less, so used he was to being ordered around. Wong maintained his usual smile, albeit slightly forced, his arm bandages soaked with blood. How much blood had he lost? Would he make it? Once we got to the cave, we had to inspect his wound and patch it up. He needed some proper rest, too, if we wanted him to move on.

"Kathy's one of us now," I said.

Georgie sniffed.

"She is one of us," I repeated for his sake and pulled the gun off my shoulder. "Let's get going. Kathy and myself first, Jim and Wladas next. Wong and Georgie in the rear. Kathy will show the way."

She didn't move, her absent stare fixed on the truck.

"Kathy?" I called. "It's time to go."

The girl stirred. "I want my gun back."

CHAPTER THREE

JIM

THE CAVE wasn't a cave, really - more like another one of those Forecomers' mysteries. The oblong entrance, too regular to be natural, barely showed in the steep hill slope. Grass grew over its top edge. A truck could pass through it easily. It opened into a tunnel a few hundred feet long, too straight and level, its walls artificially smooth with marble-like veins running through the gray stone. I tried to scratch it with my knife, but the blade left no trace on the matt surface glistening in the twilight. The beacon towers back on the river seemed to be made of the same material. The tunnel ended in a rough black basalt wall, or at least that's what I thought it was.

We were way too exhausted to start a fire. I prepared to stand guard through the night: if I got too tired, I could ask Jim to replace me. Wladas and I cleaned Wong's wound and patched it up the best we could, then did the same to Georgie's. Finally, I told everyone to get some sleep.

I sent Kathy to the end of the tunnel away from the rest. She didn't look too happy about it but chose to keep it to herself even though I could see she was dying to give me a piece of her mind. I strategically placed Georgie by the entrance hoping he and the girl wouldn't bump into each other during the night as they still kept exchanging hateful glances. Between them lay Wladas, his head resting on his bag and handgun, and the ever-watchful Wong.

Night descended onto the hills and the valley below. The black sky twinkled with stars. The silence would have driven me mad, had it not been for my men's disturbed breathing. It didn't feel real, as if I wasn't on Pangea any more; it was as if I had no mission, no FSA brass to report to, just sitting there musing on top of a hill far from civilization, and below lay the Russian steppe overgrown with feather grass, its air fragrant with lavender and filled with grasshoppers' chirping.

I woke up with a start. Had I been dozing off for long? Pangea had no moons, and the starlight was barely enough to make out the outline of the shadowless hills. I hadn't a chance in hell of telling the time.

After a moment's hesitation, I woke Jim up. He forced his eyes open, nodded and, shotgun in hand, walked toward the cave entrance.

I looked over our trophies. Two Remingtons and thirty cartridges. Kathy's gun turned out to be Italian: as I looked closer, I made out the word Benelli on the grip. The gun had an elongated magazine and a switch between pump and semi-auto. A good gun: light, trustworthy and versatile. Not a bad choice at all considering the terrain. I wasn't quite ready to trust Kathy with it, and Georgie even less so. Let's see first how they got along with the others.

I watched Jim's back as he sat by the cave's entrance. Then I walked over to Wladas and pulled the handgun out from under his bag. He kept sniffing away even as I lifted his head and took the bag itself. Wong opened his eyes the moment I approached, and it took me some time to explain to him, in a whisper, why I needed his gun.

Cleaning the guns would make the time pass quicker. It would keep me awake, too. I sat down next to a sleepy-eyed Jim and reached into the bag for some rags with Kathy's gun across my lap.

"Let me do it," he said.

He sounded like a fully grown man, not the underage deck boy I'd known. This was the first time he'd really spoken to me, and the fact in itself was weird considering we'd already been through thin and thick together.

He pulled the bag closer, took the gun and began taking it apart deftly and expertly, laying the pieces out on a clean cloth that I had put down for him.

"Where did you learn all this?" I asked. "You know how to use a gun, don't you?"

Jim looked up at me. "My uncle taught me."

He was still a teenager with his starry eyes and a pride in his voice. At this age, praise from one's father or a mentor gives you wings and makes you forget past wrongs. It feels as if life will never end.

Had he had a normal life, really? Jim hadn't seen anything yet, apart from Pangea. He'd never been on Earth. Whatever he knew about it, he knew from Pangean deportees.

"I need to ask you something," he said, serious.

"Ask away."

Jim fingered the breech staring at the valley, preparing

to speak.

"They all say," he nodded at the cave, "Georgie, Uncle Lars, Grunt... everyone says the same thing. Life on Earth is real hard, they say. Governments choke the life out of people with their laws, prisons and taxes. Before, there used to be political parties, or so I've been told. It was they who fought for power and started the war," he scratched the top of his head. "Now that they've discovered Pangea, they use it to exile offenders. To instill law and order, like. But that's something I don't understand. How come there're so many offenders? They keep shipping them in several times a month."

He looked up at me. I frowned looking for the right words to explain. But apparently, he hadn't finished.

"This is the thing I wanted to ask you. If all these political prisoners are exiled because they wanted justice for everyone, how come they start doing the same things here?" He thought and added, "Here, they're also at each other's throats fighting for power. They take advantage of the weak. It's like they wanted a better life on Earth, but here they start doing the same thing their governments do."

I stared at him, unable to answer while he went on, "People like McLean, it's pretty obvious they shouldn't have any power. So why do they all obey him back in town? Why should they?" He recovered his breath and finished, anxious, "Did you understand? You know what I mean?"

I did indeed. Talk about straightforward.

"Listen," I reached for the flask in the bag's side pocket. "How d'you know this stuff about laws and taxes? Who told you about parties and political prisoners?"

"My parents did."

"Who are they? Who were they back on Earth?"

"My dad was a neurosurgeon. My mom, a schoolteacher."

"Where are they now?"

"They died. During the plague."

He took out his knife, pushed the gun parts to one side and used the end of the cloth to wipe the breech.

"I'm sorry," slowly, I unscrewed the flask top. "I really am."

"It's all right. It's been a while."

He sat there, composed. Even his voice didn't give.

"I don't remember my parents," I took a large swig and put the flask away. "I grew up in an orphanage. I remember getting here, but not what happened to my family. It's as if I'd had a memory wipe."

I sat there, silent, surprised at my own thoughts. I'd never thought about my parents before. I didn't know who they were or what they did. Weird. Not normal.

"You," I started, "you're right what you've just said. You can't change everyone. We just don't seem to be able..."

I wanted him to understand me but I didn't know which words to use with this homeschooled boy.

"To do what?" he opened the breech and picked up the slide spring. "Able to do what?"

"Did your father tell you about his work?"

"He did. He told me a lot. I loved listening to his stories. He had a journal where he kept all his science notes."

"Then you must know that our bodies are made of flexible systems. We are decentralized."

"I know what you mean," he nodded. "We don't have one particular organ which controls all of our body."

"Exactly. Now if some system unit fails, the system would normally restructure the traffic. But if your heart or liver or kidneys are damaged, you'll most likely die."

"It still doesn't mean that those organs are dominant in the human body."

"Right. That's how they create electronic chains these days: with routers, so that if one unit fails, the others will bypass it until the failure is repaired."

"So?" Jim lowered the spring.

"Our society has a different model. It's vertical, with one control organ on top. It issues orders and decides what to do in any given situation. Every law-abiding citizen should obey the rules - called laws - imposed on them by the government.

"Yeah," he nodded staring at the valley. "If you destroy the controlling organ, the whole system will collapse."

"You got it. So they could try and build a new society here on Pangea. But it wouldn't change people's nature. Speaking genetically... have you heard about genes?"

"It's," he looked up, "it's some kind of inbred memory, right?"

"It is, it is. Generations of our ancestors have formed the current society model which is based on obedience. There'll always be a leader, and whether he's elected or an usurper doesn't really matter. Can you tell me something? Are you a free man? Think well first."

"I... I think I have some control over my life," he said slowly. "But I still can't do whatever I want. I have to..." he nodded, "yes, I do have to obey. I obey the loggers' foreman. Uncle Lars."

"And," I raised my hand, "what if there is no Lars Swenson?"

"There'll be another one," Jim said quickly. "Another leader."

"Who will head the loggers' team," I pointed out.

Jim didn't answer. But his face was different now. He'd understood.

"Shame," Jim finally said. He put down the spring and reached for the firing mechanism housing. "Does it mean things will never change?"

I shook my head. "We won't know even if they do. We won't live long enough."

For a while, Jim didn't move mulling over our conversation. Then he picked up the rag and started wiping the breech.

The stars started to fade over the horizon. The dawn was creeping into the sky. Someone grunted; we both turned to see a gasping Georgie toss and turn on the cave floor. He rose wincing from the pain in his leg and pleading for some water.

I handed him the flask. "Go sleep now." He glanced at the far end of the tunnel where Kathy slept, then lay back down, careful not to disturb his wound.

"Lars Swenson," I said when I came back to the entrance, "is he really your uncle?"

"Yeah," Jim handed me the assembled gun and reached for the other one. "On my mother's side."

He lay his suntanned hands on the weapon and started depressing lugs and twisting latches, unclicking the parts with blindfolded ease. The boy seemed to have potential. His parents must have known as much which was probably why his father had kept notes and spoken to his son about his work. They must have hoped for the much-rumored repatriation amendment. Back on Earth Jim could do well. He could become a teacher or an engineer;

he could continue his dad's research. He had the brains and the skills... but not the luck.

"Can you tell me," I shoved three cartridges into the magazine and clicked the safety catch into place. "Your uncle, what did he do before he became a loggers' foreman?"

"He was on New Pang council board," Jim wrapped a piece of cloth around his finger and wiped the filthy insides of the breech. "He was about to become head of the city administration. The townspeople liked him a lot. They still remember him. Uncle Lars was responsible for supplies and deliveries. He wanted to build new workshops in the estuary and a shipyard. The epidemic changed all that."

"I see," I stared at the sun rising over the eastern horizon. So had it not been for the plague, Lars Swenson could have become the baron of New Pang. I turned to Jim, "And who initiated this Confederation thing?"

"Initi... nitiated," he struggled with the word.

"I mean, whose idea was it?"

"Ah! I see. It was Uncle Lars's," Jim unwound the cloth from his finger, turned it inside out and continued wiping the grime off the gun.

"Thanks," I moved stretching my stiff shoulders.

So Lars could have headed New Pang, had it not been for McLean's curbing of the pandemic. I had to admit the logger had done his best to exaggerate McLean's faults in order to create the image of a ruthless gangster. He'd done it quite subtly, too, mentioning his building the water pipeline and uniting the population during the plague. And still McLean's people burned the infection victims. Having said that, what else could they have done? Here, there're no white-coat researchers capable of creating lab-produced vaccines.

I hiked my neck to my right shoulder, then to the left. Then I locked my fingers and stretched my arms. So Lars Swanson wanted New Pang for himself. That's why he needed the cyber weapons: no wonder he kept mentioning them. But the riggers wouldn't wage war on McLean. Why should they? They seemed to have a normal working relationship with the city. McLean had apparently pitted them against the loggers. Besides, he kept sending carula shipments to the Fort and he really wanted to find out why Earth needed them so badly.

What a can of worms. Just my luck to get mixed up in their local politics. All I wanted was to find Neumann, and once I did that, I'd have no business staying here.

I looked around. Two still asleep: Wladas and Kathy. Georgie groaned as he tried to turn on his other side. Wong sat cross-legged with his eyes closed, meditating, and worked his wounded hand, clenching and unclenching the fist. Only a small spot of blood showed through the bandage meaning Wladas and I had done a decent job of tending to his wound and a good night's rest had completed the healing.

I slapped my hips and got up. Time to break camp. I still had to find time to speak to Kathy on the go. We needed to discuss how better to smuggle Neumann out but first, I needed to know what the FSA had promised her for her cooperation. I had no instructions regarding my Pangean contact and didn't plan on bringing back anybody other than Neumann - but Kathy probably counted on it. So I had no idea how she'd behave once she realized we were to part ways. Then again, I couldn't make it without her.

I told Jim to finish cleaning the guns and started

waking everyone up. Wong rose without a word, took his gun from Jim and walked off. Georgie grumbled casting unhappy glances at the girl. Wladas shook his head and looked around, uncomprehending, rubbing his thin sallow face and trying to remember where he was.

A few minutes later, we sauntered out into the sunlit morning valley. A warm breeze promised a clear hot day.

"Everyone ready?" I scrutinized them one last time and commanded, "We'll move as before. On encountering the enemy, take cover and defend yourselves. In the event I'm killed, Wong takes over the command. Questions?"

"How about our guns," Georgie grumbled glancing at Kathy.

She sniffed and looked up at me. The bruises around her eyes had grown darker, a deep caked gash showing on the bridge of her nose.

"You'll have your guns," I said, "when the moment is right. Let's go," without going into more detail, I strode down the slope toward the valley.

CHAPTER FOUR

WALKING AROUND THE DEVIL'S BARN

I'D UNDERESTIMATED Georgie's condition. Within half an hour, he'd begun to slow our group down. He limped, cussing under his breath at the piece of shrapnel that had ripped his leg open.

Kathy caught up with me. "We'll have to leave him," she said in a low voice. "This way, we'll never make it to the oasis by midday."

"No, we won't," I cut her short. "He's coming along."

We moved further east as we followed the river that showed now and again through the stony hills on the edge of the plain. I turned to the girl,

"This is a funny route, don't you think? The oasis is to the south of the cave. We should be going away from the river."

"Maybe," Kathy stared right in front of her. "To the south is the tigers' pride territory. We won't survive against them. So we're taking the scenic route. Walking

---

around the barn, isn't it what they say? A car would've taken us there in fifteen minutes. But..."

I didn't hear her last phrase. The Information in my head had started up again, and I nearly jumped hearing its monotonous female voice,

Pangean tiger, the most dangerous predator indigenous to the Continent. An adult animal weighs up to a thousand pounds. Fully grown males can reach over two meters in length...

It went on about claws as thick as construction steel; about saber-shaped upper fangs and vital organs protected by a massive rib cage. You needed a pulse gun to pierce the animal's hide: regular firearms might scare it but definitely wouldn't kill it. Its head was large and round with a wide lower jaw. The Pangean tiger was capable of accelerating up to sixty mph over rough terrain.

A true killing machine. You probably needed a grenade launcher to stop it. Surprisingly, they were easily domesticated to the degree of a loyal working dog that wouldn't dream of attacking its master.

That was an eye-opener! My brain refused to believe the Information. Why couldn't you do the same with Siberian tigers? Still, I had no reason not to trust the software.

"Kathy," I ventured in order to double-check the information, "have tigers been killed in the past?"

"Sometimes, yeah. Locals hunt them for their skins. If you make a jacket out of it, it's as good as bulletproof."

"And the cubs?"

"The cubs?" she turned to me.

"Can't you keep them and their mother in a cage or something? I mean, to train them, like in the circus? Can it be done?"

"You're nuts, man," Georgie commented in the back. I looked at him.

"No, you can't," Kathy said. She wanted to add something but paused, raised her hand to her eyes and peered at something in front of her. I never knew what her 'you can't' meant.

The sky darkened over the horizon. Another thunderstorm, I thought. We could do with a bit of rain. It wasn't even midday yet, but the sun blazed down and the hot wind started to scorch our skin. If we wanted to get to the oasis, we'd better move it, and fresh rain from the east might rev us up a bit. We could collect some water, too.

"We need to go back to the cave," Kathy said. "Before it's too late."

"Why?" I said.

"Look up," Georgie said approaching.

At a distance, the air thickened, swirling, as if the horizon was engulfed in a forest fire. Still, I knew there were no forests there, just rocks and lumps of clay.

"There's a storm coming," Georgie said. "This French bitch is right. We need to leg it."

Kathy lunged forward but I blocked her way and clasped her wrist. "If you two keep threatening each other or calling each other names, I'll leave you both here! No water, no guns! Do I make myself clear?"

They sulked. Georgie's jaw moved as he ground his teeth. Kathy clenched and unclenched her fists.

"We're one team," I let go of her hand.

Georgie spat. The girl turned away. I went on, "A sand storm? What's the worst thing about it?"

"The wind," Georgie said. "It'll fucking blow you over. The sand will block your lungs and scrape your eyes out.

Unless you hit your head on a stone."

"Is it so strong, the wind?"

"It is," Kathy turned to us. "Let's go back."

I looked at the horizon, then at the south where the tigers' territory lay. When would the storm reach us? How long could it last? I didn't want to lose another day sitting it out by the river. Varlamov could take action any day now, and I didn't even know how and where he intended to use Neumann and how I was supposed to get him back to Earth.

The sand cloud grew. Now I could clearly see its edges. Still distant but visibly approaching, it was heading for the river. Soon it would cover us. Then we wouldn't be able to find our way anymore.

"We can't go back," I said. "We won't make it."

"We might," Kathy said.

"Look how fast it's growing," I nodded toward the east. "It'll cover the hills before we get there. But if we go south, we might just catch the edge of it."

"The south is tiger country," Georgie said. "Better turn back."

I looked at the sandstorm weighing up our chances. "Let's risk it. No good beating about the bush. Animals normally lie low during storms."

"You're nuts," Kathy exclaimed.

"Nuts as a clone's ass," Georgie added. "Do you think you can escape the tigers? You'll be lunch before you know it."

"This is no time to discuss it," I lifted the gun, checked the magazine and stepped forward. "Those who'd rather go back, be my guest. I won't stop you."

After a moment's hesitation, Wladas walked over to me, pale and silent, his forehead covered in cold sweat.

The decision hadn't come to him easily.

Kathy and Georgie didn't move. After a pause, Jim joined us. Wong walked past us, smiling, the shotgun on his shoulders.

"Forward, at the double, march!" I glanced back at the two remaining. Georgie spat and hobbled after us, frowning. Kathy paused and trotted behind him.

We ran watching the storm approach from the east. Very soon the swirling clouds of sand and dust eclipsed the sky. The hot wind lashed our faces; grains of sand stung our eyes as the storm choked us clogging our noses, ears and mouths. The sun glowed yellow through the murky brown haze.

This was only the beginning. "Stop!" I yelled covering my face with my hand. I grabbed Kathy's shoulder forcing her to stand next to Wladas and ordered them to rope themselves together. Wong didn't need instructions: he'd already made his belt into a noose and fastened it round Georgie's hand. Jim gave me his gun strap. I shoved its end under my belt buckle and we resumed running south, guided by the sun.

The wind grew. I was forced to slow down as our group huddled together, stumbling and burying their faces in their elbows. Still, they kept going. They had to: the moment the sun went down we'd lose any sense of direction. So we had to keep going.

A large shadow slid past. Wladas cried out. I raised my gun while Georgie and Kathy yelled at me demanding theirs.

"Jim!" I spat out the sand and called over the wind, "What's on your side?"

"Two, I think!" he answered. "Two tigers."

I took one hand off the gun and shielded my eyes

from the stinging dust. A shadow... then another... and again... how many of them were there?

"Five," I heard Kathy's finally-composed voice. "They're prowling around."

"Can someone give me a fucking gun?" Georgie kept screaming.

I was racking my brains for some way to deter five adult tigers. Even one was enough to tear us all to shreds. That's why I missed the sound that had weaved itself into the storm's roaring. First I took it for the wind singing in my ears. Then I realized it was not the wind but a whistle. A cop's whistle.

Its trill died away, then repeated, closer this time. As if on cue, the tigers legged it and disappeared in the haze. A white light came on in front of us, similar to one of those Forecomers' beams. But as far as I could remember, there were none of them there.

The bright spot of light shifted up and down as it approached. Was someone trying to send us a signal?

"Hello!" I stepped forward. "We're here!"

"We're here!" the others shouted. "Over here!"

A gust of wind pushed me onto Jim who collapsed onto one knee. Wladas behind me cried out and clasped my elbow pulling me to the ground. I wouldn't have stayed on my feet had Kathy not offered me her shoulder. With her other hand, she held onto Wong's belt who dragged Georgie along trying to brave the wind.

I wheezed attempting to take another step. Holding onto each other, we struggled toward the bright light until a new gust of wind knocked us all down.

Sand blinded our eyes and crunched between our teeth. My swollen tongue was abrasive in my dry mouth. But the light approached - not as fast as we'd thought at first, but it kept moving toward us.

Suddenly the wind abated. The storm still raged around us but it seemed to have lost its strength, as if it had had its fun playing with new toys and had left us under a falling blanket of sand flecks.

Dust floated in the air. The light went out. The sun shone brighter showing bits of sky and a tall human shape.

A man in long flowing robes and a headdress strode toward us leaning on a staff. His face was covered by a shawl.

"Ahmad," Kathy gasped. "This is Ahmad! The goat-herder from the oasis!"

A large herd of goats followed the man, about forty animals at least.

"You know him well?" I spat sand as I sat down and picked the dirt out of my ears, nose and eyes.

"Not really, no. I've seen him a couple times. Normally it was Famba who did all the talking."

Our faces were covered with so much dust you couldn't even see Jim's freckles. Wladas reached into his bag for the flask and was about to wash his face when Kathy stopped him.

"No point in wasting water. Have a swig yourself and offer some to the others. You can wipe your face with a cloth."

He complied, a silent question still in his eyes.

"We don't know if we can get more water at the oasis," she explained. "Better save it. Now don't say anything," she lowered her voice. "Leave him to me."

I nodded. Let her do it. Georgie didn't have enough strength to protest. He sat and wheezed spitting out sand as Jim wiped his face with a cloth. Wong was already back on his feet, his shotgun on his shoulders, greeting the goat herder.

Ahmad walked past him without acknowledgment. Kathy waved her hand to him. The goat herder walked toward her and stopped. The bell-jingling goats advanced a little more and stopped too. Some of them bleated, identifying themselves. Long-haired and tailless, they had black patches on their heads and short horns no more than a thumb long. Very sharp.

I swung round remembering the tigers. The storm had moved off toward the river. Had the tigers moved along? Or... I looked at the goats. Could I have mistaken these hairy beasts for tigers? Say, a few had strayed from the herd and the man had whistled to call them back. All that panicking was for nothing.

A silver whistle dangled on Ahmad's chest. On his belt he wore a lamp very similar to those I saw in the hotel and on Grunt's boat. Still, this one was different. Its base was of the same material as the cave and the Forecomers' tower supports. A glass tube sat in the base letting the light through its convex lenses. A thick cap of the same material covered the lamp.

That's how we could see the light through the storm. It didn't take long to realize that the deportees applied the Forecomers' technologies to suit their own needs. Why not use a lamp like that when you had no other option?

Ahmad's crafty black eyes glanced around shiftily. He hid the whistle in the folds of his robe and removed the shawl showing a broad furrowed face. He had a straight nose, a thick moustache and a wiry graying goatee. He must have been old but he stood straight with his wide shoulders and his hand steady on his staff, giving us a lordly look.

"Lost your way," he said in a husky low voice with a thick Oriental accent and bared his crooked teeth. "Ahmad feed goats, Ahmad see storm. Ahmad see men, come give help."

"We really appreciate it," Kathy said gracefully. "How can we make it worth your while?"

"You know price."

"But," Kathy looked back at me, embarrassed, "We..."

"Ahmad?" I produced the fabric tube with the money. "How much?"

The goat herder bared his teeth again. He shook his head, "You new here, man. You misunderstand. I take your guns. You go."

"What's that for a..." I started but Kathy hissed at me and stomped her foot.

"Who is commander here?" Ahmad gave me a crooked smile as his hand reached into the folds of his robe.

An animal roar made us turn. The storm had shifted over the river leaving a haze hanging over the hills. The visibility was good though. A large mound of rocks which we hadn't noticed earlier was piled up on the ground not far from us. The roaring seemed to come from behind it.

"He is," Kathy nodded at me.

"Then why woman speak?" Ahmad addressed me.

I looked into the man's crafty eyes. This wasn't the kind of man you could convince easily. He knew what he wanted. He had raised tame tigers for self-protection. That's why Kathy didn't want us to go through the valley. She hadn't had time to explain but it didn't matter. Ahmad would find a way to get his toll paid this way or that. This was his territory, and we'd trespassed.

"She spoke because she knew you," I finally said.

Ahmad looked at Kathy.

"He's right," she said. "I tried to tell him we shouldn't go this way..."

The herder raised his hand. "Guns."

"What's the swap?" I said.

"Your lives," the smile disappeared from his face. His eyes went cold.

I knew I could kill him, and he knew it, too. That would be the end of us. His tigers would make short work of us.

"Let's meet halfway," I insisted. "We won't make it there," I waved toward the east, "without our guns."

"Go back to New Pang. Buy more guns," Ahmad said patiently.

"We can't go there," I said. "We need to keep going."

The goat herder raised a bushy eyebrow and stroked his beard. Then he nodded, "Very well. You are Ahmad's guests. Alexie's generator broke. You fix before sunset, we quits."

"Agreed." Now I knew the raiders weren't in the oasis otherwise he wouldn't have offered us the deal. He'd have too many visitors to lodge.

Kathy stared at me open-mouthed but chose not to say anything.

"Go to village," Ahmad's hand reappeared from the folds of his robe and rearranged the whistle on the chain. "Woman will show you Alexie's house."

He nearly walked through me. I stepped aside as did Jim and Wladas. Georgie's sad stare followed the goat herder. The bells jingled and the goats bleated after their master.

CHAPTER FIVE

LONG TIME NO SEE

B Y THE TIME we got to the oasis, Georgie was in a bad way. Blood had soaked his bandage and pant leg and he was very pale, paler than Wladas who helped Jim to support Georgie's limp body.

"That way," Kathy pointed at the closest sandstone cabin with a straw roof.

The oasis consisted of three cabins fenced off with clay bricks, each with several lean-tos and outhouses. We passed through a flimsy gate under a wooden arch and entered a yard where a few gnarly trees cast shade over a well.

No one came out to meet us.

"Wait under the trees," Kathy said and went into the cabin.

Wladas and Jim helped Georgie to sit down. Wong went for a bit of a recce along the fence. I had a look around.

The water pump stood on a thick log base next to a bolted-down diesel generator, its insides rusting under bent metal covers. No wonder it had given up the ghost. You really had to take good care of these things and put them under tarps to protect them from the elements.

I raised the creaky lid and looked inside the well. The water was about sixty feet down the stone-lined shaft. You could tell that whoever had done it knew his job: in a properly lined well, the water level would stay high and clean.

Gutters snaked from the well to each house, some reaching inside the outhouses, other to water troughs and corrals. In one corral a mule swished its tail, its head low in the feeding trough. Several ostriches were wandering about in another one.

Ostriches! They must think they're back home in Africa. The third and biggest corral stood empty - had to be for Ahmad's goats that I'd just seen by the river.

One structure stood apart from the rest - a squat fenced-off barn away from the trees. Wong came to it, took the shotgun off his shoulder and motioned for me to approach. I told the others to stay put and walked over to him.

I smelled blood even before I came close. Wong kicked the door open. Guns at the ready, we cringed and stepped back. Cages stood inside on the floorboards covered with sawdust. Inside them, I saw half-eaten bones and torn animal skins. I stepped back, unable to stand the thick smell of a menagerie. Five empty water buckets stood by the barn door. No marks for telling me who they were for.

Wong nodded at the buckets and gave me a meaningful look. I didn't answer. Instead, I turned round and walked back into the shade.

By the time we returned, Kathy had come out

followed by a portly woman, a thick plait of hair dangling below her waist. Her round face was rather crimson at that moment as if she'd spent all morning cooking by the fire. I looked up at the smoke trailing from the chimney.

The woman wiped her plump fingers on a flour-covered apron, rearranged her dress and said in a deep voice,

"This one, no?" She pointed at me. "You promised our Ahmad-jan to fix the machine?"

The woman spoke in a slow Southern Russian singsong. She came to me and offered a firm handshake.

"I'm Alexie, me. I'm on duty here while the men are away on business."

"Yeah," I glanced at Kathy.

"Oh," Alexie looked at Georgie attended by Jim and a foot-shifting Wladas. "He ain't looking good. He'll bleed to death on you in a minute." She looked around and went on, "Bring him into the house. And you," she pointed at me, "go to the larder, get the tools out and see to the machine, will ya?"

After explaining where to find the larder, the woman showed Wladas and Jim into the house. They carried Georgie in while Wong and Kathy stayed outside.

Their choice of tools didn't amount to much. Three box wrenches, two screwdrivers and a pair of pliers. I scooped them all off the shelf and came back out.

"Know anything about generators?" I asked Kathy.

"I can unscrew a bolt if needed."

"Stay and help me, then. Wong," I turned to him, "go and check out direction east. See what's out there."

He checked his handgun, balanced his shotgun on his shoulder and jumped over the fence. I stared at the generator.

"Know when the raiders are coming back?" I squatted by the machine thinking how best to tackle it.

"It'll be a while. Alexie said we've just missed the work shift changeover."

"Hold it here," I dropped the wrench onto a bolt aiming to unscrew the cowling to get to the fuel line.

"It'll be at least another week," Kathy lay her hands on the wrench and held it in position. "We've been lucky. Ahmad doesn't normally bargain."

Lucky indeed. If only I could have worked out what was wrong with the generator!

"You think you can fix it?" hope shone in Kathy's eyes.

"I'll do what I can," I grunted as I unscrewed the first bolt.

Once I'd removed the cover, I squatted by the machine tapping the wrench against my leg. What had we got there? A gas feed tap. A fuel pipe. I unscrewed the tank top - empty. I pushed my hand through the hole and felt the bottom. My fingers came out filthy. So... I'd remove the tank, clean the fuel pipe and try to start it.

"Well," I turned to Kathy, "if I don't get it working in an hour, they'll need a professional."

She didn't reply.

"Not to worry," I said. "The engine seems okay, but the tank filter is probably clogged and so is the fuel pipe. Go to the woman and ask her for some rags and diesel. Tell her we'll soon be finished."

As I fiddled with the tools I noticed two children's faces in the window: a tiny tot of a boy with blond tousled hair and an older girl, dark curls framing her curious face. Both watched me with great interest.

The boy looked a lot like the landlady and the girl

resembled the goat herder. Apparently, Alexie and Ahmad didn't waste their time here.

I gave the kids a wink and started unscrewing the next bolt. Kathy returned with some rags and a can of diesel and began helping me.

"Wish you hadn't been so double fucking quick back at the coast," she sighed. "We wouldn't have been here to begin with."

"Correction," I prized the filter out of the fuel pipe with the screwdriver. "You wouldn't have been here. Neither would we."

She grinned but didn't say anything.

"When did McLean first decide to find out the purpose of carula?" I ripped a rag in two, soaked its end in diesel and started cleaning the inside of the fuel pipe.

Kathy paused. "Half a year? I honestly can't remember. Do you know its purpose?"

"Not really," I gave her a clean cloth and nodded at the filter wishing I hadn't started.

Kathy placed a hand on my shoulder. I put down the fuel pipe. "What is it?"

"Carula," she said. "When the scientists first came to study Pangea, McLean used to see Neumann a lot and also the woman, the biologist. They told him how to grow seaweed. That's when he started his New Pang farms swapping his crops for Earth deliveries.

"So what?" I shook her hand off. "Earth needs carula to make a food supplement. Too many mouths to feed."

"That's not what I mean," she shook her head. "If you compare the amounts of carula we ship and the Earth's population, we'd have to turn the entire coast into seaweed farms. Besides, the riggers still have the gold - why didn't Earth demand it back?"

"Are you talking about the Arctic goldmines transport? The supply vessel that was caught in the jump?"

"Exactly. It was packed to the upper deck with gold. Now why would they waste energy shipping carula back to earth, and leave gold behind?"

"I think I know what you mean," I frowned racking my brains for an excuse to cut the discussion short before the Information butted in. In that case, I'd have no other option but to eliminate Kathy. That would really mess up my plans.

She waited.

"Because," I started, "the energy costs much more than the gold itself."

Kathy chuckled. "Yeah right. You can tell that to the freshly arrived dumbfucks but not to me!"

"So what do you want?" I demanded.

"Just to see how the land lies," she crumpled the rag, blew through the filter and started rubbing it clean. "I knew that McLean would try to use you. He wouldn't work with the FSA. Your Feds must be really stupid, telling him about your mission. He thought that the Feds wanted to expatriate the only carula researcher; they would ask McLean to help you and leave him with jack shit. That's what I wanted to warn you about. I had everything ready, guns, money, I had a whole plan how to give it to you in my brother's house. It didn't work, did it?"

We worked in silence for a while. Then I asked,

"What did the FSA promise you for doing this?"

"Amnesty. For me and my bro."

"How do you think you were going to leave Pangea?"

"I'd go with you," She looked up at me, surprised.

"Didn't they tell you?"

I suppressed a negative answer. I'd received no instructions regarding her and her brother.

"Right," I changed the subject. "How do you keep contact with the Fort?"

"I've got a radio."

"Oh," I checked the fuel pipe against the light and took a new rag. "Where do you keep it?"

"None of your business."

So. This was getting interesting. She was probably waiting for me to answer her carula question. Or she might be wary of me leaving her behind. She seemed to have grasped the whole point.

"Kathy. I need to know where you keep the radio in case I need to use it. If you get killed, I-"

"Until I am, I'm still your contact."

I looked into her face. The way Georgie had described her back at the coast, you'd think she was a fucking Nazi. And that's what she'd been at first, but now... Now she was a human being desperate to get home, by hook or by crook. I didn't think she was putting it on. But why would George still hate her so much?

"Sorry," I tried to sound calm, "it won't work this way."

"How will it, then?"

"We've already engaged with General Varlamov's men, if you remember. And we were lucky to survive. Once we find the professor and try to smuggle him out, there will be casualties, believe me."

The kids looked out of the house. The boy walked out into the yard. The girl hid herself behind the wall, sticking her head out.

"I believe you," Kathy rose and reached into her

pocket for a flat round candy box. "Some of us won't come back."

She opened the box and stared inside for a while, then handed it to the kids.

She didn't look like a Nazi freak. Even if she'd zapped three clones. Could a cold-blooded murderess be so nice with kids? She tousled the boy's hair and told him to share the candy with his sister. Then she came back.

"What's your brother's name?"

"Philippe," she picked up the filter and the cloth.

Actually, the existence of a brother (I remembered the dark-haired French guy at McLean's place) suggested he was the one with the radio. "Does he know your collaborate with the FSA?"

"Who, Philippe? Not the slightest idea. He thinks I deal with several groups. Many raiders do so."

"What if McLean finds out?"

"He trusts me. And he's interested in making new connections. He can't be everywhere at the same time."

"Fine," I put the fuel tube aside and rose to remove and clean the gas tank.

Once I was finished, I said a silent prayer and tugged on the starter rope. The engine jerked and sprang to life. For a moment, we listened to its powerful sound watching the water trickle down the troughs into the corrals and houses. Kathy gave me a weak smile.

"Kill the wretched thing before you waste all the gas!" Hands on her hips, Alexie walked out of the house. "When the men come back, they can start it up then."

She turned to go back in, but added, "Well done, thanks. Now in with the two of you for a wash and a bit of dinner. Go have a look at your friend, too."

"How is he?" I asked meaning Georgie.

"Not good," Alexie shook her fist at Wong who was climbing over the fence. "Can't you use the gate?" she shouted, then turned back to me. "You go see for yourself. I should really leave him here for a day or two. Ahmad-jan and I will take good care of him. He seems fit and strong so he can pay us back by doing a few things about the house."

She went back in.

"So," Kathy asked picking her nails, "you gonna leave him here or drag him along?"

I gave it some thought.

"One of your men can't be trusted," she pointed out.

That was true. The cyber troopers by the river had recognized one of them, but which one? Was it Jim or Georgie? Or Kathy? Definitely not Wladas - he'd just arrived at Pangea, although...

The solution came to me naturally. "I know what to do," I said. "Wong, come along with us."

The house had only two rooms. One contained a clay oven and a table; in the other, Georgie lay on a bed. We washed ourselves in a narrow corridor that led to a lean-to. Then we walked into Georgie's room.

He looked even worse than before. Sweat trickled down his ashen face. The eyes glistened with anxiety. Without letting me speak, he hurried, gasping, begging us not to leave him "in this fucking rat hole". I asked Wladas what he thought about the wound. He didn't waste too many words. Blood loss and septicemia.

He was right there. It's not the bullets that kill in action: it's dirt. Septicemia - blood poisoning - could turn the smallest scratch into a lethal wound. Especially in the Pangean climate, rife with alien bacteria. I hadn't forgotten my carula wound yet.

I reached into my pocket for a few coins and gave them to Jim. "You stay here with him." I told him to give some money to the landlady. This way she could arrange it with the raiders to take Georgie and Jim back to the loggers.

Georgie tried to object but I didn't listen. I gave Jim's shotgun to Kathy, waved to the rest and walked outside.

Alexie was scrambling out of the cellar hatch in the hallway. I hadn't noticed it at first. She held a pitcher of milk and a packet.

"Here," she shoved the food to me. "Thanks for the generator." She turned to Kathy. "Go and get some water. Take as much as you can carry."

I took the pitcher and the packet of what turned out to be frozen meat. Apparently, the cellar had an ice room.

"Thank you," I said. "I'm leaving Jim to look after Georgie. He'll pay you."

The woman nodded and let us out into the yard. Calling for the kids to come and eat their dinner, she disappeared back into the house.

We filled our flasks and traced the fence heading east. The sun crept toward the horizon but the air was still too hot for comfort. In the tree shade I hadn't noticed it that much. I looked back. The goats and their herder were returning from the river back to the oasis.

This time the tigers trailed nearby flanking the hairy goats who paid no heed to them, apparently accustomed to the predators' company. Three of the tigers were rather large - probably, male. Their skin was a stripeless grayish yellow, two saber teeth protruding from their upper jaws. As for the rest, they looked like normal tigers back on Earth with their catlike heads, long tails and feline gait.

Kathy slowed down too watching them. "Predators

prowl at sunset."

Was it a book quote or her own sentiment? "And then they dine," I said.

The air shuddered. Our ears popped from an explosion. Another one thundered through the valley throwing us to the ground. We covered our heads as missiles flashed past us.

When the shock waves subsided, I rolled onto my back, sat up and raised the gun. The trees in the oasis crackled as fire licked their tops. Smoke billowed over the barn. Two rockets hissed through the smoke: one hit the goats, the other, the settlement.

Another blow sent me onto my back. I covered my face feeling the ground tremble. Then it rained with stones and chips of wood.

"The children!" I heard Kathy over the next explosion.

"Down, you idiot!" I kicked her feet away pushing her to the ground.

The worst thing for infantry is a rocket launcher. Once the explosions had died away, we heard the approaching roar of sand buggies. Several of them. The clatter of pulse guns was interspersed with the humming of an engine. A behemoth personnel carrier approached the settlement. His roof sported several grenade launchers.

Here we go. They'd mop us up in no time.

The launchers shuddered spitting out a dozen grenades. The heavy vehicle rocked on its suspension and rammed the fence. Two of the sand buggies headed straight for us and yet another one rolled out into the valley chasing the three remaining tigers.

The fur on the animals' heads was singed by the flames. Their saber teeth glistened in the setting sun. Incredibly fast, the tigers were catching up with the buggy.

The pulse gun flashed blue scorching the first tiger's head and ripping through his spine. Blood everywhere. The tiger tumbled; the two others sped up and raced off together, leaping at the buggy. One collapsed in mid-air but the other thrust at the moving vehicle knocking down the twin-barreled gun on the roof.

The buggy's wheels swerved under his half-ton weight. For a moment, the tiger disappeared in a cloud of dust. His teeth and claws clashed on the armored steel. The combat vehicle tilted to one side and nearly flipped over. Its brakes screeching, it slid a few more feet forward and came to a halt.

A hatch opened. A trooper emerged raising his pulse gun shooting at the attacking tiger. Still roaring, the animal reached out for the soldier. His gun went flying as the man disappeared in the hatchway. The tiger collapsed on the armor and slid off, already dead.

The electric motor whirred as the engineer tried to restart the vehicle. Kathy jumped up and started for the buggy but I stopped her as a personnel carrier appeared from the burning settlement. The two other sand buggies had already arrived. No good trying to resist: all we could do was wait.

The buggies rolled closer and surrounded us baring their twin-barreled guns. The personnel carrier towered above them, its loader casting a wide sidelong shade over us. A row of hatches opened spewing out soldiers in light gear each equipped with DSS - digital soldier kit which included a universal infrared binocular visor, portable camera sights and a terminal in a breast pocket, all connected to the optoelectronic control system.

The commander's cupola opened. A squat officer with

a raised visor peered out of the personnel carrier.

A captain, judging by his breast chevron. He raised his high-cheekboned face to me with a crooked grin.

"What did I say?" I heard.

A cyber trooper slid out onto the armor of the nearby buggy. I recognized him. He'd shot Famba that day by the river. He stood there, laid back and indifferent, resting his hands on the stock of his rifle, and stared at the fat-faced engineer.

"It's him!" the cyber trooper said. "Can't you see?"

"You don't remember us, eh?" the captain grinned. "They've done a good job on you."

"There were children in the village!" Kathy spat out. "You killed them! You've just killed innocent people!"

The captain lowered his head and spoke into the hatchway,

"Operator. What do the scanners read?"

"All clear," a voice came from the hatchway. "No survivors. All dead."

"You're right," the officer bared his even teeth and barked, "Drop your weapons. Resistance is futile."

I nodded to Wong and Wladas, dropped my gun to the ground and raised my hands. Kathy froze with her shotgun barrel down, her eye twitching.

"Don't-" I started but the girl leaned forward, her lips moving.

Wong beat me to it. He knocked the gun out of her hands, pushed her toward the carrier and threw her gun to the soldiers.

CHAPTER SIX

METROPOLIS

"**Y**OU FUCKING jerks!" Kathy yelled in an already hoarse voice and slammed the vehicle's bulkhead. "Where are you taking us?"

The soldiers in the cab didn't react. Sand pattered under the personnel carrier's wheels as it whizzed forward. An occasional stone clanked against the hull, then it was all quiet again.

They'd handcuffed us and crammed us into the reserve battery compartment - a perfect lockup that could only be opened from the outside. A tiny grill in the stanchion let in a thin mixture of air and exhaust fumes. At least they'd left us the water which had proved a lifesaver, especially after we'd dampened pieces of my torn T-shirt and wrapped them around our faces. This way at least we could breathe. From time to time, the vehicles' headlights cut through our pitch-black dungeon as they followed the commander's radio orders and changed formation. Then I clung to the grill trying to work out exactly where in the desert we could be.

Wladas kept a gloomy silence. For a while, Kathy had tried to convince him to join her screaming fit. Instead, he'd clammed up and paid no heed to her pleas and threats. Finally, she lost her voice trying to get answers from the soldiers and stopped, exhausted.

The battery compartment was far too tiny for us to stretch our legs. Kathy huddled up next to me. Wong and Wladas doubled up opposite.

I gave up my attempts to divine our destination. Instead, I thought about what the squad captain had said. He'd recognized me, even if I'd never seen him before. Apparently, the cybers knew me, too. I remembered their argument at the foothill by the river. So it looked like I shouldn't have blamed Georgie and Jim, let alone Wladas, for knowing my identity.

What the fuck was going on? Where did the cybers know me from? According to FSA analytics, General Varlamov had no more than three cyber troopers. The rest of his men were human. And? It didn't pan out. I had to approach the problem in a different way. There was this idea, something I'd remembered just as I'd arrived at Pangea...

But I couldn't breathe, let alone think. I wriggled in place trying to find a more comfortable position. The noise of the engine started to drive me nuts.

Kathy must have read my thoughts because she turned and croaked into my ear,

"What was it their officer was jabbering on about? I didn't quite get it."

A bright beam of light reached through the grill illuminating Wong and Wladas' faces. One of the sand buggies turned about and drove past the carrier heading for a body of water glistening far away.

The river. We were by the river. The carrier turned and continued toward it.

"Mark," Kathy jogged my shoulder. "You hear me? I said, what did that asshole commander say to you? Looks like you've met before!"

"I've no idea," I said watching our progress toward the river.

I recognized the characteristic clang of the wave deflector as it dropped into position on the vehicle's front. The engine revved up as the driver turned the aft waterjets onto blow. We were about to cross the river. The first buggy was already in the water. The carrier's beam hit the deserted opposite bank. Without slowing down, we rolled into the river.

"No idea," I repeated louder. "First time I saw him."

"The Chinese," she changed the subject, "he's not a chatty type, is he? Are you?" she turned to Wong.

"leave him alone," I said, my eyes glued to the grill. "He's only my cover." A wave hit the carrier's armored side splattering water in my face. The vehicle rocked gently.

"A gunman?" Kathy leaned against my shoulder trying to see what was going on.

"Sort of. A combat tactician, rather."

"Some partners you've got," I could see the smirk on her face, "Why did he stand and watch us fight, then? Back at the coast he didn't hesitate to kick our butt. Here, he wasn't so decisive."

"Why should he be," I shifted again trying to stretch my stiff muscles. "Their combat potential was his own times one hundred."

"Their what?"

"Too long to explain."

The carrier crawled out of the water and started climbing a steep hill. I fell over Kathy and Wong over Wladas. Another headbeam crossed our dungeon revealing heavy clumpy soil around. Not a grain of sand. It looked like we'd crossed the desert along the river's left bank. In that case, we had to be near the swamps. A weird route indeed.

Immediately, I answered my own question. Judging by what I remembered of the Information's map in my head, the convoy had crossed the plain to bypass the oil riggers' base and was now heading for... let me think... we were going north toward... toward the farmers' settlements and the City of Forecomers. But where exactly were they taking us?

"And this Wladas," Kathy spoke again, "what's he got to do with you two?"

"Wladas is a neurotech," I answered mechanically as I tried to guess where we were going. "He specializes in cyber troopers."

Varlamov had given the farmers plenty of notice to relocate. He was after something, and that something was near the old city.

"You mean," the girl insisted, "he knows how to kill these tube-headed monsters? Is that what he does?"

"It is," I nodded. "He knows how to kill them."

"So why was he too fucking slow to catch a cold back at the river?" she snapped.

I couldn't take it any longer. "Because you need custom weapons to take them out! Do I look as if we have them? So do shut up and help me think. Have you ever been in the swamps? You think one could camp there? And if you can, what would General Varlamov need there?

She sat silent for a moment. Then she said,

"By the swamps, there're some alien ruins. We went there a few times. Just some rock fragments and a few tunnels, all collapsed. Nothing interesting. We didn't find any artifacts there. Just a hole in the wall.

"Good to make camp?"

"A temporary camp, yeah. Vehicles easy to camouflage. Actually, if you dug yourself in by those ruins, a hundred guns couldn't touch you."

"I see," I said but the truth was, I didn't see anything. The swamps covered a lot of ground. Farms, famous for their fertile soil, ran all along the swamps' edge. It had been Neumann who'd brought his biologists to Pangea to study its various regions. I rubbed my wrists under the cuffs. "Enough now. We need some rest. Go and sleep."

I sat back and closed my eyes. Kathy next to me shifted trying to get comfortable.

I didn't know how long we'd sat side by side. I'd lost count of time and drifted into a restless slumber. When I opened my eyes, the darkness outside had started to dissipate. The carrier's engine groaned a couple of times and, amid the hiss of the air pumps, we jerked to a stop. Wong and Wladas awoke with the impact.

"There we are," I said looking through the grill.

The buggies and the personnel carrier were parked on a flat stone platform - or rather, a granite slab half the size of a soccer pitch. Beyond it I could see a grassy plain and... just some mist - so thick that the sunrays couldn't penetrate the murky fog.

Now I finally got my bearings. We were in the old city. The fog swirled around over the swamps. I turned to Kathy: the farms should lie behind the carrier.

A hatch creaked open, then another, followed by

talking and the stomping of feet. Guns clattered. I looked through the grill at the cyber troopers hurrying away from their buggies with a stretcher. The small angle of vision didn't allow me to see where they were taking the wounded soldier.

Metal-plated combat boots stomped overhead. Locks clicked and the lockup hatch moved aside. I had to shut my eyes from the unbearably bright morning light.

"Get out," a voice ordered. Kathy rose first but groaned and collapsed on top of me. Wong managed to spread his numb legs. Soldiers grabbed his shoulders and yanked him out, then pushed him down to the ground. They repeated the same with each of us.

A couple of minutes later we had warmed our muscles up a little. At least we could stand up under the indifferent stares of the squad captain and two more guards. I, in the meantime, made my first observations of the area.

The first thing that really jumped out at me were some huge structures I decided to call gasometers. Two enormous octagonal buildings loomed in front of us eclipsing the sky. I was sure their rough moss-grown stone walls guarded one or two of the old planet's secrets. On the roof of the one closest to us stood what looked like a crane jig complete with a gear hoist and some cables. Apparently, they'd been very recently used to lift something heavy to the top and left there. Along the roof's edge I noticed the ends of a camouflage net stretched over it.

It had to be my imagination, but for a second I thought that the sky over the structures gleamed with a whitish blue shimmer. Ancient foundations lay behind the buildings, arranged checkerwise for whatever good it did them. Behind the foundations was another granite platform with a mobile solar power system installed: five squat panels on wheels glistening with photo cells faced west. They reflected the rays of the rising sun making me squint with their light. Fat cables ran from the panels to a power converter and then further to the nearest gasometer disappearing in an opening guarded by some troopers.

Apart from soldiers, I noticed several civilians. At first I thought they were captured farmers. Then I saw guns in their hands and remembered Lars Swenson's stories. Clones. Oh well.

The clones had their own camp by the power station with three tents and a rusty truck tractor hooked to a ten-ton trailer. That was about it. Some of the humans guarded the outside perimeter: I could see several figures spread out along the border with the plain.

Someone shoved me in the shoulder. "Forward march," the captain motioned us. The soldiers took us to the opening in the nearest gasometer's wall, the one with the cables. I glanced in the direction of the swamps and noticed mountain peaks rising over the toxic mist.

A patrol carrier drove past with a soldier sitting on its armored turret. Now there were only three vehicles left at the platform: the personnel carrier and the two buggies one of which had been damaged by the tiger. Mechanics were already busy laying their tools out by its front wheels.

As we walked to the gasometer I tried to estimate their battery inverter's capacity. If I wasn't wrong, it could power half of New Pang. They could bring electricity to half the city's homes plus light the streets with their battery reserves!

So what was it that General Varlamov - or Neumann with his backing - had discovered in the City of the Forecomers? What had the general been up to all this time as he'd lain low off Pangean's authorities' radar? And why had the said authorities done nothing about it?

My head swam with questions, each more important than the last. Watchful and alert, I walked down a dimly-lit passage trying to remember every ledge and turn, every apparently useless detail like a dented bucket in a niche by the wall, or an air vent twenty paces to the right from the gasometer's entrance, or the number of the steps leading underground.

The staircase seemed to last forever. I noted some three hundred-something steps until I finally lost count. Wladas walked in front of me. The passage narrowed as it descended so that the captain and the guard behind my back kept catching their weapons and gear on the stone ledge. The fat cables snaked along the wall to my right. Good. If the lights went out, it would be easy to feel our way back.

"What a place," Wladas whispered. "Sheer Metropolis."

"Sheer what?"

"Metropolis. The city caught between heaven and hell."

"No talking!" the captain ordered.

A gun barrel dug into my spine. I cringed but didn't talk back. There'd be plenty of time. I followed Wladas through a doorway and found myself in a large hall crammed full of machinery. Humming transformer cabinets touched the low ceiling. Thick cable bundles snaked and looped over the floor and the walls so you would have a hard time sorting them out. In a far corner, in a cubicle staked out with console tables, an operator in officer's uniform watched several monitors, his strained face illuminated by the screens' glare.

The captain walked past us, intent like an animal chasing his prey. Not the gait of a typical man: his body had to be cram full of implants. We walked past the cabinets and the cubicle and found ourselves between what they call "clean rooms": two glass cubes stuffed with expensive lab equipment.

Wladas glanced back at me, and I nodded. He knew what these machines were for; I'd never had a chance to see anything like them. Apparently, Varlamov had orchestrated his Pangean exile scenario well in advance and arranged the delivery of all this special-purpose apparatus and their staff sworn to secrecy. Our analytics had misjudged him badly. They didn't have the slightest idea about all this shit.

I remembered the hoist machine on top of the gasometer. That's how they must have brought the machines inside. The hallway was just about wide enough to get the cables in.

Disinfecting lamps burned in one of the two glass cubes. There, two neurotechs in white "clean suits" stood over a cyber trooper sprawled in a hospital chair.

His chest was pried open. Ridged tubes and catheters disappeared under his ribs. A drainage machine reverberated on a stand by the chair pumping lymph through the body. Blood dripped onto the floor under the chair. The neurotechs paid no attention to it. One spoke to the patient in the chair who answered calmly, his face relaxed.

But of course - the cybers' complex nervous architecture allowed them to shut off certain body areas and stay insensitive to pain.

The other neurotech seemed to be tuning a portable mentoscope. The machine differed a lot from the stationary one they used in the Fort for mind scans. This one looked like a small tomograph with an additional console and a few plugs on the side panel for power and auxiliary equipment.

"Are they torturing him?" Kathy asked aloud.

The guards smirked.

"No," Wladas whispered with a cautious glance at them. "Just maintenance."

"Maintenance?" she winced.

"The tiger mauled him, remember?" I said. "It has to be serious if they've opened up his chest. They're changing his combat modules or even reinstalling the software."

"No talking," the guard snapped behind me.

I swayed. His gun barrel hit the air. The guard stumbled and nearly fell face down. "Halt!" he shouted regaining his footage.

"Hands on your head!" the other one raised his gun.

I'd done it on purpose. I wanted the guards to stop us here so I could have a good look at the lab. Hopefully, Wladas had done the same. Wong's observational skills didn't need to be questioned.

While the guards trained their guns on us, I studied the lab equipment. How many cybers did Varlamov have? Two were out on patrol, and another one was lying here in intensive care. The captain had to be a cyber, too. That's already four, plus Varlamov himself - their mastermind and control center.

I glanced over my shoulder at the other glass cube. Two labs for five cybers was a bit over the top. It meant there were others I hadn't yet seen.

"What's going on?" I heard the captain's voice from the hallway.

"This one," the guard pointed his gun at me. "He didn't obey orders."

'Liar," I gasped biding for time. "You nearly lost your gun."

"You fu-" he struck out with the butt of his rifle.

"As you were!" the captain ordered. "Shut up, both of you!"

For a moment, the officer studied me and the others, suspicion in his eyes. "Carry on,' he finally said. "I'll join you in a moment."

He walked past us. The guards took us in the opposite direction into a wide stone hallway dimly lit by glowing wall lamps. I followed Wladas along more cables snaking along its walls. The guard's angry stare burned a hole in my skull.

The neurotech cried out and stopped. I nearly walked into him. All three of us froze next to an open-mouthed Kathy.

Oh well. Wladas had to be right about Metropolis.

We stood on the doorstep of an enormous hall divided by a transparent sheet of either glass or plastic. The nearest half of the hall was packed with all sorts of machines I'd never seen before. Chart recorders ticked, cooler fans whirred inside server boxes; lights flickered on control panels; lidless casings exposed more lengths of cables.

An officer at a console station in the center glanced up at us and went on tapping at his keyboard. This part of the hall reminded me of a combat control center. But the other half... I took in a lungful of air and let it out slowly as I gazed at the stuff dreams are made of.

Behind the partition lay a fragment of an alien world.

The sheer size of it defied human imagination. Spherical vaults of gray marble-like stone came together at an impossible height, too high to see. Their circumference was studded with long rods slanting downward, their ends almost meeting above the center of the hall forming a truncated cone narrow end down.

About a meter below, on a pedestal, lay a black ribbed semisphere. It was covered in small black blisters as if the sphere had been made with bubbling hot tar and then refrigerated at just the right moment.

A group of people stood around the sphere: a tall broad-shouldered man in a military uniform and two civilians: a submissive white-haired old man and a woman with her chin in the air. Both wore lab coats.

Above their heads, weak bolts of lightning sparked from the lower ends of the rods reaching for the semisphere. Something prevented the lightning from touching the ribbed surface - some protective field or other - causing the lightning bolts to diffract and change direction. They climbed back up the rods like spiders and exploded high above sending a rain of sparks down onto the researchers' heads. They talked, indifferent to the phenomenon. Or rather, the man in the uniform spoke while the other two listened to him.

The captain reappeared next to us. He stepped toward the partition and froze with his fingers to his temple. I was right, then: he too was a cyber, tuning his communications channel.

The woman habitually repeated his gesture. This was getting interesting. Was she a cyber scientist? She turned her head toward us: a narrow face, a straight nose, thin lips and long fair hair. Her wide-open eyes sparkled with recognition when she saw me. She touched the old man's shoulder, her lips moving silently behind the soundproof partition.

The captain shook his head and pressed his fingers tighter to his head, his face strained. It could be that the partition was not just sound- but also radio-proof. I'd heard of those security shields before although I didn't know much about their technical aspect.

The old man and the one in the uniform turned around simultaneously. I nearly jumped as the Information identified the former as Boris Neumann. The voice in my head said a few words and stopped. The old man removed his glasses and wiped them squinting at me shortsightedly. Then he put them back onto his aquiline nose and vaguely waved his hand, open-mouthed.

Had he recognized me?

The next moment my eyes met the other man's. This time Information chose to remain silent, but judging by his chest chevron replete with two large black stars, I was looking at General Varlamov. A broad face, determined chin, the dented bridge of his nose - a souvenir of an old fight, - gray-tinged temples and a stiff dark mustache.

For a moment, his eyes glistened betraying the avalanche of emotion. Blood flushed his face. Then the general pulled himself together and walked to the partition, his hands behind his back.

What was going on here? How many times did I have to ask myself that question? Why were they all staring at me as if I'd risen from the dead?

Varlamov stopped in front of the partition and moved his lips. The captain turned to us and repeated his words aloud,

"So you're back, son."

The captain's voice was devoid of emotion, his stare vacant. He acted as a transmitter for the general's speech.

Varlamov turned away. "Proceed," the captain repeated his last words. Gradually, the officer's eyes grew more cognizant as he recovered from his apparent stupor. He signed to someone behind our backs, and guards rushed in to apprehend Kathy, Wong and Wladas. Two more soldiers - the captain must have fetched them when he'd left the room - raised their guns. A neurotech in a mask and clean suit stepped up to me and buried a syringe in my shoulder.

"What's going on?" My legs grew weak.

"You'll soon find out." The captain nodded to his men. "Move it!"

The Information in my head screamed red alert. My knees gave. An agonizing pain pierced my temples and the back of my head. Information started a countdown. I couldn't care less.

'What did the general say?" I shouted.

The soldiers supported me underarm and dragged me along the hallway to the vacant clean room. The other neurotech was already busy in it hooking up the mentoscope.

"What did he say?"

They laid me into a chair. Steel bracelets snapped shut on my wrists and ankles. A copper band pinned my head to the back rest.

"Tell me!"

"He told you the truth," the captain leaned over me. "Surely a traitor like yourself must remember something?"

The neurotech came over to the chair and raised the syringe. A thin jet of fluid squirted into the air.

"What?" I croaked shaking with pain, "Remember what?"

"He's your father."

CHAPTER SEVEN
THE TABLES TURN

THE INJECTION into my neck relieved the pain for a short while. The neurotech told his assistant to prepare the catheters and plasma containers when I started gasping for air. For an instant, everything darkened before my eyes. They gave me another shot and jerked the back of the chair down. Sharp cold steel pierced my ribs.

I struggled and wheezed as I spat blood. The electronic clock on the mentoscope showed 5.07 a.m.

"Too early," a voice spoke by my side. "Turn it off. We need to reset the system."

"He'll die if we do," a confident voice replied.

A blurred silhouette blocked out the bright lamps above me. Latexed fingers touched my eyelids.

"Dilation is still normal. We can carry on."

"Too much risk. The general won't-"

"We'll proceed! The biocyne in his blood will pull him through."

The silhouette disappeared. The light seared my eyes

bringing the pain back. The agony in every cell of my body seemed to cleave my heart. I didn't have the strength left to cry out. Tears gushed from my eyes. Next to me, a drainage pump turned on. Catheters stung my body piercing my lungs and reaching for my liver and kidneys, then entering my stomach. The semispherical module of the mentoscope loomed above me.

"Probe readings?" I heard the senior neurotech's voice dampened by his mask.

"Normal," the assistant answered.

"Scanner?"

"Mnemocapsule clamp confirmed."

"Commence with the extraction."

I felt it even though the pain overpowered all sensation. As if a hand had slipped into my skull, squeezed my brains and pulled them back out slowly and deliberately.

My teeth ached. My eyes bulged out and my mouth filled with blood. It trickled down my nose into my throat. I wheezed trying to spit out the clots and didn't understand what was happening.

"All done," the assistant's voice pierced the droning in my ears. "Do I update the wetware or..."

My brain erupted. I lost control of all sensation balancing on the cusp of pain and pleasure. My consciousness separated from my inner being escaping the glass room with its equipment and neurostaff. For a second, I hung in a void. Then everything changed.

Varlamov looked down on me from above, his eyes smiling. There were no general's stars on his chest: instead, he sported a lieutenant colonel's pips. He eased up the legs of his pants and squatted in front of me. It turned out I was sitting on a stool in a corridor with light-colored walls and a threadbare carpet runner. A desk stood next to me. Behind it, with her hands clasped together, the principal sat patiently waiting.

The principal of what?

"Take it, Mark," Varlamov smiled as he handed me a toy gun. He looked younger - a good twenty years younger. He patted my cheek and pinned an elite paratrooper's badge onto the pocket of my favorite checkered shirt.

I beamed with joy and glanced at the principal - the principal of the orphanage - and gave her a goofy smile. "I now have a father. Finally you've come!"

His face looked at me again but now he wore a dress tunic with rows of medal ribbons and glistening general's stars on his epaulettes. His white-gloved hand jerked into a salute. Inhaling the fresh ocean breeze, I, Master Specialist Mark Varlamov, commander of the cyber troopers section, having graduated from infantry school with honors, heard my own resolute voice as I reported my arrival at the Fort for further military service. My father was proud of me and the successful start of my career. We were back together again.

The breeze was still here, but now my father was gone. I stood on an open platform observing the Fort's construction from above. They were pouring concrete into the shuttering around the atomic reactor. The arms of cranes and scaffolding towered over the Fort's outer wall which was just starting to grow.

The platform offered a good view of the ocean, the Continent and the L-shaped pier. A ferry boat with prisoners had just cast off. Below, the projected territory of the Fort resembled an ant hill. Workers in bright safety vests and construction helmets busied themselves with jackhammers; excavators and bulldozers roared as they cleared the space for the new base buildings. Officers were issuing orders to the workers; armed soldiers and combat vehicles were moving along the coast.

A new face now. This time a woman's. We lay in bed, her fingers touching my shoulder as she whispered sweet nothings, words of love. I was overwhelmed by the feeling of warmth toward Mira. Mirabella Neumann. She was a chemist-biologist and the Professor's daughter. She'd arrived at Pangea not long before and my father - as if he knew beforehand that we would be together - entrusted her to me. I resisted his decision in every possible way. Idiot. Now I was laughing but when I had gotten his order I'd very nearly submitted a transfer request. I seriously believed that it was better to go back to Earth than be a babysitter for this cyber she-nerd who only showed interest in test tubes and chemical reactions. That way I could easily lose all my combat skills. But I was mistaken and now I was grateful to my father for his wise decision. Because Mira proved to be different. She liked the military; she was interested in guns and told me that she dreamed of an officer's career. We became friends and even closer. Now I couldn't imagine myself without her. I wouldn't want to part with her even for one moment.

She stretched and laughed, then threw the edge of the quilt over my head.

Darkness. Light. Bright lamps, flashing. Far-away voices. A total confusion in my head. Where was I? Where was Mira? What had happened to her?

For an instant my eyesight became clearer. The figure of the masked neurotech loomed before me, stapler in hand.

"He's come around," his assistant said. "This boy's tough."

Without further ceremony, he took me by the chin and turned my head aside, then pierced my cheek with an injection gun. The stapler touched my chest and clacked a few times fastening a deep incision.

There was practically no blood. The air stank of surgical spirit. I tried to unglue my lips and ask them about Mira's whereabouts. But my head swam.

We were together again, me and my father, standing on the Fort's walls leaning against the parapet. I listened to him, shattered by the truth about Pangea. No one was going back to Earth. Neither the deportees nor the military garrison. Even he, the general, didn't have the right of return. We all had a one-way ticket: the Professor, Mira... why her?

The reason was simple: the government was afraid of infections and pandemics. The swamps deep on the Continent were rife with incurable alien viruses which could wipe out humanity in one fell swoop. The Central Public Health Inspectorate had analyzed Mira's reports and concluded that the New Pang pandemic had been provoked by malignant bacteria brought in by people from the swamps. A secret order had arrived at the Fort forbidding all servicemen and civilian personnel from returning home to Earth. An open-ended quarantine was declared while the Inspectorate developed vaccines against the unknown disease.

There was a way out though. A universal solution: biocyne. Mira had proven that biocyne was capable of not only identifying and repairing DNA breakage and chemical damage, but that it also showed resistance to all alien viral activity. The only problem was to extract the pure biocyne from carula in a field environment. Mira's laboratory needed the latest equipment but Earth answered in the negative to the base commander's request. We'd become prisoners of Pangea through no fault of our own.

Father had told me about it in order to hear me out although he already knew what he was going to do. He was the only person with the key to the jumpgate and the possibility of a unique communications system with Earth that engaged his cyber modifications. Which meant that he, General Varlamov, was the only person on Pangea who could send and receive messages to his associates among the top brass.

After having consulted his sources, he learned that only society's elite used biocyne on Earth and that it was impossible to produce it in sufficient quantities. Which was why the government had taken this tough but efficient measure.

The Fort found itself between a rock and a hard place. On one side, the Continent with its thousands of deportees. On the other, Earth that kept sending them new prisoners. We both knew that sooner or later this information would leak out to both sides resulting in a stalemate; the garrison could mutiny and the outcome would then become unpredictable.

Father couldn't accept the government's policy that left his men stranded on Pangea. Neither was he planning on spending the rest of his days there. He had never abandoned his soldiers in the field of conflict. He was a professional who could foresee complicated situations and preempt them. He'd planned and accomplished dozens of secret missions. Also, he only trusted himself and believed in me. He'd always said that I'd become the best - a new caliber in cyber staff evolution.

I had high neural functionality criteria in all four classifications. Varlamov didn't have a family. He'd spent a long time scouring children's homes for a unique kid like myself. In any case, that was what he impressed upon me when he'd picked me up from the orphanage. Then came college and infantry school. Father wanted me to continue his cause and his dynasty. He wanted me to be worthy of General Varlamov's name and take pride in bearing it.

"What course of action are you going to take now?" I asked him.

My own voice resounded strangely echoing and distant. It dawned on me that we were communicating through the memory chips using a closed narrow channel switched off from the signal amplifying network that connected all the base's cyber staff to the general. Third parties couldn't listen in. That's why the words reached us with a delay creating the echoing sensation.

The general glanced at me and continued his story. Apparently, Professor Neumann had not received government funds for a long time. It was my father and his highly-placed associates who had financed his research. They planned to overthrow the government but in the event of failure, to find shelter on Pangea.

To that I objected that we couldn't just shut the jumpgate down. The two worlds could collapse and we'd all die. The government, too, wouldn't tolerate this turn of events. It would send in troops to obliterate the garrison and hunt us down all over the Continent to exterminate us.

Father calmly listened to me and told me that Neumann had found a Forecomers' machine in the old city. All we needed to do was to start it up but we needed to hurry and find a way to do it. He didn't let me in on the details of its construction and purpose. He only said,

"It's our trump card. We'll sever contact with Earth and deprive them of biocyne. That way we'll play for time."

He had everything ready for that scenario. A camp had been set up in the old city in strict secrecy and the necessary equipment had been installed. Clones were drafted in for this purpose. They still hadn't built their republic in the foothills and were gallivanting around in the eastern part of the Continent bushwhacking, risking being wiped out at any given moment by local clans.

Captain Rustam Blank, the general's confidant and the camp foreman, as devoted to Varlamov as a puppy, pulled the wool over the clones' eyes by promising them the latest sequencer that could extend their limited lifespan. He provided them with weapons and rations, and things got moving.

The next day after this conversation with my father, Mira, myself and a squad of cyber troops set off for the old city in order to accomplish two objectives. First, the squad had to strengthen the security of the location where the Forecomers' machine was situated. The second objective: someone had to risk his life and venture out into the swamps in order to retrieve fresh samples of the malignant bacteria from which Mira would then try, under field conditions, to extract the vaccine. We had literally one drop of unpurified biocyne and now we had to decide on a volunteer to administer it to before sending him to the swamp.

So there we were in the City of Forecomers. It was my first time on the Continent. Mira stood next to me and I didn't need anything else. The cyber staff patrolled the area in three shifts. Clones were sent to guard the camp's perimeter. The ubiquitous Blank kept ordering neurotechs and operators around growling at them to hurry them up with the equipment installation and tuning. We had to get it all done within a week. Professor Neumann alone was thoughtful and spoke little but instead spent a lot of time by the Forecomers' device - the rods under the gasometer's dome, directed toward the matt black semisphere underneath. The sparks from the exploding bolts of lightning above showered his gray head. The device functioned even though it seemed to be idling.

Once we'd finished installing the equipment, the engineers commenced with the building of the optical membrane which had to divide the gasometer's hall in two and protect the Forecomers' machine from unauthorized access. I had little idea of how the membrane worked. It appeared to be made of fiberglass, only crystal clear, its fibers less than one micron thick invisible to the human eye. The fibers integrated a communications network that could be tuned to a specific cyber trooper's personal channel allowing the signal controller to let a particular person through to the machine. If you attempted to get through the activated membrane without authorization, the best scenario was that you could lose a limb, and the worst, you could be killed.

I thought that father would entrust the membrane control to me. But Blank told me it was none of my business. He booted the professor out of the hall and cast a predatory glance at me when reprimanded. He didn't risk answering me back knowing that if ever we came to blows he'd lose: what with my latest implants, my combat potential was two units higher than his.

Temporarily put on the sidelines, Neumann and myself went out for some fresh air (I wanted to check the sentries and get the patrols' reports). The professor became talkative. He told me of the purpose of the rods being scattered all over the Continent and their connection to those installed in the gasometer's dome. But first he speculated on the origins of the Forecomers on Pangea. It was only a hypothesis, of course, but I believed him. It sounded plausible enough.

He started his story from the swamp which the volunteer was about to enter. The swamps appeared to be the Forecomers' doing who used to travel between worlds. For these alien Gods, Pangea was some sort of manmade intermediary station that housed the portal machine we'd discovered.

He didn't actually call them Gods, of course, replacing the religious term with some euphemism like "reason" or "the almighty Force", or whatever.

"The Forecomers had achieved a certain technological threshold, just like humans are about to do now. They'd learned to control the device."

Neumann called it a portal machine. It opened doors to other worlds serving like a router while the rod towers on the Continent worked as beacons used to enter the coordinates of your destination. The entire installation worked much as a GPS module, only instead of receiving a satellite signal, the beacons sent and received frequencies from outer space. So one day either through a fault of their operator or for another reason, a wormway opened on an unknown new world letting in all sorts of toxic alien matter. The professor chose to call them "the intruders". The Forecomers realized they had to leg it.

And leg it they did, just in time, because we didn't find any of their remains next to their portal machine. Neumann, too, had studied the Continent up and down during his years of research but had failed to find any alien burials or other evidence of their demise.

I was about to suggest that they could have cremated their dead but I bit my tongue. The old man was too engulfed in his story. The installation must still have worked at the time of their exodus, otherwise it wouldn't have been possible. But for some reason, it hadn't been shut down afterward. This drew Neumann to suggest that it was controlled by a limited-intellect program which kept the machine operational in order to preserve the global beacon network from destruction.

The machine had allowed the professor to discover Pangea. After the electronic bomb test explosion on the Kola Peninsula, the portal device had detected the resulting perturbations and sucked part of the peninsula onto Pangea, complete with the Samotlor tanker on its way from the Arctic gold mines. About a hundred Kola garrison personnel and various equipment had also found themselves jumped to Pangea. Raiders were still busy hunting for all the junk and taking it to New Pang to sell.

The professor described the state of the two worlds as a collision of two soap bubbles.

"Imagine a straw connecting an Earth bubble and a Pangea bubble. It created an enormous surface tension so perilous I call it Point Apocalypse. So what caused the connection to stabilize without destroying both worlds? The portal machine, of course."

The professor nicknamed it "his bubble theory". Now he wanted to find out how he could open portals to other worlds - any worlds. Knowing how to do it would allow him to disconnect the Earth from Pangea, then create a new wormway if needed.

It all seemed to come together. If this world was indeed nothing more than an artificial docking station, then it explained the fact that the environment was so limited: its creators had only bothered to include the elements they needed. The absence of mineral resources now explained itself: the Forecomers had had to be humanoid or at least catered for such, while the toxic swamp had to be the result of a near-human error.

The toxic intruders' world had to be entirely different both in its structure and environment. Mirabella Neumann couldn't give a concise description of the swamp life forms, so deadly to humans. By now, the area had capsulated forming its own habitat and a breeding ground for new colonies of mutated viruses and bacteria. Some of them had adapted to life outside the swamp; others penetrated the ocean. That's why you had to treat all local food produce with care for fear of poisoning or even death.

It was possible that the Forecomers had realized or even known what they were dealing with. So they'd sealed Pangea and left. But now, people had arrived instead. Neumann especially belonged to this species of science fanatics: the race that would stop at nothing until they got the answers to their curiosity. According to him, science had finally stumbled onto the right path and made the first baby step toward our extraterrestrial brothers capable of traveling through time and space. The similarity of our technologies had allowed for this first contact promising more progress ahead.

Neumann hadn't even noticed the wasting of his and his daughter's life on research which until now had brought no tangible results worth mentioning. Okay, so he'd put forward his bubble hypothesis and worked on his Point Apocalypse theory suggesting, in part, that the Earth-Pangea wormway could be destroyed by exploding a nuclear charge inside the wormway itself. That seemed to be the only way to destroy the portal that consumed indecent amounts of energy threatening to collapse Earth.

But Neumann didn't want to be known as an armchair theorist. A man of practice ready to embrace the unknown, he wanted to take his ideas to their logical end. Just as my father did.

I felt sorry for the old man. Everyone seemed to be using Professor Neumann: my father as well as the government.

I arched my body and heard a dull snap as my sinews and vertebrae spasmed. I opened my eyes and collapsed onto the bed. My heart drummed in my chest. Reality came back just as quickly as it had taken them to remove the memory chip. The clock showed 5.24.

"He's come to," the neurotech threw the electrodes onto the defibrillator stand.

"Where are we taking him now?" his assistant pulled my eyelids down one after the other and nodded.

"Blank told me to take him to the general as soon as he could walk," the neurotech glanced at me. "Think you can do it, Master Specialist?"

It's been a while since anyone called me by my rank. Ever since I'd left Pangea, to be precise. How long had it been, two years? Something like that.

Gingerly, I bent my elbows and sat up trying to adapt to my body.

"You'll live," the neurotech concluded. He lay his hand on my shoulder and leaned closer. "We've implanted you a fourth-generation memory chip, standard upgrade, three channel coms. Sorry we didn't have anything more state-of-the-art. In your left eye is a monitor lens with a built-in infrared camera. In your cardiac muscle you still have a burnt-out stabilizing stimulator. That's it."

His assistant handed him a measuring tube filled to the brim with a cloudy liquid.

"Drink this. It'll make you feel a bit better," the neurotech took the tube and nearly brought it up to my lips but held his hand. "Apparently, the Feds fitted your aorta out with a chemical blocker. You'd think it's nothing much, and then... Had we known about it straight away, it wouldn't have taken us so long. The fucking thing activated so we were forced to give you CPR. I thought that was the end of you, Master Specialist. You were lucky we had a defibrillator at hand. The stimulator screwed up, naturally. We'll give you a new one when we have time."

He brought the tube up to my lips. Mechanically, I opened my mouth and swallowed the liquid, all the time trying to remember the names and identities of these two. I couldn't possibly remember all the camp staff but they certainly knew me as General Varlamov's son.

Father, I sent him a silent call, are you waiting for me? We're back together again.

The stone walls dampened my signal. The memory chip's operating range without the amplifier didn't exceed a few dozen feet.

My bare feet touched the cold floor. I inspected my staple-patched chest. The scar was still stinging like hell but I knew it wouldn't be long before its edges knitted together. Then I'd pull out the staples myself: not for the first time, I might add. Still something felt wrong. I couldn't quite put my finger on it but the world around me seemed to have somehow changed. I sensed it but I couldn't explain it. It could be post-op grogginess... I needed to recuperate. I had my false identity removed; they'd unblocked my memory but those Federal experts had very nearly done for me with their heart blocker. It had to have been their analysts' idea. Either they knew the general would try to recapture me or they were afraid of me changing camp. So they covered their backs. It may look like nothing much, just as the neurotech had said, but the delayed-action chemical blocker couldn't be detected with a scanner. And it's pretty pointless to try and open the aorta to look for a clot when the patient is about to croak. That's why the lab staff used the defibrillator. It had worked a hundred percent: they had broken the growing clot down with electric pulses despite the obvious risk. Had the stimulator not burned out, my heart would have gone into overdrive, and then...

I raised my head and met with Captain Blank's gaze. He had several soldiers next to him - regular guys, not the cyber type. Blank had already tuned to my frequency and kept his channel open and receiving.

Oh well. I sent him a return impulse, rose from the bed and walked out of the "clean" room. Blank handed me an army jacket. I already knew where to go: the monitor lens showed my route in every detail.

So! The tables had turned. The mind games were over. They had given my memory back but it didn't change very much. The only thing that remained was to speak to my father. I had to stop him at any cost. It had to be possible because without me, he'd never get anywhere. I was the only one who could start the portal machine.

PART THREE

CHAPTER ONE
THE DREAM IS ONE STEP AWAY

STILL, I WASN'T quite right. The hallway seemed to be the same but when you looked at the stone walls, they seemed to emit a weak glow. I squeezed my eyes shut and opened them again. Now they were ordinary walls of dark uneven basalt.

But... wait up!

My feet froze to the floor. Blank gave me a rough shove in the back and I lost my train of thought. Barely staying on my feet, I turned round and glared back at him. The guards raised their rifles and glanced in alarm at the captain waiting for his orders. He said nothing. His face relaxed and he waved us through.

I still would have found the road even without the monitor lens. I remembered it too well. We were heading toward the stairs that led down to the closed level under the gasometer. There Mira had built her laboratory two years ago when we'd just arrived in the old city. The place was quite well-chosen, with a large room below and a wide shallow-sloping hallway leading to the exit upstairs, perfect for bringing in equipment. We'd had to widen the stairwell with a jack hammer but the former miners among the clones had made short work of that. Mira had also asked them to build a stone partition to divide the room into both working and living accommodation. Naturally, I'd been more than welcome in the latter.

The guard in front turned into another passage and started down the stairs. The walls seemed to be gleaming again. I thought I saw some sort of grid shimmer appear on their surface. It flashed red and died away leaving a vivid imprint on my retina.

I glanced back at the captain. He kept walking as if nothing had happened and gave me a quizzical look. That was weird. Did it mean that neither he nor the soldiers had seen anything?

We walked down the stairs and along a wide hallway. The guard in front stopped by Mira's laboratory door. My palms broke out in a sweat as my heart pounded in my chest and I knew that Mira was behind the wall waiting. I detected her frequency, open and free, but my father seemed to be there with her. They were bouncing messages off each other and it seemed that the discussion was quite heated. At that moment I couldn't say which one of them I wanted to see more. All previous speculation was obliterated by my emotion.

Advance, Blank ordered.

Slowly, I entered the silent room. Practically nothing had changed there. A cot, a small table, two stacks of plastic containers in the corner. To the right, the stone partition and sliding glass doors. A light burned in the lab.

Of course, after two years I wasn't used to the

memory chips any more. I'd forgotten the idea of the thought communication. My eye caught sight of some shelves that hadn't been there before. Baby blankets were stacked on the top shelf, next to a folded bedspread. On top of it lay some homemade dolls made of plastic tubes, the kind that wounded soldiers used to fashion in hospitals during their convalescence.

I stepped to the door and again glanced at the shelves. The lower one was occupied by two clean little plates edged with a cute drawing next to a baby bottle half-filled with white liquid. None of this belonged here. I walked toward the door, and the glass panel slid noiselessly aside. I entered the laboratory.

Mira sat by her work desk staring at the opposite wall. A lamp was lit on the desk lined up with test glassware next to her electronic tablet journal where she normally entered her test observations. A refrigerator hummed in the corner. Behind it I noticed the ultracentrifuge she used to separate liquids and mixtures. Next to it, stood the general.

He put his hands behind his back and kept clenching and unclenching one strong fist as he stared at the sliding glass door in front of him. It lead into the airlock and further into the "clean" room. Only this one was not meant for the cyber staff but for Mira's studies. There, she worked with viruses - the viruses that had started the whole thing and prompted Blank to accuse me of treachery.

Mira's stare shifted to my side. To stand there and not reach out to her was more than I could bear. I so wanted to hug her and run my fingers through her fair hair burying my face in it.

General, I tuned into the open channel and stood to

attention.

What did you tell them, Mark? father asked calmly without moving.

Everything.

Mira could hear us speak. She looked at me, her eyes moist. The general turned around. *Why?*

I couldn't hold it in any longer. I tried to resist the impulse as I really didn't want to explain anything to him. But my emotions got the better of me. I blurted out everything I'd bottled up since I'd made the decision to change sides. I didn't want millions of innocent victims on Earth to die as the hostages to a handful of ambitious conspirators.

You tricked me! You extracted the virus without telling me what it was for. I risked my life in vain back there at the swamps thinking that I was helping people to get the vaccine. And you... You understood everything beforehand. You were aware that I wouldn't go along if I knew your real plans. You taught me how to defend my country and its people and how to kill its enemies, but you yourself decided to wipe out all life on our planet. What do you say to that?

The general remained silent. He stood there with his head tipped forward, his hands still clenched behind his back.

I lost it, *Are you still hoping to build a new society here on Pangea? Those flexible decentralized systems of yours without irreplaceable links?* I shook my head. *I'm afraid you can't. People don't change. And you-*

I stopped and looked at Mira's tearful face. Blank came into the room. The general nodded. In one smooth practiced motion the captain drew his handgun from its holster and placed it against the girl's temple.

I see. Now they would command me to power up the

portal. Father wanted to sever all connections with Earth for one simple reason: the deadly assault virus that Mira had extracted in vitro could easily annihilate humanity which was the general's main goal. Once the virus had wiped out all human and animal life forms, it would gradually lose its potency and would allow new settlers to return to the planet. But if the portal wasn't closed, the virus could work its way back to Pangea through new prisoners or soldiers, and then...

If you hurt her, I looked at the captain but my words were addressed to my father, *you'll never go back home.*

Mira, tell him, the general said.

She ran her hands across her cheeks wiping away the tears and raised her blotchy face to me. She stared at me without saying a word.

Mark... her lips trembled. She glanced around in desperation. *Mark, they've taken our daughter.*

I felt as if somebody had hit me with a sledge hammer. I hadn't - I couldn't have - misunderstood her because the mental channels transmit every word loud and clear. Vocal chords don't participate in the exchange and the ear doesn't need to detect any oscillation so no spoken phrase depends on the wave length.

I've got a daughter? I remembered the crudely made plastic toys in the room next door. The little patterned plates, the baby blanket...

Yes, you do.

Tears flowed down her face. She pressed her hand to her mouth to suppress her sobbing. Blank looked at me grimacing. He always enjoyed humiliating others. But he derived even more pleasure from cornering his adversary and enjoying his own superiority as he watched them suffer.

We're together again, my father said to me. *We're in it till the end.*

Smothering the desire to throttle Blank, I closed my eyes. How I wished that the general hadn't called off the two cyber troopers by the river. It would have been better that they had killed us there and then without having recognized me. The only reason they had left their posts was in order to give us a decent reception. When they'd reported to my father, he hedged his bets and sent an armored personnel carrier and a mobile escort group in three combat vehicles. He was afraid that my motley crew of friends could have a high combat potential and, not knowing our possibilities, wanted to take me alive.

I've got to see my daughter.

Later, the general said. *When the job's finished.*

No, I insisted. *Give the girl back to Mira. This way I'll be certain that they'll be all right. Then we'll carry on.*

Blank grinned wryly staring into my eyes, his gun still at Mira's temple.

I'll deal with you later, I said, suppressing my anger. *After I've solved the main problem.*

The smile disappeared from his face, replaced by a bitingly cold glare. I wanted to put him off balance. Blank flicked the safety catch off.

As you were, Captain! the general ordered. *I'm in command here, and I decide when and who dies. Put your gun away.*

Unwillingly, Blank obeyed.

Leave us, father added.

Mira didn't move. The captain grabbed her elbow but she pulled her arm free and thrust her chin in the air as she rose and stepped toward me. *I'm sorry.*

She touched my cheek and walked out of the lab.

General, Blank gave him a cursory nod and left.

We looked through each other without seeing anything. The general was hiding his hands behind his back. I stood to attention opposite him, mechanically following the regs.

Stand easy, Master Specialist, father stepped toward the desk and leaned against it knuckles down. *Let's put rank aside and speak as equals.*

He blocked his mental channel and straddled Mira's chair folding his arms on its back.

I waited patiently trying to block out emotions. I needed to know how the general was going to begin because this would affect our later actions. Firstly, I wanted to know how he'd send the virus back to Earth. He had to have a mole among the Feds in the Fort - he must have, otherwise how could you explain that they'd started preparing their mission a week before my arrival on Pangea? The general had most likely used his contact to plant disinformation about his supposed new actions against Earth's security. He then started to demonstrate his strength causing the FSA to start worrying. That's why they'd acted in haste. They'd chemically modified my identity, given me Wong for partner and sent me on a mission to find Neumann and stop the general.

He rested his elbows on the back of the chair and interlaced his fingers, looking up at me. Probably, second-guessing me too. The longer we were playing this silent waiting game, the further each of us was advancing in his own calculations conceiving a new plan of action.

So - secondly, the general's and the FSA's objectives overlapped at least on one point. They both wanted me to use the portal machine to disconnect the Continent from the Earth and prevent the Neumann-prophesied apocalypse. The difference was that the general wanted to return to Earth and use the human-free planet as a clean slate to build a new society. The FSA, on the contrary, wanted to isolate Pangea and forget about it for the sake of Earth's security: after all, the unstable wormway and the Forecomers' obscure technologies had instilled terror in many, including governments. No one could foresee the consequences of having Pangea stuck in our back yard and few were eager to maintain relations with the Continent at this cost.

What did it leave us with? Once Pangea was lost, Earth would lose biocyne, too. But the rich and powerful still wanted to live long so they were now stocking up on biocyne sending out-of-date technology and written-off military equipment to the Continent in exchange for new shipments of carula. Deportees had no idea of its real value and kept sending it by ferry to the Fort, content with what little they received for it.

I glanced at the glass airlock door. Crossing the room, I looked into the lab and turned back to my father. He raised his brow watching me. A weak smile danced on his face.

"You've worked it out, haven't you?" he said. "Yes, that's the capsule. The one with the virus inside. It's been here for almost two years now waiting to be put on the boat and shipped to the Fort."

I peered through the glass. A fat orange tub sat there, looking very much like that of a tactical nuke, only the markings on its sides were different. Orange and yellow, they warned of chemical and nuclear contamination.

How fucking typical. Varlamov didn't even have to attack the base in order to send the virus back to Earth. The deportees themselves would do his dirty work. The shipment inspections were lax so no one would pay much attention to the virus-containing capsule buried within the seaweed. At the appointed hour, thermite charges would melt the aluminum shell and let death fly. The first ones to die would be the medical staff who dealt with biocyne. They'd spread the virus around their clients in administration. The minister would be one of the first to be affected, and then... then it would be too late.

"Who do you have an agreement with?" I asked. "McLean? His ferry's taking it to the Fort?"

He nodded.

So that's why McLean was so interested in carula. Varlamov had probably hinted to him that carula shipments were important and valuable. He'd planted this idea in his head leaving McLean to ponder over it until he'd driven himself to a frenzy. So when I had come... "Your man in the agency. Can you give me his name?"

"You're professional, Mark. Let's do it this way: once the shipment clears the corridor, I'll give you the mole's name. Happy now?"

The general seemed uneasy - worried probably of me throwing a monkey wrench into his works. I nodded to him. Varlamov wasn't Blank. Which was why he'd become a general to begin with. He'd never departed from the rules when he followed his own designs; he'd thought several moves ahead and disposed of unnecessary steps in order to avoid ad-libbing whenever possible. His reasoning was non-standard, his body was modified, his experience was superior...

"Don't you try to outgame me," Varlamov said. "Your reactions are faster but your abilities are not yet fully developed. You're now one step away from your dream - my dream. Think well what opportunities it will open up to you once we carry it through."

"What you gonna do?" I chuckled. "Stuff me with more implants? Replacing regular army with cyber troopers was your idea, but no one will need it when you kill off all your men. Who do you want to defend yourself against, anyway?"

He looked at me calmly, his eyes blank.

"You're quite prepared to kill my own daughter, my own flesh and blood. It means nothing to you, does it? You never had a family. You scoured orphanages for a child with a unique nervous system and you found me. Then you forgot I was human and turned me into another means to suit your own ends."

"You're a soldier," his voice was stern. "You're a natural master specialist, a born officer. Don't make me think less of you."

Wrinkles formed under his eyes. He clenched a fist, ran his knuckles along his mustache and rose.

"Sure," I stood up and straightened my shoulders. "You always put the end above the means. The only thing you forgot was me and that I was human..."

"All words," he fobbed me off and stepped toward the door. "Words, and nothing else. It's only actions that matter."

"They do," I nodded. "You're right. Actions do matter."

"Guards!" the general shouted into the doorway and turned to me. "By tomorrow night the shipment will be in the Fort. Do what I ask and you'll get Mira and the baby back."

He walked out. The guards arrived. One of them motioned to me with his gun, and I followed Varlamov along the hallway.

CHAPTER TWO
NO WAY OUT

I AWOKE and sat up, unable to understand what had disturbed me and how I could see in the dark. My brain, exhausted by sleepless nights, refused to cooperate. My head swam, my belly rumbled, and all thought was suppressed by thirst and hunger.

I finally pulled myself together and remembered that I was in a cellar under the gasometer. The general had told the guards to bring me here. The memory chip in the back of my head had woken me up after five hours as I'd programmed it to do. The infrared camera lens seemed to be working. "System check," I gave a mental order. The memory chip reacted making me realize that there were no other implants in my body. Okay, I'd have to do with what I had.

I stood up and did a couple of toe-touches and arm circles, then a few squats to get my blood going. The stapled scar on my chest didn't trouble me that much. I was about to pick the staples out but reconsidered. Let it heal a bit more.

I was alone in the room with rough stone walls, a floor but no doors. Instead, a guard hovered on the threshold.

"You gonna feed me?" I asked him.

He didn't answer but waved to another soldier in the corridor. They exchanged a few quiet words and the guard came back alone.

"Apparently, you are," I mumbled and sat on the floor listening to the dying footsteps in the hallway.

Five minutes later, they brought me a pack of field rations without a spoon or a fork or even a can opener. The soldier used his bayonet to rip open a can of beans, freed up a plastic container from some candy, hardtack crackers and what-not, and poured the beans into it. He filled my mug from his flask and left.

They seemed to be seriously thinking that I'd want to escape. They were right. The top of a can in skilled hands like Wong's, for instance, could become a very effective weapon. I shook my head, took a pinch of cold beans, threw it into my mouth and started slurping slowly. Then I reached for the mug and froze.

Apparently, the remains of my slumber were finally swept away - or maybe the food helped as it's well known that one thinks better on a full stomach. In any case, what was worrying me was the fact that the general didn't just chance on mentioning the cargo or McLean. He never did anything off the cuff. I didn't think he'd lied to me. More likely, he'd said it to distract me and make me concentrate on a way of stopping the ferry, thus overlooking other important details.

Mechanically, I sent another handful of beans flying into my mouth and washed it down. I'd never make it out of here alone. Without a car, I couldn't get to the city. Besides, I had to take Mira with me and I had no idea where my daughter was.

Phew. I listened to my stomach rumbling. Wong, Kathy and Wladas had to be somewhere nearby. If I freed them and explained to each what to do next, my chances of success would improve greatly. Kathy and Wladas could be trusted to guard Mira and her daughter while Wong and myself could deal with the general's men.

I nodded and decided to leave only Kathy with Mira and the baby, adding Wladas to Wong and myself. To stop the cybers, we needed a neurotech and Wladas' qualifications allowed him to do just that. There was little left to accomplish: leave the room, acquire some guns, kill most of the guards on my way upstairs, find my friends, Mira and her daughter, split up, find a safe place for the latter and win.

Easier said than done. I glanced up to where the guard stood in the doorway, took a large gulp and attacked my food. There was no knowing when I'd be fed again but my body would need fuel. I finished off the beans, wiped my fingers on my pants and shoved the crackers into my hip pocket. I might need them later.

Varlamov was sure I'd start the machine. I had no choice: I had to do so for Mira and the baby unless I managed to free them earlier and fuck off out of the old city. But: I still had to intercept the cargo, stop and ferry and let the Fort know about the possibility of the virus reaching Earth.

I still couldn't believe that the general would embark on mass murder. It wasn't like him. Otherwise he wouldn't have tried to lead the Feds up the garden path luring me out to Pangea.

The sentry in the doorway adjusted the rifle strap on his shoulder and jumped to attention, chest out. Hurried steps issued from behind the wall, followed by a loud snap and the sizzling of an electric current. Something popped like a blowpipe. A breech clacked shut. Surprise on the guard's face gave way to a grimace of pain when the needles of the taser sank into his cheek, a spasm doubling him up. The once-sagging spiral leads of the taser grew taut, the needles ripping skin from their entry points. The soldier fell face down, his head thudding on the stone floor. He convulsed a few times and fell silent.

I sprang to the door and recoiled. I was looking down the barrel of a silenced handgun. In his other hand, Captain Blank held the taser.

Freeze! I heard in my head.

Blank stepped out into the corridor, lowered his hand and shot the guard in the neck. Then he trained his gun back on me.

What does that mean? I asked soundlessly.

I'm letting you go.

You killed the soldiers. Why?

No, a predatory grin appeared on Blank's face. *You killed them both. You shot them. Mira brought you a gun and you decided to leg it. Hands up.*

He motioned me with the barrel to follow him out of the room. His gun still trained on me, he stepped over the body and walked backward along the hallway.

What do you want? I bent my elbows keeping my palms up.

The second sentry lay by the wall with a shot wound to the head next to a pool of blood.

I want to finish what we started, Blank stopped by the fork in the hallway letting me onto the stairs. The passage behind his back was covered in darkness.

The general thought himself so smart that he'd

outsmarted himself.

He glanced back. *Now run. You might still have just enough time to say good-bye to him.*

He spoke in riddles. What was happening?

Blank ejected his clip and the round up the barrel and threw me the gun on its last round catch. Then he pointed the taser at me, the flashing red light on its side signaling maximal charge.

Now run, he repeated. *I'll give you a minute's headstart. Then I'll raise the alarm.*

I bolted up the stairs two steps at a time trying to remember the detailed plan of the gasometer's layout. Five stairwells converged on a central wheel that housed utility rooms and the central hall with the Forecomers' machine. From there, there was only one way out, the one we'd been brought in through. Where could they keep the prisoners, Mira and her daughter? What had Blank meant speaking about the general?

I took the safety catch off the gun. Just in time. A soldier stepped toward me from above. He didn't have time to raise his rifle: I slapped his cheek with the butt of the handgun and pushed him up against the wall pressing my elbow into his neck.

I shoved the barrel into his cheek and hissed, "Move and you're a dead man."

But he did move. Either he'd noticed that there was no clip in it or he knew it from beforehand. He whacked me in the liver, moved one step below and got a pulse charge in his back from Blank's gun.

The soldier clung to me with a suppressed cough spattering my face with blood. The charge had passed through the back of his vest. The chest armor expanded but contained the charge. We fell onto the stairs.

Blank's steps came from beneath. I grabbed the dead man's shoulders and raised myself up slightly. Shielding myself with the body, I took one step up and stumbled. A new shot rang out. This time, the charge hit the soldier's head and blew half his skull away, splattering me with gray matter mixed with blood and shattered bone.

I crawled into the hallway on my back. There, I turned on my stomach and jerked myself away from the stairwell. One sole thought beat in unison with my pounding heart: What was Blank's goal?

Using an open communications channel, the captain sounded the alert. I ran along the rounded hallway past the rooms crammed with equipment in boxes on prefabricated stands, all the time hearing behind me the growing tramping of feet and the sound of excited voices. Finally I came to the right exit and turned into it.

Father lay on a cot between the cabinets. He was already dead. His glazed eyes glistened on his pale face under the ceiling lamps. His lips slightly parted. A silver cord from an army pendant that had been hanging on the wall was drawn taut around his neck.

I leaned toward him, slid my fingers under the garrote and pulled. A silhouetted figure moved in from behind the cabinet. A blow caught me on the temple but as I turned my head at the last moment, it glanced off me. I shielded myself with my elbow from the fist aimed at my cheekbone and chopped at thin air attempting to counter attack. Immediately, I got two swift and painful pokes to my solar plexus and stepped to the wall gasping. I kicked my assailant in the knee and forced him to move aside and pause.

A pause that lasted only a second, but in that second a barrage of thoughts stormed through my head. In front of me stood Wong. Wong who'd protected me ever since we'd arrived at Pangea; Wang who'd obeyed my orders and helped me all the way. And now...

He behaved like a machine. With a smile on his face he stepped closer, parried my lunge and smashed his fist into my chin. I'd foreseen the combination and ducked. Sticking my knee out, I stamped on his foot nailing it to the floor and tried to elbow the Chinese to the ground. But I missed. He squatted and pushed my arms up, sliced into my armpits and kept hitting me in the stomach, groin and thighs.

Too late I felt the pain and realized that the Chinese was more experienced and better trained than myself. With his combat potential of six units against my three, he was a professional killer, a puppet that the FSA had programmed to eliminate General Varlamov. I had led him to my father, and all Blank had to do was to unleash him at the right moment.

My arms dangled lifelessly. My body was paralyzed: I couldn't move or catch my breath and my legs felt wooden. Wong pressed his hand against my chest and slowly moved the other arm toward his waist preparing a coup de grace. Unclenching his fist, he twisted his hand concentrating and sucked in the air.

My father, like a giant, rose up behind his back and gave the Chinese a bear hug rendering him unable to move his arms. Struggling, Wong jumped up and backheaded him breaking the general's nose. And again. But father restrained him with all his weight, constricting him.

Circles flashed in front of my eyes. Wong and the general merged into one unproportional figure. Somewhere in the back of my mind the memory chip signaled an insufficient oxygen level in my blood. The infrared lens kept changing from one spectrum to another trying to calibrate the image when something in the room changed unperceivably.

The air thickened like a sponge, sticking to my body as a diver's suit. Crimson threads lit up on the walls and reached for me outlining all the objects and people in the room and filling them in with colorful pulsating auras. Among them, I recognized the clear receding signal of the general's memory chip. Having activated the stimulator in his aorta, it started up his heart which was now on the point of stopping again. His combat implants didn't function any more and God only knew what it had cost him to hold Wong in his grip.

I breathed in. Then out. And in again, gasping for air. My shoulders still hurt but my muscles could contract again obeying the signals from my recovering nervous system. The crimson threads entered my body pumping it up with strength. Another moment, another split second, and I'd crush Wong with a single blow. His aura breathed fire, its nucleus searing with overflowing energy in his head.

I realized that I could extend my father's life for a few moments by redirecting the flow of force emitted by the crimson threads. But then I wouldn't be able to kill Wong whose blazing energy had already reached its peak. The Chinese whooped and threw my father off raising his hands.

All I did was to put my palms together. I don't know why. It was as if I was controlled by someone on the outside who was prompting me what to do before I could even think. The crimson threads wound around Wong's neck. His scream turned into a croak as his aura started to fade slowly like the filament in an unplugged electric bulb receiving the last weak voltage.

The room before me came back to normal. The general lay dying on the floor. Wong stood with an unnaturally twisted neck, the back of his head touching his shoulder. A smile frozen on his dead face.

I pushed him hard, lost my balance and sank to the floor next to my father. I reached out to him but the room was filling with soldiers. They grabbed my shoulders, threw me toward the wall and kicked the shit out of my ribs winding me.

I shielded myself with my arms and kept looking at my father through my fingers. Life was leaving his eyes. His lips moved weakly but because of the soldiers' noise and swearing, I couldn't hear what he was saying.

If Blank hadn't appeared in the room, they would have beaten me to death. He blurted out a command and the soldiers stepped aside. One of them slapped me across the face but was shoved away by cyber troopers. Obeying the captain's order, they grabbed me under my arms and dragged me off along the hallway toward the main hall where the portal machine stood.

The unknown force that had allowed me to terminate Wong had now left me. My ribs ached, my jaw smarted and the eye with the lens in it practically didn't work. The memory chip kept signaling for me to go urgently to the medical center for a checkup. I tried to comprehend what had just happened in that room but couldn't concentrate; instead, I kept seeing the faces of Wong and my dying father who'd saved my life. He had proven to be a different person from what I'd recently believed him to be. He'd wanted me to live; his emotions had given him away during our first encounter yesterday. He just hadn't spoken of his plans in detail, or rather, he'd tried to but had seen I wasn't ready yet. I hadn't wanted to listen to him, I hadn't even wanted to try to listen to him. He was a stern strong-willed individual not taken to praising people, but he always had a particle of love within him and he used to share it generously with me at every opportunity, hiding warmth and tenderness behind the Spartan mask of severity. What a shame I'd grown up so quickly and forgotten about it.

Now I couldn't bring anything back. Time moved on relentlessly. I had only two important things left to do: free Mira and my daughter at whatever cost and take Blank out.

Neumann was by the portal machine alone when the protective membrane opened in the hall letting us in. In the last twenty-four hours, the professor had taken a turn for the worst. He seemed to have aged another ten years. An ancient old man stooping in a lab coat looked at me with pity and compassion, and also with what wasn't quite fear in his eyes but rather the agony of wishing to be in my place and die not seeing what was about to happen next.

The cyber hurled me onto the floor and stood on either side of the pedestal that supported the black hemisphere. Blank walked in. The transparent membrane sealed noiselessly behind his back and clouded over concealing us from the eyes of the soldiers manning the light-flashing equipment in the control center.

"You two," Blank pointed his finger at me, then at old Neumann, "power up the machine, now."

I struggled to my feet, ran my hand across my face and stared at my fingers sticky with blood and some weird goo.

"What are you gawking at, Master Specialist?" the captain stepped toward me and knocked my forearm. "Have you never seen blown-out brains before?" He pointed at the hemisphere covered in solidified little bubbles. "Explain to the professor how this thing works!"

The stooping Neumann looked up at me, pleading. His narrow line-furrowed face had turned gray. His eyes begged, do what they say, boy, let's get it over with and then at least the soldiers will kill us.

"Step aside, everyone," I said.

The cyber looked at their captain. He nodded. When Neumann and Blank stood at a distance, I stepped up to the hemisphere. I raised my hands over the uneven surface preparing to feel both the soaring heat and cold at once.

A long-forgotten memory stirred up something unknown and powerful that had as yet lain dormant inside me. It sharpened my perception making my fingers shake with the effort. If I touched the surface, it would flash up crimson. A radiant sphere would appear overhead under the rods' lower ends shooting lightning...

Blank drew forward and grasped Neumann's elbow pulling him along.

"What are you doing?" the captain gasped. "Tell him! Teach him how to use this thing!" He pushed Neumann toward the pedestal.

I couldn't explain anything even if I wanted to. The professor wouldn't be able to do it. The Fore comers' machine worked by itself. For some reason it had mistaken me for one of its own believing me to be part of itself - or its master, or creator, whatever it was. It could be some peculiarity of my nervous system or it could be the biocide that Mira had injected me two years ago before my trip to the swamps. This was where I'd found the fifth beacon.

Back at the swamps, I'd gotten lost in the murky mist and had decided to take a break. I didn't mean to get inside. I squatted by the beacon's metallic wall splattered with mud. High above in the mist I saw the black silhouette of the beacon's receiving rod.

I had touched the wall and slumped into nothing.

At first I'd thought I was hallucinating with the swamp's toxic fumes. I searched my belt for the cartridge pouch where I kept gas mask filters when I realized I was actually inside the beacon tower. The floor was rough and basalt-like. The light-colored walls veined with gray emitted a weak glow. Part of the rod showed in the ceiling overhead.

"Atmosphere suitable for breathing," my protective suit's built-in gas analyzer reported to my helmet monitor. Just in case I rebooted it and repeated the tests. They produced the same results: the air inside the beacon was good and clean. After a moment's thought, I took off the helmet, pulled off the mask and took a deep breath. I coughed as the dry close air tickled my throat - apparently, the beacon didn't have any air vents.

I took my bearings, then looked up at the ceiling and touched the rod. Everything changed. A cold breeze chilled my face. My spine and the back of my head exuded heat. I happened to stand in the way of two energy currents, short-circuiting them. The currents lashed out at me from both sides trying to connect, but my body stood in their way like a resistor in an electric circuit. Rerouted, they then flowed into nothing - a beckoning abyss that for an instant opened before my inner eye, showing countless paths to distant worlds that until then I'd believed to be the shimmering pattern on the beacon's walls. I realized I was seeing a 3D diagram, a map whose scale was inconceivable to human imagination.

The map was crossed by a short protuberance that pulsated red: the wormway connecting Earth and Pangea. By now overcharged with energy, it threatened to explode at any moment like a boiler in need of letting off steam.

It had ended before I got scared. One thought of Mira, and I had found myself not at the swamps but under the gasometer, teleported to the hall by the portal machine. My hands lay on the red-hot semisphere. Neumann opposite stared at me speechless. Above our heads blazed a bright-white globe whose sparks and flashes suppressed the halogen lamps around the pedestal.

When I had pulled my hands away, the semisphere had grown black again. The globe overhead had disappeared leaving little bolts of lightning crackling at the ends of the rods that reached out for me although some force pushed them away redirecting them upward.

"Talk!" Blank's voice brought me back to reality. "How do you control it? Tell him what to do!"

I could touch the semisphere and choose any of the paths it offered. But then the captain would keep Mira and my daughter. He knew it well. He remembered not only my return from the swamps, but also my escape from Pangea on the day I'd learned of General Varlamov's real plans. His plans...

Two years ago I had acted on impulse. I'd run away from Pangea like a little boy without first talking to my father. I'd wanted to warn people on Earth about the danger they faced. Instead, the Feds had gotten their hands on me straight away. They started studying me like a guinea pig; they disemboweled my memory; and once the general had bluffed them into thinking he'd discovered some new course of action, they'd modified my identity and sent me and Wong back: him, as a killer to eliminate the danger - my father. Me, as a guide to lead him to the general.

In the silence that followed, I heard weak mumbling. The professor's lips moved as he repeated, "We need to stop it immediately. Immediately. Stop it. We.."

"I'm the only person who can control the machine," I finally said to the captain. "We need to come to an agreement. You bring Mira, the baby and my friends. I'll start the device."

"Non-negotiable," Blank snapped.

I shook my head. "Tell me what you want. What's your objective? Do you want to go back to Earth? Or do you want to travel in space?"

"I want to finish what we started," he articulated. "Your father turned out to be a coward."

I cracked my clenched fists.

"Stand still," Blank smirked. "The general bluffed all the way. He didn't intend to exterminate people. It was just his way of blackmailing the government. He used to say that threats were the best form of pressure." His face strained, eyes glaring with hatred. "We've been stuck here for two extra years, all for the pleasure of rescuing you." He stepped toward the pedestal and shoved the mumbling Neumann aside.

"You're going to disconnect Earth from Pangea," Blank pointed at me, "as soon as the cargo clears the jumpgate."

"What are my guarantees?" I wasn't going to let him browbeat me. "Mira, my daughter and my friends must stay alive. Otherwise..."

"I already told you. It's non-negotiable. You choose," he made a fist and untucked his thumb. "You either do what you're told and wait for us to come back from New Pang or," Blank unbent the index finger and made a gesture as if pulling a trigger, "all of your so-called friends, your daughter and your broad are history."

I gnashed my teeth and leaned forward.

"They'll all die," added the captain, "each and every one of them, right in front of your own eyes.

CHAPTER THREE
AN IMPORTANT LINK

I HAD TO ADMIT my defeat. In the first round at least because I knew that Blank wouldn't give up. He'd keep Mira and my daughter hostage while he still needed me, and then...

Keeping my cool, I again told the captain that the machine wouldn't obey anyone but me. No one but me could sever the link between Earth and Pangea.

For a few seconds, Blank fell silent, thinking. Then he drew his gun and shot the professor in the head. The bullet went through the old man's temple; he flapped his arms and fell face down onto the semisphere.

Blank shot Neumann three more times. The bullets left ragged holes in the professor's bloodied lab coat. Then he slid down onto the floor next to the pedestal.

"It's up to you if you want the others to live," Blank put the gun back in its holster. The protective membrane cleared up. An opening started to grow in it.

"Clean it up," the captain nodded at the body and stepped into the opening.

The cyber troopers lifted the dead professor like a rag doll and dragged him out after Blank.

I couldn't understand why Blank killed Neumann. The old man had probably known too much about Pangea and the Forecomers. Blank didn't want to leave us two together fearing that the professor might have come up with a way out for us both. Or maybe he'd wanted to break me: if now he told Mira that I'd caused her father's death, she would see me in a completely different light. No, he wouldn't go that far. Blank wasn't that stupid to alienate me: if I lost Mira and the baby, I wouldn't do jack shit for him.

Once the cyber troopers passed through the opening, the membrane sealed shut. Within a minute, the command center was empty apart from the operator by the control panel, his face illuminated by the glow of his monitor.

Now what? This simple question drove me mad. I had no idea how to get out of this trap. If I stayed behind the membrane, I wouldn't be able to stop Blank.

Wait up. Who said I couldn't?

I glanced at the semisphere. The 3D map of the universe reappeared in my mind. Immediately, the memory chip zoomed in on it and sent the plan of Pangea to my lens monitor.

Oh wow. I shook my head. It looked like the late Neumann had been right and human technologies did indeed resemble the Pangean ones - or rather those of the Forecomers. The portal machine and the chip in my head exchanged data like server-based protocols. Apparently, either my nervous system had somehow linked up with the machine or the device itself had tied itself to my memory chip and studied the software in my head while

I'd been busy bargaining with Blank. I sort of divined the symbols on the plan but I still had no idea exactly how my brain communicated with the portal machine.

I sat cross-legged on the floor and started staring at the equipment in the command center. The cabinets, the control panel and the monitors' glow swam before my eyes. I tried to relax and see the crimson threads that had helped me to defeat Wong.

There could be a fault or two in my reasoning but I didn't care anymore. Apparently, the device and the program that controlled it - which was possibly an artificial intellect for all I knew - had mistaken me for some part of itself, a main link within a flexible system. Yes, link was the right word. This was why two years ago in the swamps the fifth beacon had activated sensing me inside. This was why the machine's preprogrammed protective shield hadn't allowed me to die when the Chinese was about to deal me a lethal blow. Now we were one and the same, and if danger threatened me, the portal machine would protect me. Now that nothing and nobody posed a threat, the defensive program had gone on standby so no matter how much I concentrated, it wouldn't respond.

From the corner of my eye I sensed a movement in the control center. I got up off the floor. Behind the membrane stood Blank, Wladas, Kathy and their guards - the very same cybers who had shot the raiders at the river.

The captain's lips moved soundlessly as he gave orders. Then he opened the entrance through the membrane and stayed there while letting in my friends and their escort.

"We're leaving, Master Specialist," he pointed at the officer at the control panel. "We'll keep in touch through the operator."

"Where's Mira and the baby?" I stepped toward the opening.

"They're going with us," Blank turned away and ordered the soldiers to prepare the mobile reserve group to set off.

The membrane between us sealed up and clouded over.

I looked at Wladas. He looked surprisingly calm, content and relaxed. He stood by the wall, away from the rest, fondling his sharp stubbly chin and didn't even pay me any attention as if lost in his thoughts. Kathy, by contrast, was looking around everywhere staring open-mouthed at myself, at the semisphere and at the rods showering sparks as the lightning died away overhead.

"Quit gawking," I walked over to the girl. She turned her back to me and raised her hand to touch the membrane. "I wouldn't do that if I were you."

"Why?" Kathy gave me a surprised look.

I led her away from the membrane.

"You'd lose your arm before you knew it. This is the latest means of defense which Blank controls."

"That miserable scumbag?" She motioned her head toward the membrane.

"His name's Blank. Captain Rustam Blank, a cyber officer. General Varlamov's adjutant and bodyguard. And his assassin," I added in a whisper so that the guards couldn't hear.

We stepped behind the pedestal.

"And they told us you'd killed the general," Kathy whispered quickly.

I turned to her.

"They didn't really say it to us," she admitted. "The

soldiers were discussing it among themselves."

One of the cybers came toward Wladas and pushed his shoulder motioning him to rejoin us. Another pulled the backpack off his back and slammed it to the floor. "Here's a flask of water and some dry rations."

I remembered his name. Badry. Aquiline nose, hazel eyes, a broad forehead, black curly hair escaping from under the raised visor of his helmet. Badry had served in Blank's section ever since the building of the Fort. He was the garrison's veteran often mentioned in dispatches by the general.

"How long are we supposed to hang out here?" I asked squatting by the backpack.

"To the bitter end, Master Specialist," Badry answered and stepped back to his men.

I unvelcroed a flap and pulled out the flask.

"Hey," Kathy called out to them, "and what if I need to go for a piss?"

"Hold it," Badry barked over his shoulder.

His dog-faced associate grinned and guffawed. "Why not," he said in a deep voice. "Let her grin and bare it. That would be a sight for sore eyes."

"Shut the fuck up," Badry cut him short. "This isn't a summer camp, you pervert. You're not in the Fort anymore."

Dog face sulked under Badry's heavy glare but didn't say a word. Kathy, too, swallowed her pride and kept mum. Clever girl.

I took a swig and splashed my face with some water to wash off the caked-on blood and bits of brain. Wladas sat next to me, asked for the flask and whispered quickly, "Soldiers were saying that you killed the general. I don't believe them. This Captain Blank, he came to us and let

Wong out. You should have seen his eyes when he did it..."

"Where did they keep you?" Whether Wladas believed me or not mattered little to me at that moment. "Downstairs or up above?"

"Downstairs. In some kind of room, like a cave. We had to go down a long staircase to get to it. I remember there was a strong smell of food there and all along the hallway. As if there was a kitchen next to it."

I nodded mechanically. They'd kept them next to the mess hall.

"Did you see a woman and a baby?"

"Nah," Wladas shook his head. "They put all three of us in that room. Then they let Wong go, and then... we heard a noise, and..." He clung to the flask glancing at Badry who was casting us an attentive eye.

Then Kathy distracted him. She also wanted to drink and sat on the floor next to me. The cybers stood there for a while in silence and then strode over to the opposite wall speaking in hushed voices. Wladas went on,

"From what I heard, they had all left. Almost all of them. A few guards hung about upstairs. Blank took all of the clones with him. Where they went to, I don't know."

"To New Pang to see McLean," I whispered.

"Oh really?" the girl raised her eyebrows.

"McLean is going to send another carula shipment to the Fort," I took out the rations and tore the pack open glancing at the cybers. "They've already come to an agreement. The shipment contains a capsule with an assault virus which will open at a preset time."

"And?" Wladas frowned, uncomprehending. "Okay, so a few people will catch it..."

"Not so," I shook my head. "This is a swamp virus

from an alien world that leaked onto Pangea."

"What do you mean?" Kathy took the pack from me and rustled open the crackers.

"Let me finish," I hissed. "It's a long story. You'll have to believe me. They've modified the virus so that it kills slowly to make sure it spreads everywhere on the planet. And when the pandemic gains momentum, it'll be too late because by then, I'd have disconnected Pangea from Earth."

Kathy and Wladas stared at me without saying a word trying to take it in.

What an idiot I was! They didn't know anything! Not about biocyne nor about the fact that it was extracted from carula produced at McLean's seaweed farms. Neither did they know about the portal machine nor the beacons.

"In short," I said, "don't ask questions, just believe me that if the capsule with the virus in it reaches Earth, there'll be hell to pay."

"I don't give a fuck," Kathy said out of the blue. "Let them all croak. I don't have anyone there."

"But I do have family," Wladas transfixed her in dismay.

"Eat," I hissed and shoved a cracker in my mouth. I took a can opener which was included with the rations and ripped open a can of beans. "I don't want the cybers to suspect anything."

"Yeah right," Kathy opened a pack of disposable spoons. "Can you tell me Mark why you're fussing so much? Is it for the Feds?"

"It's for my wife and daughter," I answered nibbling on a cracker. "Blank keeps them hostage. And will continue to keep them until he doesn't need me anymore."

"Wait," Wladas grabbed my hand preventing me from taking another bite of my cracker. "Did you say, disconnect Earth? How are you going to do that?"

He looked at the semisphere on its pedestal, then raised his eyes to the rods protruding from the impossibly high vaulted ceiling. "Do you know how this thing works? This machine?" He scratched his cheek and lowered his gaze. "You think it can take you back?"

"It can," I whispered before swilling down the rest of the cracker with some water. "I can go back to Earth. I can travel to other worlds. I can..." Now that was a thought! I could use the machine to travel across Pangea itself. If the machine had been able to teleport me from the swamps back to the gasometer, I could now try to get closer to New Pang - either to the beacon in the bay or to the one in the estuary, by the loggers' camp. In the latter case it would be quite a hike to get to the city but nevertheless. I could still catch up with Blank and meet him fully prepared to free Mira and my daughter. He'd never get the virus to Earth.

"Why would you want to disconnect Earth and Pangea?" Kathy asked.

"To make sure the virus doesn't find its way back," I said. "Here in the swamps... how can I tell you... the swamps are part of their natural habitat..."

"You mean the swamp was sucked in here just like the Kola Peninsula was?" Wladas ventured.

"Exactly," I glanced at the cybers.

The soldiers sat on the floor backs to the wall, their legs outstretched. Dog face busied himself with his pulse gun: something was malfunctioning in his video sighting unit. Badry leaned against the wall and closed his eyes.

"Now," I said as quiet as I could, "listen up. We can handle these two. But the operator," I motioned with my eyes at the communications officer by his equipment stand, "he's behind the membrane."

"There's another way," Wladas interrupted without turning to me. "Let's say I know how to turn off this membrane for a while."

For a few seconds I stared at him unblinking. Then I said, "What do we need to do?"

Wladas paused twisting the plastic spoon in his hands.

"We'll have to kill one of the cybers."

"I can smoke 'em both if you want," Kathy shot the guards a prickly glare.

"Wait a sec," I said.

Wladas went on, "Whenever one of us goes through the optical membrane into the opening, it is in fact activated, but in an integral part the protective field registers a security code which only Blank knows. While letting us pass, the membrane reads our neural parameters. Just like the mind scanner at the jumpgate exit, remember?"

I nodded. I thought I knew what he was implying.

"The processor's memory," Wladas whispered in excitement, "controls the membrane. It contains the data of everyone who passes through it."

"But that data is unique," I butted in. "Our nervous system, our brain, our conscience..."

"Exactly," Wladas' eyes glistened. In his excitement, he waved his spoon around. "The membrane identifies all who attempt to cross the field as enemies, even if they possess the key. By the key I mean the code that can increase or decrease the protective field's intensity."

"Yeah," I promptly shoved a cracker in his mouth

because he had suddenly sat up straight staring at us.

Kathy who'd all this time been stiff with tension, open-mouthed, turned sharply back to her food and dug her spoon into the beans. Dog face nudged Badry with his elbow and asked him aloud to turn on his laser range finder in order to check his sights' settings.

They busied themselves with their guns while we stuffed our faces, pointing their lasers at various points on the vaulted ceiling. Finally they stopped and started yapping again.

"Carry on," I whispered to Wladas who sat with his back to the soldiers.

"So. The membrane only reacts on the living."

I shook my head, unable to understand what he was driving at.

"It kills all life that passes through it if it doesn't receive the correct security code," he said rapidly. "We've all been in its field. The system remembered us and stored the data in its memory cells. When we cross the field, the system compares the parameters and sends a request to the processor. Then it either lets us through or eliminates us."

"Do you mean," I tapped his shoulder with my spoon, "that a dead cyber could open the entrance? You think his body could cross the membrane and nothing would happen? The field's status would remain unchanged and its potential wouldn't grow, right?"

"Yes, that's right. But only for a second, not more, because the processor's brain would come into discord with the sequential algorithm. My colleagues from the Defense Ministry labs still haven't found the solution to this problem. They didn't think much of it and accepted the membrane as is. Who would think of killing themselves one step from the membrane only to get to the other side as a dead man?"

"Yeah," I glanced at Kathy. She wrinkled her forehead in thought chewing on her spoon.

"So," I started, "we need to get hold of a gun, kill a cyber, throw the corpse into the membrane and shoot the operator?"

"We'll only have a second," Wladas reminded.

The girl shrugged. "So let's try."

And before I could suggest a plan of further action, she got up and said angrily,

"That's it, I can't hold it any longer! Open this thing of yours before I piss myself!"

The cybers stared at the girl who stepped toward the semisphere demonstratively unbuttoning her combat pants. She squatted disappearing from their view.

"But," dog face started.

"Wait!" shouted Badry.

Both soldiers shoved their guns behind their backs and leapt up.

I hate adlibbing. You can never be sure of the outcome.

The cybers split up. Badry ran around our side of the pedestal and happened to be with his back to Wladas and myself. Without a moment's hesitation, I grabbed the collar of his bulletproof vest and his neck with my other hand. I kicked the back of his knees and pulled him sharply toward me, my chest pressing at the back of his head.

It was a perfect lever. His vertebrae snapped. Badry didn't even have time to cry out. Kathy shot up like an uncoiling spring toward dog face and buried her plastic spoon in his eye.

Dog face squealed in pain, his scream resounding in a multi-voiced echo under the vaulting. Clutching at his face, he stumbled and made an instinctive step toward the membrane trying to retrieve the gun from behind his back.

Now every second counted. Kathy grabbed the barrel of his gun and tugged it toward her knocking his feet from under him. He was still alive when he hit the membrane which started rippling from the impact, one moment transparent, the next opaque. His scream was cut short when blood gushed from his severed neck as his head, lopped off by the protective field, rolled over toward the operator in his control center.

It took the duty communications officer some time to realize what was going on. As he started from his stool, I jerked the gun off the dead Badry's shoulder but failed to drag his body to the membrane in order to shoot. I just didn't have enough strength: the cyber trooper weighed over two hundred pounds in full gear.

Wladas came to my aid. He grabbed hold of one of the corpse's arms while I pulled the other. We dragged the body close to the membrane and threw it in. I raised the gun and squeezed the trigger.

The first pulse struck the stand next to the officer burning a hole in it and spattering blue flames. The officer cried out and collapsed on the floor. I shot again but the membrane had closed the gap. With a loud hiss, the pulse hit the murky membrane and shattered into flakes of fire enveloping us in a hot wave.

"Shoot, Mark!" Kathy shouted forgetting that I couldn't hit the target through the membrane. "Can't you see he's getting up! Shoot him!"

The operator grabbed at the stand and heaved himself

up. Rising to his knees, he reached for the keyboard - apparently, trying to press the emergency button to warn Blank.

"Come on!" the girl gasped. "What the fuck are you..."

She finally understood that shooting was useless.

I slung the gun's strap over my head and shut my eyes feeling my heart flutter in my chest. I took a deep breath and lunged forward.

"What are you doing?" I heard Wladas and Kathy call after me.

There wasn't time to explain anything to them. I only hoped that the portal machine's intellect that had included me in its flexible structure wouldn't incinerate me in its protective field. My death couldn't be in vain.

Heat enveloped my face. The air thickened as the crimson grid reappeared around me. The memory chip screamed signaling an overload and the cracked infrared lens prickled my eye. Then the membrane arched preventing me from stepping through. It shuddered and burst with a crackle like a window pane. Losing my balance, I fell onto my knees and tilted my head back when the dumbfounded officer was just about to lay his hand on the keyboard.

That was it! I didn't have time to stop him!

Claps from an pulse gun behind my back made me duck instinctively. Shimmering trajectories traced over my head. Part of them hit the operator's chest and sent him sprawling over his stand. The other part went higher up.

I turned round. Kathy sat next to the pedestal, her legs akimbo, staring in amazement at dog face's gun in her hands.

"Now that's a recoil," she said with unconcealed admiration. "Now that's a gun!"

Wladas wheezed out loud. Pale, he opened his mouth, pointing at me and at the place where the membrane had just been.

"How? How did you do it?" Finally, Wladas overcame his excitement and approached cautiously the invisible line and the two dead cybers next to it. He reached out with his shaking hand and felt the air. "But..."

I jumped up and ran across toward the stand behind which lay the dead operator. The monitor was broken. A ragged hole gaped in the stationary radio with its molten slide gauge dripping black plastic onto the desk.

I thumped the useless radio with my fist and spat on the floor in anger. Now we couldn't contact the Fort and warn them of the arrival of Blank's cargo. In killing the officer, Kathy had ruined the communications unit. Now we had to find another solution.

Steps and voices came from the hallway behind the equipment.

"Hide!" I prepared to fire my gun and started moving along the equipment cabinets. "Kathy, cover me if I need it."

I didn't think it was the upstairs guards. Probably, just someone from the former base personnel: laboratory neurotechs who'd heard the shots and had hurried to find out what was going on.

When I took up my position behind a humming server rack, two men appeared in the hallway wearing light-colored protection suits and masks pushed up onto their foreheads; The lab assistant was persuading the chief neurotech to call the guards. But the neurotech hurried ahead, not listening.

I let both of them pass me and stepped into the hallway. When they stopped dead in their tracks staring at the corpses, I shouted,

"Stick 'em up!"

The two startled but obeyed.

"Slowly. Now turn round."

They did.

"How much more personnel left in the camp?" I asked without letting them get their act together. "And how many of them are guards?"

I glanced across my shoulder listening. Had the shots been heard up above?

The neurotechs didn't answer. They just blinked, dumbfounded, keeping their hands raised above their heads.

"Well?" I lifted my gun.

"Three left," the assistant hurried. "They guard the entrance."

His partner bobbed his head.

"Yes," he swallowed, "plus us two, and the communication officer with the cybers, but you've already..."

"Have the guards got a car?"

Both shook their heads. The assistant mumbled that Blank had taken all the transports and told them to wait and keep their heads down.

"Kathy!" I said. "Keep them in your sights. Not a step out of here until I get back!"

I wanted to turn but reconsidered and added, "Don't touch anything here. Is that clear?"

"Yes!" The girl got up from behind the pedestal and trained her gun on the prisoners.

I ran to the staircase trying to pick out the cracked lens from my eye socket on the way. I passed the "clean" rooms, turned into a doorway and ran upstairs two steps at a time.

I reached the long hallway and headed for the exit illuminated by the crimson rays of the rising sun. Suddenly I stopped dead in my tracks.

Shots rang out on the surface. Carbines pinged, machine guns clattered and pulse rifles whooshed. Judging by the latter, the neurotechs had lied to me. There were many more guards there.

The light in front of me faded. A long shadow lay across the floor. Someone had breached the hallway and was barking orders. I was halfway to the exit next to where the deformed bucket still lay in the niche. I'd completely forgotten about it. My foot got caught on it sending it rattling and I stumbled hitting my shoulder on the wall.

Now I could use the infrared camera! I infinitely regretted not having taken the cyber's tactical helmet and vest. The element of surprise was lost. The soldier who'd backed into the hallway was in full combat gear. We raised our weapons simultaneously and fired.

He sprang back toward the exit. I ducked onto the floor banging my hip on a stone. The soldier's bullets whizzed a meter above my head; mine also hadn't found their target. I sat up and pushed myself back into the niche with my heels when still more shots rang out in the hallway.

This time the soldier was more accurate. I was saved by a stone ledge. Bullets sprayed it chipping bits off one and scratching my cheek. The enemy had changed the fire rate and were shooting single rounds moving along the hallway not letting me stick my head out. I pressed my back to the stone and pulled my legs up hugging my gun, unable to do anything.

The soldier's gun fell silent. The magazine clattered to the floor as it fell from its catch. I jumped up and made a dart for my adversary squeezing the trigger...

I heard the dry click of the electric discharger. My magazine was empty too. I lunged at him with the barrel of the gun aiming for his neck and jabbed him.

The soldier tilted his head forward. The anti-recoil system of my barrel had pierced his visor. I swung the butt of the gun into his shoulder and kicked him in the groin when an explosion boomed behind his back. My eyes went blank.

The shock wave sent us reeling to the floor. Tongues of fire roared along the hallway burning up the oxygen. I held my breath and shut my eyes. The dead soldier's body shielded me. For a few seconds, the flame raged above us and then died away.

I heaved the burnt corpse off me, turned onto my stomach and crawled toward the exit on all fours. The memory chip started ranting again urging me to report to the medical block. My eye was stinging from the recently-extracted lens. My head rang like a bell and my nose bled.

Forcing my limbs to move, I crawled to the exit, hugged the wall and pulled myself up. Gasping mouthfuls of burned cordite-filled air, I threw myself out of the building.

I couldn't hear any shooting, only faraway voices and the shuffle of hurried steps. I wanted to turn on my back and take a lungful of air but I only had enough strength to lift my head and place my cheek on the sand.

"Look, it's Mark!" a familiar voice came from beside me. "Jim, it's him! Big as life and twice as ugly!"

On my left-hand side, Lars Swenson's thick voice was bellowing commands.

Finally it dawned on me that the guards' resistance had been broken. Most likely, all the soldiers had also been eliminated. A bit too late, if you'd ask me. I wished Swenson had made it here earlier. But then things could have taken a different turn and Blank with his cyber troopers, combat vehicles and with a squad of duty guards could have made a short job of the loggers' militia.

Someone grabbed me by the shoulders and turfed me onto my back. Jim's freckled face loomed over me. He was smiling.

"Oakum, what're you waiting for?" Georgie croaked, approaching. "Lift him. Fritz, help him!"

A lank man in a pea-coat with faded silver-lace patches on its shoulders pushed Jim aside and bent down to me. He grabbed the lapels of my jacket and jerked me into a sitting position. He had fiery red hair, a mustache and a neat little beard. The still-smoking mouth of a grenade launcher hung on his back.

I poked his chest with my finger. "Are you Havlow? The tanker engineer?"

He cast me a surprised glance and shrank back, chewing energetically on his tobacco, the epitome of how Lars Swenson had described him to me. Go to the riggers and find Fritz Havlow, he'd said.

"How d'you know me?"

"From them," I nodded at the loggers.

The giant Swenson was busy ordering his men around. He bellowed commands and swung his arms as he motioned them each to their own place on the platform in front of the gasometer, telling them what to collect as trophies and what not to touch until he'd had a moment to inspect it.

There were more people buzzing amid the ruins,

commanded by a tightly built stocky man in a sooty captain's cap.

"Any guards left in the building?" Fritz asked.

"None," I looked at Georgie limping toward us.

He looked considerably fresher than during our last meeting, except for his leaner frame and sunken eyes on a gaunt face.

Leaning on Jim's arm, I got back to my feet. "How did you get out?"

"Remember the cellar at the farmers'? The ice room?" Georgie slapped my shoulder. "We took cover there. In the morning, we got to the river and caught the New Pang ferry on its way to the riggers'. So..." he massaged his injured leg.

"I see," I paused and cleared my throat. "And the farm woman? Her children?"

"All alive. Akhmad died, though."

"I know."

From under his pea-coat, Fritz produced a Parabellum handgun. He stepped through the entrance and peeped down the hallway but recoiled and waved his hand in front of his nose.

"You can't..." he swallowed, "you can't breathe in there! How did you survive?"

Without answering, I took the flask offered by Jim and gulped down half its contents, then cleaned my face and eyes with the rest.

"I fired a thermobaric round down there! At twenty paces," Fritz said.

"Leave him alone," Georgie said. "The guy needs a breather."

"Later," I handed the flask back to Jim and pointed toward the entrance. "There're Wladas and Kathy down there."

"No! That ass of a clone is still around!" Georgie stepped toward the opening but I held him back by his shoulder.

"She is, and she's saved my life."

"Long time no see!" I heard from behind my back. Lars Swenson approached us accompanied by a few young armed militiamen.

"You've done it, Private. Congrats!" he shook my hand without stopping.

"Too early to congratulate," I squeezed his broad palm. "Clones and the cyber troopers are now heading for New Pang. They're driving to see McLean who's going to help them ship their cargo to the Fort. The cargo contains an assault virus destined for Earth. It'll cause the death of millions. We need to contact the Fort and warn them about it."

Lars' face didn't twitch. After a moment's thought, he said,

"There's only one option, right? We have to stop the cybers, is that what you mean?"

I nodded. He was quick on the draw. No need to give him the details.

"When and how did they leave?" he asked.

"They left before sunrise, in combat vehicles."

"We just missed each other," he turned and shielded his eyes looking at the sun hovering over the horizon. "We won't make it," he turned back to me and shook his head. "If they have combat vehicles, we'll need an airplane to catch up with them."

"Don't you have the radio? You can contact the jumpgate and pass the information on to their commander."

"Won't work," Lard shook his head. "It's not strong enough. I'll need a signal amplifier to reach them. And the amplifier is at McLean's place."

I cursed through clenched teeth and looked at the militants crowded around me.

"Be prepared to defend this place, just in case. When cybers don't receive the next guards' report, they might come back."

"What do you suggest?" concern clouded Lars' face.

"Just dig in and hold the entrance. Make sure not one of the motherfuckers gets into the building."

"And you?"

"I have an idea. Bur first, I need to get to the tanker. How far is the riggers' base?"

"Twenty-five miles or so," Fritz said.

"Are there any emergency exit systems left there?

Fritz nodded.

"You think you can spare a fast car?"

Again he nodded.

"Let's go then," I stepped toward the platform. "Shit," I stepped back. "I have two people left inside. A man and a woman. Georgie and Jim know them. Also, two neurotechs we've taken prisoner and a hell of a lot of equipment worth keeping."

Lars' eyes glinted when he heard about the equipment. He glanced at Georgie. Fritz chuckled: he, with his technical and entrepreneurial skills, didn't want to let this booty slip through his fingers. The last thing I needed was a loggers and riggers' squabble over the loot.

"Best not to touch anything until I'm back," I tried to sound convincing. "Don't try to turn anything on or off. Apart from the lab equipment, they also have the Forecomers machine that could take us all back to Earth."

Georgie's jaw dropped. Fritz cleared his throat. Lars ran his strong hand across his face and beard.

"Jim," I continued. "You go down first. Tell Kathy and Wladas that they're safe."

"Sure."

"Lars, you make sure our Georgie here doesn't smoke the girl. They feel too strong for each other."

Georgie darkened.

"Promise to make sure they're okay?" I asked him.

Lars grunted. "The word of the King of the Forest."

"Let's go, then? " I turned to the red-headed Fritz.

He stared at the ruins and the remains of the solar panels scavenged by the riggers. The guy in the captain's cap was dishing out orders.

"I'll give you a thousand gold pieces," Lars said unexpectedly. "We can deal with your captain later. Now go, we don't have much time."

Fritz nodded with a lopsided grin.

"Take Georgie with you," Lars added, winking at him.

He knew where his interests lay, I thought as I followed Fritz out to the car. Lars tried to keep everything under his own control. He knew the stakes had risen very high indeed.

CHAPTER FOUR
AS THE CROW FLIES

I T TOOK our open-top Willys less than an hour to get to the desert. I thought at first that the ragged brown outline that caught my eye behind the smooth dunes was a far-off mountain. Then I realized that it was in fact our destination.

Fritz drove. I kept glancing back from my passenger's seat checking for Blank's reserve combat vehicles. Georgie sat in the back. The old Army jeep groaned as it rocked over the dunes. The windshield was folded forward but the desert air flow didn't bring relief as the sun stood high at its zenith beating down like a blow heater. We were approaching the riggers' base, or rather, the stranded Samotlor tanker that I had mistaken for a mountain.

I'd seen a few large vessels in my lifetime. Atomic cruisers and submarine missile launchers, and even Chinese intercontinental clone carriers. But they'd all been sitting in the water hiding the bulk of their body from view.

Now it was different. The slanting aft of the ship had grown into the sand. Its stem rose above the dunes that concealed half its body. When we drove closer, Fritz made a sharp turn and instead of driving between the dunes toward the ship's rusty side and the deck structures, steered the jeep at almost a right angle to it. The worn-out painted digits of the tanker's draught markings still showed on its bow.

I stood up in my seat and craned my neck trying to make out the hatches of the emergency exit systems' launching tubes. I knew they had to be somewhere under the cabins. But the jeep swerved again, and the dunes swallowed up the ship.

"Sit still. You'll see it all in a while," Fritz said.

I'd already told him on our way there what exactly I needed parts of the launching systems for. But I hadn't yet explained how or where I was going to use them. These days, all superships were equipped with two-seat ejection capsules, located aft, that allowed the crew to abandon ship in case of fast fracture.

My idea was to remove the capsules' gunpowder engines and use them to make a quick copy of an assault jetpack. I'd studied them at army school and knew that the thrust principle was the same in both. I also wanted to use the drag chute to decelerate in case I rocketed too high in the air. The riggers' base had everything necessary for my purpose: a workshop, tools, a welding machine and even a savvy mechanic in the shape of Fritz himself.

The jeep mounted a shallow crest and drove along a narrow wadi between the dunes. The well-used tracks ribboned down into a deep crater.

Its shallow front edge was shaped like a horseshoe. That's why Fritz hadn't driven straight on. We'd have simply toppled down. The tanker's enormous side loomed up from afar serving as the rear wall of the crater. The paint was peeling off in many places. Below, rough wooden ramps led to ragged openings cut into the ship's side with welding torches. Bent pipes protruded from the widest opening and led underground.

Squat sandstone structures crowded the bottom of the crater. Closer to the entrance, two tents stood away from the rest with a swing gate between them. Further on, a rectangular platform fenced-off with barbed wire was studded with the straight rows of filler spouts of the oil containers buried below. I counted almost two dozen of them. In the center of the platform stood an unusual machine with a pivoted rod and a spool of thick ridged pipe.

"Is that the oil tank?" I turned to Fritz pointing at the platform.

"Exactly," he said slowing up and shifting down.

"And where's the rig and the supply vessel?"

"I have a funny feeling you've been here before," Fritz cast me a quick glance.

"It's not important. Just answer the question."

"They've dismantled the rig," he said after a pause, shifting up. "Its remains are still lying on the shore. When this shit landed here, the tanker and the tug were luckier than the rest of it. It took us five years to dig the rig out of the sand bit by bit. Finally we built the tank and pumped most of the fuel into it.

"Wise move," I nodded. It's best to keep fuel underground in this heat. The old rig could have exploded, God forbid if they hadn't done it.

"All right, then. And where's the supply vessel?"

"The bulk carrier? It's far from here," Fritz thumbed

behind his back.

"Yes," bored by the whole trip, Georgie poked his head out from between the seats pointing back. "It took the raiders a long time to find it. We only recognized it by the mast housing above the cockpit. It stuck out of the sand in the middle of the desert."

"And how did it end up underground?" I asked.

"How do you expect me to know?" Georgie answered.

"Can you see how the tanker's standing?" Fritz nodded at the behemoth in front. "Why are you asking?"

"Fine," I sat back. "So did you dig the carrier out?"

"You bet your life we did," Fritz grinned. "We worked three shifts shoveling sand. There was gold there. Haven't you heard? The convoy was on its way back from the Arctic gold mines when Pangea had appeared."

"And what about the tug?" I was surprised I couldn't see any people down in the crater. Two lookouts hovered on top of the cockpit studying the terrain through their field glasses. Another one - apparently the watch commander - leaned on his elbows against the window's ragged steel edge staring at us.

"Are you talking about Svyatoslav Norg? The icebreaker?"

"Exactly."

"It landed right in the middle of the river. Just sat there rocking on the waves as if it had always been there. The crew didn't even know what had hit them. They stopped the engine and jumped ship, and then.."

"But where is everyone?" I interrupted him. "Why are there no people down there?"

"Look at the sky," Georgie answered as Fritz steered the jeep along the tanker's side toward a steep long gangway. "The work shift are busting their asses at the river. The others are chilling out in the cellars waiting for the heat to subside. And the rest," he nodded at the road, "are in the old city with the loggers. They're the ones who got you out of the shit."

"I see."

Fritz killed the engine, jumped out of the jeep and hurried up the gangway. We followed.

"Slow down, will ya," Georgie limped up the steps behind us mentioning clones under his breath. "I can't keep up with you two!"

We were met by a gaunt gray-haired little man in knee-long shorts, a torn sailor tank top, a pair of thongs and a faded bucket hat with a greasy rim.

"Why are you back, Fritz?" he demanded casting suspicious glances at me and the wheezing Georgie behind our backs.

On his belt hung an ancient yellow-leather gun holster. A revolver handle peeped out from under the flap, a thin leather strap hooked to a ring on it. The man, as if accidentally, lay his hand onto the gun and moved a finger unbuttoning the flap.

"Relax, Stepanych," Fritz swept his arm pointing at us. "They're friends. We only need to get to the safety capsules. We need to remove a few things."

"Does the captain know?" Stepanych, squinting, distrusted us. "I know you, Fritz. You want to sell the damn things. It's all right but what if we need them capsules later ourselves?"

"Listen, old man," I stepped forward. "The safety capsules up here can save our asses. Yours, mine and everyone's. Everyone on the Continent."

"What the fuck is that? Who are you to raise your voice here like that?" the man's hand moved to draw but

Fritz grabbed his wrist, shoved discreetly a couple of coins into his other hand and stepped closer, whispering in his ear.

When Stepanych moved away, he wrinkled his nose and scratched his head. His lips moved in silence. His face reflected the strain of mental work.

"You there," he rotated his index finger at his temple, "you'd better think before you open your mouth."

"We only need to get to the capsules," Fritz said. "Then we'll pop into the workshop and we'll be on our way. The work shift will still be at the river. They'll never even know we've been here."

Stepanych glanced at the lookouts on top of the cockpit and fingered his long gray mustache.

"All right, damn you. Go," he stepped back to the railing to let us pass and added at our backs, "I'm afraid I've got to report to the captain anyways."

"Be my guest," Fritz waved him off and walked toward the cabin deck. Without turning, he said, "Georgie, you've been on the lower decks, you take the customer to the safety capsules."

"And you?" Georgie asked.

"I'll get some tools from the workshop."

We split up. As Georgie and I descended into a stifling darkness, he tried to draw me on my plans and suss out what I needed makeshift jetpacks for. But I didn't have time to explain. Together we opened the hatches that led to the capsules. I showed him the sequence in which we had to pry the levers open in order to release the capsules in their shafts and send them sliding down the rails toward the deck.

I had to hurry. Blank must have been approaching New Pang and he knew that he had trouble back at the camp, in the gasometers. He might have dispatched a reserve squad already for all I knew. It was a race against time.

When the safety locks clicked and the rockets' nozzles clunked onto the fireproof tiles inside, Fritz returned. He threw me a screwdriver, hurled another to Georgie, put the toolbox down, and we got working. We unscrewed the bolts that kept the tiles in place, then took them off their mounts and set them aside. I inspected the jets' nozzles and panels and nodded to Fritz. The capsules couldn't have been in a better state of repair - I'd even noticed traces of original lubricant on the panels. Why would it be otherwise? No one had any use for them here. The hermetic shafts with their hatches and heatproof tiles worked as natural sarcophagi offering the best conservation imaginable.

It took us another ten minutes to remove the jets and extract the drums that contained the brake chutes. Afterward, sweating like pigs, we took everything to the workshop and I used all my welding skills to shape a jetpack frame.

While Fritz and Georgie busied themselves making mountings for the thrusters and cutting stabilizers out of pieces of tin, I made leather hand and ankle straps and, once the contraption was assembled, attached them to the frame.

We fumbled around with it for about forty minutes, no more. The jetpack turned out to be awkward and heavy - nothing like the original Defense Ministry kit - but I didn't care. I was more than pleased with the result: the thrusters hung on the frame on either side of me and between them sat two brake shute drums. I could have added a safety deflector to make sure the blast didn't burn my feet but I didn't want to lose more time than absolutely necessary. At any moment, Blank's reserve squad could have arrived at the City of Forecomers.

So we decided to go back. I still had to assemble the fuses and wire them in to the gunpowder tubes. I couldn't use the original fuses: to be able to get to them, you had to eject the capsules from the shafts and open them. You couldn't do that without a crane.

We set off on our way back. Georgie sat next to Fritz while I took the back seat and started fiddling with the wires. I leaned the jetpack against the backs of the front seats so that the tubular handles of the stabilizer controls faced me. I used some insulating tape to attach two button switches and fed the wires through the tubes.

There'd been no portable batteries at the tanker but Fritz had unearthed a flashlight with a hand generator. I could use it to power the fuses. In the workshop, I'd borrowed a pair of safety goggles which were now hanging around my neck.

"Fritz? What was it you told Stepanych to make him let us through?" Georgie's voice cut through the hum of the engine. "I'd rather fuck a clone than do something like that. I'd never let us go in."

I looked up. Fritz tilted his head at Georgie and gave him a sly grin. But Georgie rose in his seat, leaning against the dashboard.

"The thing is, he-" Fritz started but Georgie didn't let him finish.

"Over there!" he stood up, then slumped down again as the Willys hit a stone. "Look!"

By then, we'd almost reached the rocky plateau. There, far in front of us, two combat buggies were racing toward the City of Forecomers raising clouds of dust from the road.

Fritz hit the anchors. I grabbed at the jeep's side just in time, my chest very nearly ramming the jetpack's frame.

"Looks like one has turned round to meet us," Georgie croaked. "What do we do now?"

I lifted the jetpack, stood up on my seat and put my arms through the straps.

"You haven't tested it!" Fritz raised his red eyebrows staring up at me.

"Never mind," I said fastening the ankle straps. "If it's stable, that's all that matters. It sure can fly me from here to the ruins."

I finished and wiggled my shoulders adjusting it, then put on the goggles.

"But what about the wiring? The fuses?" Fritz said seeing two disconnected wires hanging off my shoulder.

"Splice them," I lay my hands on the stabilizers' handles that traced the shape of my arms.

"Can't you see we're toast!" Georgie exclaimed. "We need to get the fuck out of here."

"Wait," I moved one hand onto a handle and turned my head watching the right stabilizer change the gradient. "They'll have better things to do with their time in a moment."

Fritz adjusted a twisted strap and slapped my shoulder, "All ready."

I nodded to him and stood with my feet wide apart, then crouched and leaned forward. The jetpack pressed on the small of my back. I rearranged it and took the handles again.

"Now duck."

I grasped the hand generator's handle and pressed the button. Loud crackling and hissing noises came from behind my back. With a swoosh, tongues of fire issued from the two nozzles lifting my feet off the seat. For a second, I hovered about a meter above the jeep in a cloud of sand and dust raised by the jet. Then it jerked me up so hard that the acceleration knocked the stuffing out of me. The straps pulled hard against my chest. The air roared in my ears.

I slightly spread my arms changing the stabilizers' angle and looked down. I was sliding along the valley gradually descending. Fritz and Georgie in the jeep had stayed far behind. I glimpsed a combat vehicle below making a sharp U-turn: it must have noticed me.

The next moment fiery projectiles criss-crossed the sky, launched from the pulse gun on the vehicle's roof. They didn't seem to have any guided ones: in a cyber's hands, one would be enough to hit any target.

Changing the stabilizers' angle again, I rose higher to overtake the second vehicle of the reserve squad. It was racing toward the gasometers that loomed into view far ahead. If only I had enough fuel! If I burned the two remaining stages, the jetpack would become a useless pile of junk. Then I could forget saving Mira and my daughter.

The thrusters had been designed to lift a much bigger weight than mine, but unlike combat jetpacks, they weren't made for repeat ascents that battlefield situations demanded. It meant that the fuel in the stages would burn out completely in about two minutes creating enough thrust to accelerate to nearly two hundred miles an hour. That would allow me to glide for a while using the stabilizers and then...

The gasometers approached rapidly when the engines died. I estimated the distance and started to drift down. I had to find a place to land. The chutes would kill the speed but as I had little control over them, they wouldn't prevent a hard landing.

I used the stabilizers to slow down my descent a bit hoping to make it to the gasometers. And I could already see below the yellow and brown spots of a cam net stretched over the roof of one of the buildings.

Shots were ringing out below. Both riggers and loggers fired away at me with their carbines mistaking me for one of Varlamov's troopers. This was the last thing I needed, to get a bullet in the guts from one of their snipers and go tumbling down from a height of two hundred meters. Not my idea of fun.

When I arrived at the gasometer with the portal machine, I dived down and reached behind my back to activate the chute. I pulled a brace releasing the drum and, grabbing at the stabilizers' handles, drew them close to turn the stabilizers parallel to the ground.

The chute billowed open jerking me up. My legs shot forward like those of a marionette. I let go of the handles and pulled the chute's webbing as I tried to increase the surface area of the chute hoping to slow down my descent. I barely missed the roof and flew chest first into a stone wall.

I got the shit knocked out of me. Dozens of fireflies exploded in my brain. Circles flashing before my eyes, I grabbed at the edge of the cam net and hung gritting my teeth.

"Don't shoot!" I heard Lars' strong voice. "It's one of ours! Get him down before he falls!"

I glanced over my shoulder. I hung about thirty meters up. To my right, I noticed the end of a crane hoist protruding above the wall at slightly more than an arm's distance. Fragments of a disintegrated wire rope were still stuck in the crane's block. The heavy jetpack prevented me from climbing up, but I could always try and reach the crane's arm.

Below, people fussed about shouting at me to hold on; someone urged for a tarpaulin to be stretched under the wall.

Yeah right. By the time they found one, the cybers would have been here and then the settlers would have had more important things to do with their time, leaving me hanging until I dropped, exhausted, from the height of a twelve-story building. Then they could scrape me off the concrete if they wanted.

I took two deep breaths and pushed away from the wall to gain some momentum. As I swung back, I reached out for the crane's arm and scratched its surface breaking my nails but at least catching hold of its edge. Now I hung sprawling in the air like some kind of crucified martyr.

My shoulders shook with the strain. My neck muscles were cramping.

"Get to the crane!" I heard. "Climb down the rope to the ladder!"

It was Lars shouting but I couldn't even turn my head for fear of letting go of the wall's edge.

Not breathing, I released the net. My right hand slid off the edge while my left one grabbed the wire rope. But instead of the jolt I expected, I started falling with it. The block overhead rattled with the unwinding rope. The people watching me on the stone platform below grew closer with every second.

A man on the ladder jumped off just in time to avoid my legs kicking his head. At the last moment, the block jammed. The rope jerked and stopped. My fingers slackened; not expecting this turn of events, I kicked the ladder as I tumbled head over heels flailing my arms in the air. Then I was hanging head first wondering why I'd stopped.

"Get him off!" Lars ordered. "Quickly!"

Grunting from the pain in my chest, I doubled up grabbing at the ladder's sides and finally realized what had happened. The ladder's lower rungs were caught on the funnels of two engines and that had prevented it from falling. But I couldn't get down on my own.

Strong hands grabbed my back. A deep voice told me to hold still. I let go of the ladder and entrusted myself to my helpers.

The next moment, I was standing down on the platform.

"Prepare to fight," I told Lars when he stepped toward me without going into details.

I unstrapped myself, put the jetpack down and squatted next to it studying the stabilizers and the nozzles.

"What's all this?" Lars asked. "Where're Georgie and Fritz?"

"Back at the base," I stood up and lifted the jetpack by its frame. "You have two combat vehicles bearing down on you. Things will get pretty hot here in a minute."

Rubbing my aching chest, I went toward the gasometer's entrance.

"Where are you going?"

"Down," I ducked into the opening and hurried toward the stairs hearing Lars wheezing behind me.

The stench of Fritz's thermobaric round still hung thick in the hallway. I hauled the jetpack onto my shoulder and covered my face with one hand. As I walked down the steps, I nearly ran into two burly bearded men.

"Who are you?" one of them asked suspiciously raising his carbine.

"Let him through," Lars ordered. The loggers stepped aside.

Wladas and Kathy waited for me by the portal machine.

"How is it?" the girl asked and then shook her head, unbelieving. I must have looked a sight.

"Fine," I turned around. "Where are the cybers' bodies?"

"We've put them in the room where they kept us," Wladas explained.

"Get in there, quick! Take a uniform off one of them and his gear. Hurry it up."

He blinked, confused.

"Didn't you hear?" Lars boomed as he stood next to us.

'Kathy," I said, "help him. It'll be quicker with two people."

"Right," she nodded and motioned to Wladas. The pair of them disappeared down the hallway.

"I need a pulse gun and some ammo," I told Lars as I walked toward the pedestal with the semisphere on it. "A knife and a handgun, as well."

I put the jetpack down and glanced at the rods vibrant with lightning.

"Mind if I ask where you're off to?" Lars asked once he'd given the orders to his men.

"I don't know yet," I wiped the sweat off my forehead and unbuttoned the jacket. "Either to New Pang bay or to your tollgate. Which one is closest to the town?"

He coughed. "Are you serious," he nodded at the

pedestal, "about using this thing to teleport yourself to one of the beacons?"

"I am," I turned to him. "So which one can take me to town faster?"

Lars thought stroking his beard.

"Depends where in town you want to be."

"McLean's farms."

"Then it's definitely the bay beacon. But they'll see you."

"That's my problem. I absolutely have to send a message to the Fort. And..."

I didn't finish. I couldn't start telling him about Mira and our daughter. Or about my father.

Kathy and Wladas returned bringing a uniform, a harness, a pair of boots and a tactical helmet. I took the jacket from Wladas and glanced at the name tag over the breast pocket. The uniform had belonged to Badry. I started to undress.

"Mark," Kathy said.

She stepped toward me but had to give way to Lars' men who'd just come back with a pulse gun, seven rounds of ammo, a knife and a handgun. They put their goodies down next to the jetpack while one of them was reporting to Lars about the combat vehicles approaching the site.

"They're about to attack," the man's voice quaked with excitement.

"I'll be up there," Lars dropped before leaving the hall.

"Mark," Kathy started again. "Can you take me with you?"

"You'd better stay here," I put on the harness, adjusted the straps and took the helmet from her hands.

"Why?"

"Because I've no idea if I can teleport myself alone.

What if the machine," I pointed at it with the helmet, "kills you or me, or both?"

Kathy glanced at the semisphere and looked up. I went on, "Let's not take unnecessary risks. I know Blank. I know how many of them are there and I know what tactics they use. I think I can do it."

I put on the helmet and connected my memory chip to its interface, then checked the work of the information terminal and its interaction with all the harness and weapons modules. Everything was in perfect working order.

"Stand aside," I said to Kathy and Wladas as I heaved the jetpack onto my back. "Even better, go out into the hallway."

They exchanged glances and walked out of the hall. I waited for a moment watching them leave. Then I buckled up and stepped toward the pedestal.

"Mark!" the girl called out. "Just in case, the radio is with Philippe, my brother. First house downtown from McLean's. The one with the red roof. It's in a stash under the bedroom floor. If you move the bed and lift the floorboards, it's all there."

"Thanks!" I turned back to the sphere, touched its surface and closed my eyes seeing dozens of shimmering little dots.

CHAPTER FIVE

POINT APOCALYPSE

M Y MIND plummeted into a void. The dots had scattered in the dark which grew until it filled the universe, the corridor between Earth and Pangea blindingly bright just out of range of my vision. Below me stretched a grid of crimson threads with the five beacons pulsating on their edges. I was in its center and the beacons made the five points of a star inscribed into the grid. The beacons sent their signals to the glowing corridor not letting it snap and disconnect the two worlds preventing the universe from collapsing.

All this I realized when the beacons' power had entered me. Now I was part of their system - a speck of light capable of channeling energies and restructuring connections.

It felt weird. In the outer world I was a soldier, a master specialist who knew how to fight and kill. Bound by the most elementary parameters, I could predict a situation's outcome by using my knowledge of the enemy's combat potential and measure it in standard units. But here... Here I held sway of the powers of the Gods who had created Pangea. To lord it over the worlds is far too much temptation to resist. The corridor could disappear at my first whim cutting Earth off from the portals and excluding it from the net, just like the Forecomers had done to their unwanted guests cutting them out like an abscess whose toxic remains still rotted away in the swamps.

But I wouldn't do that. Not until I'd rescued Mira and our daughter.

The grid, the beacons, the handfuls of bright dots all lit up together and then went out. I shook my head in confusion and closed my eyes to get used to the darkness. When I opened them again, I realized that I had teleported from the hall with the portal machine...

Teleported where?

The flashlight in my helmet lit up. A rod protruded out of a vaulted ceiling. The beacons must have all had the same design. In order to find out where I was, I had to go outside. I stepped forward sensing a slight resistance in the air, as if I'd walked through a gossamer film. It reminded me of the moment when I'd stormed the optical membrane back in the gasometer, only then everything had happened much faster and firmer - more vividly.

Light poured in. The sea wafted brine in my face. Waves splashed against the rocks at the cliff's base. I looked around. The large round dome glinted like steel, the twisted rod in its center boring into the sky. The dome stood on top of the cliff, bound by the ocean to its left and the rocky shore to my right. Further on, soft sunlight poured through the drifting clouds where McLean's estate stood on the bay.

I took a cautious step down onto the wet rocks. Facing the beacon, I made my way around the cliff's base toward the water and looked south.

The Fort loomed black on the horizon. A barge was approaching it at full steam, smoke belching from the funnel over the wheelhouse. I raised the rifle and looked through the sights. A rusty container took up all of the barge's deck - the very same one that had been mounted on the trailer in the clones' camp.

Too late. I hadn't made it. Blank and McLean had already shipped their cargo to the Fort. Why was I so sure Mira and the baby were still alive? The captain could have killed them and left for the gasometers to join his reserve squad which was fighting the settlers even as I stood here.

After a while, I dismissed my premonitions and began preparing for the flight. Most likely, Blank would rather temporarily cede control of the portal machine than lose the hostages and with them, the possibility to manipulate me. While the captain didn't know that I'd reached New Pang, I still had a chance to rescue Mira and the baby. And this chance was by a surprise attack from the sea from which they weren't expecting us.

Standing firmly on a flat rock, I estimated the wind's direction and strength and took off. But not as successfully as the last time: one of the thrusters was retarded, spinning me around in the air. I had to maneuver the handles in order to straighten myself up and avoid falling into the water.

Fighting for my life, I flew far from the shore which I'd planned to follow in order to penetrate McLean's estate. Now there was little left to do: if Blank (and I didn't doubt that he was at the estate) wasn't monitoring the area with his armored vehicle's radar, they would detect me within a minute or a minute and a half at best. But if things were like I thought, then...

Two small figures appeared in the air over the bay: two cyber troopers in Centurion suits had launched from the roof of McLean's place. Too bad. The element of surprise was now lost. They might shoot me down as I approached and I'd lose speed and be unable to free the hostages in time.

What is a minute of dogfighting to an observer? He wouldn't have time to understand anything. Amid the flashes of firing and the swift maneuvers, a rookie wouldn't be able to follow who was attacking and who was defending. But a trained soldier always acts concisely and by the book: he knows the enemy's combat potential and follows the situation, applying procedures already refined in training. Only now the two cybers were about to face a master specialist. Despite the makeshift jetpack on my back and the absence of a combat suit, these two who were now flying toward me had lost too much time. They should have taken off earlier.

Just as I expected, they split up. This was a standard trick: one of them flew above me while the second one tried to flank me in a wide arc from the shore leaving me an open space over the sea to maneuver. This was a mistake: the cybers lost out on speed.

I banked into a sharp turn to scan the bay. Data on the enemy flooded onto the helmet's monitor. One of the buggies took up a position on the pier while the other raced along the edge of the cliff toward the tip of the cape. They wanted to prevent me from landing there. The memory chip detected several more targets: a group of soldiers in McLean's courtyard. Carrying digital gear, they were in intense radio communication with the armored vehicle whose radar had locked on to me. Its operator could at any moment have launched a guided missile at me. But for some reason, he hadn't done it yet.

A second later, I got all the answers. Blank sent me a message via an open channel requiring me to land and surrender before they shot me down. He hovered in the air high above me mercilessly burning his fuel - apparently sure that I wouldn't dare challenge him. This was why the operator in the armored vehicle hadn't shot at me: they needed me alive. Oh well. The captain had just freed my hands.

The cyber who had flanked me from the shore realized his mistake too late and was tardy to turn around. I fell in behind him and shot him just once from close range with my pulse gun.

His jetpack exploded in a fountain of sparks, flames shooting in all directions. I zoomed up. The soldier, enveloped in flames, tumbled into the sea. I didn't look any further. I straightened out and headed for McLean's estate paying no attention to Blank's attempts to intercept me.

While I was dealing with the cyber, the captain had time to descend and was now heading toward me at the same altitude intending to head me off. The distance between us decreased. The memory chip sent new calculations to the monitor: we would collide some two meters away from McLean's verandah on the cliff.

I swerved trying to reduce the distance to Blank and fired a long burst sending the pulse downward. The captain soared up avoiding the shots. Not quite what I'd had in mind.

The sensor in my helmet bleeped as a missile shot up above the estate and headed toward me trailing smoke.

I turned and went after Blank trying to catch up with him. Having lost me, he had nothing else left to do but to shoot me down. The only safe place now was next to the captain. The flames from the nozzles of his jetpack kept oscillating as he tried to save fuel and make it to the shore.

Blank flew a sine wave pattern and I had nearly caught up with him when all thrust disappeared behind my back.

Extending my body, I reached in front of me trying to grab Blank's ankles. Our speed leveled out: on the armored car's radar screen we must have looked like one dot.

I had guessed it right. A bang came from behind me. The operator had activated the missile at the last moment - most likely, on orders from Blank himself who was afraid to die with me.

The shock wave propelled me forward. I got hold of Blank's foot when his thrusters came back on. Covering my face with my elbow from the blast, I pulled my knees to my stomach and kicked the air below.

We were swirling a couple of meters away from the water. I glimpsed the familiar jetty that separated the seaweed farms from the pier and the verandah suspended on the cliff by its support beams. There, a group of people leaned over the railings watching us.

Blank's jetpack rattled as it burned the last drops of fuel. I reached out with my other hand and grabbed the sheath on his side pulling the knife by its handle. Together, we tumbled into the water between the jetty and the shore.

We both sank to the bottom like stones: me, dragged below by my makeshift jetpack and the gun, and Blank, by his Centurion suit. I would much rather have killed the captain and then tried to get rid of the weight. But I couldn't take such risks: I might not resurface.

My right hand got caught in a net. Carula's long stalks rippled in front of my face. I had to kick myself free from my opponent, cut through the net and surface for a breath of air.

When I dived again, our automatic flashlights on our helmets cut through the murky water. Blank who'd by now got rid of his suit and gear, was frantically moving his arms rising to the surface. When he noticed me, he drew his handgun and leveled his arm at my chest.

I stuck the knife out in front of me and slashed ay his hand grasping his forearm to deflect the gun. Three shots hissed past leaving lines of bubbles - two barely missed my shoulder while one grazed my helmet. I slashed again, this time at his elbow. Blank let go of the gun but grabbed my wrist trying to draw me in.

Our visors collided with a thump. The captain constricted me in a bear hug disabling my arms. But immediately, he let go of me and shot upward as his air supply was running out. I stabbed his hip.

He'd already resurfaced and now he dived back down. I forced him below, stood on his shoulders and kicked with all my might to get back to the surface gasping for air.

A voice came from the pier. I turned my head and met the gaze of a soldier who sat on his buggy's armor plates. He pointed at me shouting something and looking up. The next moment, shots came from McLean's verandah.

I disappeared under water, dived under the jetty and came back to the surface looking for Blank. He was nowhere to be seen.

Had he drowned?

A bullet pierced a plank over my head missing my temple by an inch. Another tore through the jetty right opposite my face and hit the water changing its trajectory and stinging my side.

I took a deep breath, dived down and swam toward the pier and the buggy.

It could be that the trail of air bubbles betrayed my location. Either that or the soldier on top of the buggy happened to have a good eye but in any case, the water behind my back foamed with his pulse charges. But I was already nearing the pier. His pulse pierced the water like tiny fireballs without changing their direction, then lost speed, exploding with a resounding crackle.

Damn it! I nearly went deaf while the soldier emptied his magazine into a spot where I no longer was.

Once the shooting subsided, I came back to the surface by the pier and grabbed at a clamp that joined the trestle and the deck. I pushed myself up and found myself by the buggy's back wheel.

The gunman who was reloading his weapon saw me and fumbled with his clip. When he realized he wouldn't have time to fire, he crouched jabbing at my head with his gun. I dodged and grabbed the stock pushing the soldier into the water. Had he been a cyber, I'd never have managed to do it.

Not losing a second, I climbed onto the buggy, stuck my upper body through the open hatch and clasped the engineer's shoulders. He too proved to be a regular soldier and screamed when I pushed his head against an angular flange inside the vehicle. His scream died halfway and the engineer slackened dropping his head onto his chest. I dragged him away from the steering stick and jumped into the buggy. I locked the hatches and pulled a sleeve of wires out of a socket on one side of the dashboard, then connected myself to the vehicle's terminal. Starting the engine, I put it into gear and reversed, simultaneously activating the fighting unit.

The machine gun on the buggy's roof turned toward McLean's estate and rattled spitting out bullets. The camera sent the image to the monitor: the burst of bullets hitting the cliff under the verandah collapsing one of the support beams in a cloud of chipped wood and rock. The spiral staircase sank and careened toward the cliff; two men fell with it one after the other.

When the buggy rolled out onto the shore, I ceased to fire, turned the vehicle round and pushed the control column. Tires screeching, the buggy sped uphill. After a couple of bends, I rammed the fence barely missing the personnel carrier in the middle of McLean's courtyard. I opened fire again sending the few remaining raiders scurrying to the house's entrance and scorching the empty personnel carrier's wheels. Then I rolled back to the gap in the fence positioning the burning vehicle between the estate gate and myself.

I hadn't forgotten the other buggy which had escaped as soon as I'd seized the one I was now driving. My current position might seem disadvantageous as the burning vehicle wouldn't allow me to open fire on the second buggy arriving. But by the same token, the buggy's thermal viewer wouldn't be able to detect me behind the burning vehicle, and when the enemy had to drive past me, I...

The sand buggy's squat tortoise shell-painted shape loomed up between the crosshairs from behind the personnel carrier. I jabbed the fire control button on the control column and darted forward to draw near to it.

Their machine gun burst into a cascade of fire before it had a chance to turn in my direction. I rammed the other buggy's side smashing my own front valance and the cowls. I reversed and did the same again, only this time I didn't have to shoot.

After the second ramming, the enemy's buggy tipped on its side. The front hatch opened, and a shell-shocked engineer fell out onto the ground. I didn't wait for the gunman to appear from the rear compartment and sped up the courtyard into Mclean's wide front doors. My right wheel got caught on his lounge table and dragged it along for a couple of meters before I stopped the vehicle, its deformed panels butting up against the staircase.

I got out onto the armor plate and had a quick look around wincing from the bullet scratch on my side. Then I jumped off onto the table and up the steps. In a flash, I was upstairs. Here, a thick cloud of dust hung in the air. The room was in a shambles. Part of the verandah's scorched floor and roof supports were missing. The chipped remains of floorboards faced the ocean. The banister was gone, but the serving table by the verandah entrance had survived the impact, complete with the tray, the bottles and the cigar box.

In the far corner of the room, a heavy cabinet leaned against the wall. I heard a faint rustle coming from underneath it. Then, a groan. I leaped to the cabinet and looked under it.

The mute steward - the one who'd very nearly shot Wong during our first meeting - stared at me groaning, his eyes pleading for help. Sitting sideways, he kept pointing on the floor under his arm.

Another person lay there, one with an eye patch and a scar across his cheekbone. McLean.

I nearly screamed in despair realizing he was lying there motionless and probably unconscious too. In his hand Mclean clenched a cracked earpiece and a microphone whose cable reached inside the cabinet.

I bent down and peeked inside it. On a shelf, a disemboweled army radio gaped at me with its rusty insides. The only reason it hadn't crashed against Mclean's head was because of some hefty old bolts holding it to the shelf.

Its front and the tuning scale were peppered with bullet holes. Through the radio's dislodged side panel I could see the corner of an exploded battery and a scorched circuit board drenched in battery fluid.

McLean had tried to contact someone. I recovered my train of thought and grabbed the steward's collar.

"Where's the girl and the baby?"

He made a muffled noise. I gave him a good shake and repeated my question, adding, "Just point!"

He shook his head as if trying to explain something. I let go of him and he started crossing his hands in front of himself pointing at the door. It was as clear as mud.

"They're are not here, are they?" I grabbed his collar again. "Where are they?"

Thoughts flashed through my mind, one worse than the other: what if Blank had left Mira and the baby in the personnel carrier I'd just smoked? Fucking idiot! What if they'd been standing on the verandah when I'd splattered it with bullets from the captured buggy? No, I hadn't - I'd aimed at the cliff, I really hadn't wanted to hurt anyone...

Mclean seemed to have stirred. I crouched next to him, grabbed at a shelf and tried to lift the cabinet wincing from the pain in my side under its weight. I managed to push it to one side and bent over McLean shoving the steward away.

"Tex," I wheezed, "You think you're all right?"

I couldn't move him or even turn him on his back for fear of a broken spine. I leaned toward his ear,

"Where's the woman, the cyber biologist, remember? The one who taught you how to harvest carula? She has a baby with her. Blank brought them to you this morning. D'you know where they are? Tell me!"

I touched his shoulder. McLean forced his eyes open and whispered something.

"I didn't hear," I pulled the helmet off and drew my head close almost touching his cheek. "Say it again."

"Phi- At Philippe's," his voice was barely audible.

"Philippe?" I sat up. "Which Philippe? What's he got to do with it?"

McLean stopped breathing. His stare fixed on the floor.

I wailed in despair and slammed the helmet against the wall. Where's Mira? Where's my baby? How could I stop the barge from delivering its deadly cargo to Earth?

Then I remembered what Kathy had told me about her brother. About... Philippe. He was apparently the one with the radio transmitter. And now McLean had mentioned him, too. What if Mira and the baby were indeed at Philippe's?

I sprang up buckling on the helmet as I took the stairs back down into the courtyard. I jumped over the banister and into the buggy and drove off without closing the hatch heading for the city. Red-roofed houses lined both sides of the road.

Kathy had said that his house was the first from Mclean's. But was it to the right or to the left? Houses here didn't have numbers but logically, it had to be the one on the left. I drove on and parked up by the roadside. A dark-haired man with a carbine stuck himself out of the first-story window and shot at me twice.

The bullets ricocheted off the buggy's hull.

"Philippe, don't shoot!" I shouted as I got out of the buggy. "Please don't! I'm unarmed!"

I raised my hands and jumped to the ground.

"Kathy's alive!" I went on. "She saved my life and I helped her survive, too! You have my girlfriend and baby. I'll just take them and go."

Philippe reappeared in the window aiming his carbine at me. Behind his back I heard a baby crying.

"You're saying my sister's alive. Why should I believe you?"

"Because Kathy told me about the stash. It's in this room under the bed! The transmitter's there. Go look!"

I turned back to McLean's house. Over its roof, the setting sun struggled through the clouds of smoke from the burning personnel carrier. No one was trying to follow me. The port and the bay seemed deserted.

A loud screech came from the window as if someone was dragging a metal object across wood. Something was clanking.

"Come in," Philippe called out.

My heart raced. Forgetting the pain in my side, I took the dark stairs three at a time, pushed a door open and froze in the doorway. Mira sat on the floor in the far corner holding the swaddled-up baby. She looked at me, tears welling up in her eyes.

I stepped toward them and stopped. Philippe stood by the window next to the displaced bed. He kept a bead on me, distrust in his stare. Some of the floorboards had been removed and the transmitter's steel body glistened between the beams.

"Get the radio out," I walked to Mira and squatted next to her, looking into her eyes and smiling. "Give me one moment... then we'll leave, all of us. I only need to warn the Fort's commander and then-"

"Why should I believe you?" Philippe repeated. "How do you know about the stash? Did you torture my sister?"

"Yeah right. And went straight to you to tell you about it. She hid the radio from you, don't forget."

"What's it all about?" Philippe wasn't in a hurry to retrieve the radio from under the floorboards.

"Later," I knelt beside the stash. "Help me," I got hold of the transmitter's corner and tried to lift it. "Are you helping or what?"

My wounded side exploded with pain. Blood drenched my already wet jacket and I tried to compress the wound with my elbow while lifting the heavy radio transmitter out of the hole.

Philippe leaned his carbine up against the wall, pushed me aside and grabbed the steel box with his strong hairy hands.

"Where d'you want it?" he asked standing up.

"On the window sill," I glanced at Mira and nodded. "In a moment. We'll leave now."

"Where did Kathy get it from?" Philippe heaved the box onto the window and turned to me.

"She used to work for the FSA."

"For the FSA?" Philippe raised an eyebrow. He opened his mouth to speak but didn't have time to say anything.

His head exploded splattering the ceiling with blood and brain fragments. A burst from a pulse gun hit the room through the window shattering the walls and setting the bedclothes and floorboards on fire. In a cloud of dust from the ceiling, I rushed to Mira and covered her and the baby with my body.

The gun kept rattling until it shot off all the ammo inside the buggy I'd parked by the house. It looked like one of Blank's subordinates had decided to avenge his death.

"We need to get out of here," I urged, pulling Mira's elbow. "The ceiling could collapse any moment. Come quickly before they change the clip."

I helped her up and we ran out into the dark stairwell. From the street came a rustling of tires and the buzz of an electric motor. They must have moved the buggy to face the house's front door.

"The lamp's on the wall, Mark," I heard behind me.

"What about it?" I turned round. Mira pointed with her eyes to a glass bulb hanging on the wall. "Take it and let's go! Quick!"

She didn't let me take her hand and stepped back saying, "Don't take me, take the lamp."

I swallowed an expletive, then took the lamp off its hook. "Are you coming now?"

"I am. Turn it on."

"That's enough!" I lost my patience. "Let's go!"

I literally forced her down the stairs. I was afraid we wouldn't make it out of the house before the assailants got to us. If they met us by the exit, I wouldn't be able to defend us.

We walked downstairs and I headed for the window opening into the back yard when a voice stopped me.

"Master Specialist!" I heard from the street. "Come out now!"

I motioned Mira to the window and started noiselessly

for the door.

"Don't try to escape! You don't have enough time!" Blank's voice kept shouting. "If you don't come out in three seconds, we'll take the house to bits stone by stone!"

What a jerk! How had he survived, I'd love to know? It must have been his somatic module reacting in time to inject an emergency adrenaline shot into his bloodstream allowing him to reach the surface.

"The lamp," Mira whispered behind me.

Her and her lamp! I looked back. Mira hadn't moved. She stood by the staircase pressing her daughter to her chest.

"One!" I heard from the street. "Two!"

"Don't shoot!" I shouted. "I'm coming out."

"You only need to turn the ring," Mira whispered at my back. "Then throw it at him."

I walked to the door, looked at the lamp and turned the ring on its base. A soft bluish light licked my face. The bulb heated up.

"Three!"

"I'm coming!" I swung the door open and hurled the lamp into the buggy where Blank sat in the driver's seat, the hatch open over his head.

He managed to leap out head first, like a champion swimmer in an Olympic pool, and somersault back onto his feet. The lamp hit the armor plate and the bulb cracked letting out a splash of bright light. With a loud hiss, the buggy disappeared in a cloud of steam.

Or not steam, maybe. A couple of seconds later the cloud was gone leaving oily stains on the armor. Blank was now ready for war, his body in a fighting stance, his hand squeezing a knife - the one I'd buried in his leg.

"I can't believe it!" he spat out. "You, throwing a

thermite! It had to be your girlfriend who told you how to use it."

I had no idea what a thermite was, and I certainly didn't care.

Blank winced and pulled his head toward his shoulder as if stretching his neck muscles before a fight. But I didn't think that was the reason. He didn't look good. Not good at all. He'd lost his helmet; his pale face and neck were covered in swollen blue bumps, and the blood vessels forcing his thickened blood around looked like worms crawling under his skin.

I clenched my fists. Blank leaned forward but his tourniqueted thigh shook and he barely kept his balance, his knees giving way under him. He suppressed a cough and clenched his teeth. Then he breathed out spitting bluish blood clots.

"Remember biocyne and carula?" I asked lowering my hands.

He staggered and shuffled one foot trying to step forward.

"What do you know about their properties?" I insisted.

He collapsed onto his knees and tried to take a swing at me but let the knife go and dropped his head.

"You're as good as dead," I looked down at him. "The slime has killed you."

His eye vessels burst. Black blood poured out of his nose; more vessels were bursting darkening his face while veins as thick as a finger bulged on his neck.

Blank wheezed and fell on his back.

"You scumbag," I said quietly. "You've deserved this kind of death."

The sky shattered. Behind my back, Mira cried out in surprise - despite my orders, she'd walked out into the courtyard. I ran out into the street looking in the direction of the beacon and the Fort behind it. When I reached the turn for the port, I stopped, open-mouthed.

A fiery mushroom cloud rose over the Fort. It resembled a nuclear explosion but not quite: it lacked the initial flash and the shock wave that normally would blow the clouds away as it encircled the sky. It was as if the explosion had occurred somewhere else - not here on the island but between the worlds...

Point Apocalypse, the thought flashed through my mind. Neumann's theory had proven to be true. But - who had delivered the missile to the jumpgate?

The mushroom over the Fort had grown, changing shape and turning into a funnel. A low hum spread in the air as the clouds started moving slowly toward it as if someone had turned on a gigantic vacuum cleaner. The earth shook. The horizon began to fold.

I backed up and shouted to Mira telling her to take cover inside the house. I had no idea what was going to happen next: our continuum could collapse, or we'd be blown to smithereens or sucked into a black hole...

A moment later, the vortex had disappeared leaving a dark stripe in the sky. Claps of thunder came from the sea. The deformed horizon straightened up and took its usual place. The clouds diffused over the sky. I stared, bewitched, at the ocean where the island used to be. I could see nothing but waves.

The beacon stopped pulsating and went out. Immediately, the dark stripe in the sky disappeared. Slowly, I turned around. Mira hadn't had time to take cover in the house. She stood in the doorway holding our daughter.

"Mark? What happened?"

"Looks like your Dad was right."

"Right about what?"

"About his Point Apocalypse theory," I walked toward the house. "He suggested exploding a nuclear device in the jumpgate to disconnect Earth from Pangea."

"How is it possible?" Mira opened her eyes wide. "Can you really destroy the wormway with a bomb?"

You could have blown me over backward. Everything fell into place. My father had outsmarted them all.

"Remember the supposed container with the virus?"

She nodded.

"There was no virus. The container held a bomb - a tactical nuke. General Varlamov was the Fort's commander so it was part of his responsibility to nuke the Fort and its garrison in case of an emergency. If, for instance, Earth faced some sort of deadly threat."

I came to Mira and gently took the baby from her. My little girl was fast asleep, sniffing peacefully in her wraps.

"What's her name?" I sat on the stone doorstep.

Mira smiled. "Era," she lowered herself onto the step next to me.

"Era," I nodded looking into my daughter's face. "A new creature in a new world."

We heard surprised voices in the street and raised our heads. People were walking out of the city, lots of them; they stopped on the hill before the turn for the port and looked west where the Fort used to stand.

I knew we were all thinking the same thing: Continent Anomalous was entering a new era.

THE END

ABOUT THE AUTHOR

Alex (Aleksei) Bobl is a Russia-based science fiction writer, author of 14 novels. An ex-paratrooper, he used his military knowledge and experience to write his debut novels for *S.T.A.L.K.E.R.*, a bestselling science fiction action adventure series set in a post-apocalyptic Chernobyl.

After his initial success, Alex Bobl teamed up with his friend and *S.T.A.L.K.E.R.* co-author Andrei Levitski to create a SF project of their own. Entitled *TechnoTma: The Dark Times*, this action adventure series is set in a post-apocalyptic future where the Black Sea has dried out and the Crimea has become a major desert. The eight books of *TechnoTma* had a total print run of over 250,000 copies and have been translated into German and Spanish. Talks are now under way about translating *TechnoTma* into English.

Point Apocalypse is Alex' second novel translated into English. The first one, *Memoria. A Corporation of Lies*, is also available on Amazon and in bookshops. Alex Bobl lives in Moscow with his wife and two boys and is currently working on his next science fiction novel. You can follow its progress in Alex's blog, *Obviously Incredible*, as well as on Twitter and Facebook:

http://boblak.blogspot.com/
https://twitter.com/AlexBobl
https://www.facebook.com/Alex.Bobl.fans

Want to be the first to know about our latest LitRPG, sci fi and fantasy titles from your favorite authors?

Thank you for reading *Point Apocalypse!*
If you like what you've read, check out other LitRPG books and series published by Magic Dome Books:

Our latest releases:

Stay on the Wing (The Dark Herbalist Book #2)
by Michael Atamanov

NEW LitRPG Series!!
The First Player (AlterGame Book #1)
by Andrew Novak

NEW LitRPG Series!!
The Beginning (Dark Paladin Book #1)
by V. Mahanenko

NEW LitRPG Series!!
The Crystal Sphere (The Neuro Book #1)
by A. Livadny

Save $5.98!
By buying all three e-books of
Phantom Server LitRPG Series
by A. Livadny
or
Perimeter Defense LitRPG Series
by M. Atamanov
as a Boxed Set for $9.99 instead of $15.97!

The Way of the Shaman series by Vasily Mahanenko:
Survival Quest
The Kartoss Gambit
The Secret of the Dark Forest
The Phantom Castle
The Karmadont Chess Set

Galactogon LitRPG series by Vasily Mahanenko:
Start the Game!

Phantom Server LitRPG series by Andrei Livadny:
Edge of Reality
The Outlaw
Black Sun

Perimeter Defense LitRPGseries by Michael Atamanov:
Sector Eight
Beyond Death
New Contract

The Dark Herbalist LitRPG series by Michael Atamanov:
Video Game Plotline Tester

Mirror World LitRPG series by Alexey Osadchuk:
Project Daily Grind
The Citadel
The Way of the Outcast

The Game Master LitRPG series by A. Bobl and A.
Levitsky:
The Lag

The Sublime Electricity series by Pavel Kornev
The Illustrious
The Heartless
Leopold Orso and The Case of the Bloody Tree

Moskau (a dystopian thriller)
by G. Zotov

Memoria. A Corporation of Lies (an action-packed
dystopian technothriller)
by Alex Bobl

Point Apocalypse (a near-future action thriller)
by Alex Bobl

The Naked Demon (a paranormal romance)
by Sherrie L.

More books and series are coming out soon!

In order to have new books of the series translated faster, we need your help and support! Please consider leaving a review or spread the word by recommending *Point Apocalypse* to your friends and posting the link on social media. The more people buy the book, the sooner we'll be able to make new translations available. Thank you!

Till next time!

www.ingramcontent.com/pod-product-compliance
Lightning Source LLC
Chambersburg PA
CBHW070542260626
47161CB00002B/475